A
GRAVE
CALLING

A
GRAVE
CALLING

Wendy Roberts

WORLDWIDE®

TORONTO • NEW YORK • LONDON
AMSTERDAM • PARIS • SYDNEY • HAMBURG
STOCKHOLM • ATHENS • TOKYO • MILAN
MADRID • WARSAW • BUDAPEST • AUCKLAND

All the words in this book are fiction except these:
I love you, David Cain.

Recycling programs
for this product may
not exist in your area.

A Grave Calling

A Worldwide Mystery/January 2018

First published by Carina Press

ISBN-13: 978-1-335-50643-6

A
GRAVE
CALLING

ONE

THE FIRST TIME I picked up dowsing rods I knew I was different. Gramps said that if you had the knack, they'd help you find water. But I always found bodies. Buried deep or shallow, long ago or yesterday—put the rods in my hands and I was drawn to the dead. A damn corpse magnet, that's me.

I sat at my kitchen table eating a dinner of tomato soup thickened with crumbled saltines. My Rottweiler was a heavy and comforting weight across the top of my feet but, abruptly, Wookie was on his feet with the rumble of a growl low down in his throat and his ears pressed flat against his sizable noggin. Seconds later, headlights flashed across my window, followed shortly by the sound of a car door slam and the crunch of footsteps on the gravel path that led from the weed-choked drive to my door. Wookie's snarl became a raucous, thundering bark that reverberated inside my mobile home. I got up and reached for the shotgun that leaned casually against the wall next to the wastebasket. I held my breath and waited.

The footsteps grew closer and climbed the two wooden steps to my door. There was a single, sharp knock.

Wookie went ballistic. He would've torn right through the flimsy aluminum door and torn the ass off the visitor if I'd given the word. And he really, really wanted me to give that word. Spittle from his teeth sprayed my bare legs as he wailed and bayed at the door.

"Hush."

The dog offered me a reproachful glance and woofed a couple times more for added measure. He wanted to continue his rampage to protect me from the unseen bogeyman, but when I hushed again in an implacable tone and placed a firm hand on the top of his head, the barking stopped. Still, his obsidian eyes never left the door and his defensive stance did not change.

"State your name and business." My voice was brisk and I swallowed anything near fear that would've caused the tone to tremble.

There was no immediate response. An uneasiness crept under my skin during the brief pause. I released the safety and pumped the shotgun. The ratchet sound was an unmistakable warning.

"State your name and business," I repeated, shouting this time. Now my voice wavered a little around the edges of the words as I pressed the butt of the gun snugly against my shoulder.

Please do not make me reach for my inner Annie Oakley because she often hangs out with my inner Calamity Jane.

"Special Agent Garrett Pierce with the Federal Bureau of Investigation. I'm here to talk to Delma Arsenault."

A hand appeared in the window and pressed official identification between the gap in the faded Priscilla curtains.

"Well, damn," I muttered on a loud exhale of air that hissed between my gritted teeth.

I clicked the safety back on and lowered the shotgun just as my cell phone rang in my pocket.

"Yeah, Gramps?"

My gaze automatically skipped out the kitchen window and a quarter mile down the gravel lane to his house mostly hidden by a cluster of cedars. In stark contrast to the dusky evening, I could just make out the soft glow of light from his kitchen window.

"You've got a visitor. Sorry, I was in the crapper and he got by me. Want me to come over?"

"No, I'm good."

"You sure? I can be there in a heartbeat."

"Nah, I've got this, Gramps."

"Is it a cop? Looked like it might be an undercover-type vehicle."

"Something like that. I'll call you once he's gone." I ended the call and blew out a long, frustrated sigh when there was another pounding on the door.

"Delma Arsenault?"

Wookie resumed barking, his back coiled muscle and his broad face lifted to the ceiling.

"Just a sec!" I shouted back.

"Lay down," I told Wookie and pointed to his worn foam bed in the far corner near the washroom.

The dog grumbled, walked over to his bed and stood on top of it with his head low and watchful. He refused to lower his body onto the bed and, as he watched me go to the entrance, his body was taut muscle waiting to spring. This Garrett Pierce of the FBI better behave or else Wookie was going to take a hunk out of his ass.

When I opened the door the man who stood in the doorway took a step forward and nearly filled it. A hundred acres of inky darkness from the onetime farm beyond filled the void behind him as he held his identification a couple inches from my face. A damp breeze whistled in around him as I took the leather badge holder and stared at the picture and then at him. It was an awkward photo of the agent, all serious, clean shaven, in a suit and years younger. The man who stood in front of me was in contrast wearing a T-shirt and stiff new jeans and sported a scruff of coarse black-and-gray bristle on his chin. The dark bags under his eyes said that he didn't sleep well. My guess was that he had at least twenty years on top of my own twenty-five.

"What can I do for you?" I tossed his ID back, and he caught it smoothly midair and it disappeared inside the back pocket of his designer denim. He closed the door behind him with his elbow, not taking his eyes off mine.

He stared pointedly at the shotgun still in my hand. If he knew what a bad shot I was he wouldn't look so concerned. I couldn't hit an elephant if I was riding one. I turned and put the gun back in the corner, then picked up a stack of old newspapers covering the seat of the vinyl booth.

"Have a seat." I slipped back into my own spot and casually resumed eating my soup as if I didn't give a rat's ass who he was but, honestly, my heart was pounding so loud in my ears I could hardly think straight.

When Agent Pierce took a step toward the table, Wookie growled.

"Wookie, down," I ordered. The mutt dropped with a heavy *fwump* into his bed while he released a sullen and derisive snort.

"Wookie?" The agent smiled as if this was the best joke he'd ever heard. "Someone's a *Star Wars* fan."

"The name came with the dog." I slurped a spoonful of soup. "It wasn't my business to change it."

The agent slid into the booth across from me. I ate my soup while he discreetly glanced around my small two-bedroom trailer; his watchful gaze paused at the pile of newspapers I'd placed on top of others on the counter, and skipped over the sparse decor and the worn lino. His keen eyes unnerved me when they returned to my face.

"So you *are* Delma Arsenault?"

"Nobody calls me that." I lifted the bowl to my lips and drank the last of the tomato soup, then got up and put the bowl in the sink.

"Right. They call you by your middle name. Julie. And by your grandfather's last name. Hall."

"You're just a frickin' Wikipedia of knowledge, aren't you?"

He shrugged and stared hard. I became keenly mind-ful of the fact I was in short shorts and a low-cut tank top. Not exactly the attire I would've chosen for a meet-ing with the FBI. I crossed my arms over my breasts and returned to my seat.

"Sounds like you made it your job to know every-thing about me."

"Not everything," he admitted.

He glanced warily to his left and I smiled. Wookie was sneaking over as stealthily as a hundred-thirty-pound dog can sneak. He flopped down on my feet be-fore the agent continued.

"I know you're twenty-five. Raised mostly by your grandfather who lives in the house up the road. You graduated from the local high school and work at the gas station in town."

I could feel a defensive nerve twitch in the edge of

my jaw. He thought he knew me. Was going to try now to wow me with his expertise. I didn't like it one bit but I leaned back in my seat and waited.

"Also," he added, "you have a reputation for finding dead people."

I didn't even blink. Did he expect me to deny or confirm? I did neither, just let it hang in the stuffy air between us. He did nothing to fill the awkward pause and finally I had to say something.

"So where are you from? Seattle? You didn't drive two hours up the I-5 to tell me what I already knew. With all your FBI know-how—" I flicked my hand contemptuously in his direction "—I'm sure you could've used some of that skill and expertise to find my phone number."

"I tried. You didn't answer any of my calls."

A loud snort of laughter escaped my lips before I could swallow it, and I covered my lips quickly with my hand. "Of course I didn't answer. Who the hell answers calls from an unknown number? Not me."

"And you don't have voice mail."

Are we seriously going to sit here and discuss my cell phone plan?

"Thought about texting you. But I got the feeling you wouldn't have replied. Besides, this is something better discussed in person." He folded his hands neatly on the table in front of him. There was a distinct indent on his ring finger where a wedding ring used to be, like it had cinched the skin and bone for many years before being yanked off.

I stared at his hands and waited.

"Maple Falls. Arlington. Alger."

My throat tightened as the town names fell like hot

irons and sizzled in the space between us. Three different Washington towns. Quiet places. Where three different teen girls had been abducted. For weeks the news had been filled with morbid conjecture and grim suppositions while search parties scoured the state, and families held candlelight vigils pleading for information.

"You caught him then?" I couldn't keep the hopeful expectation from my voice.

There was a flicker of something across his face before he nodded. "We have someone in custody. He's given us a possible location of…"

"The bodies," I finished. I drummed my fingers anxiously on the table between us. "So you know where they are. Why can't you just go and get them?"

"The location is vague and it could easily take a week for a crew to dig up someone's property. There are acres of land, and he claims he doesn't know exactly where so it was suggested this might be more expedient…"

His gaze faltered then and a flash of vulnerability flicked across those dark eyes before they cooled. He felt guilty. Like it was his own fault he hadn't been able to squeeze the precise location from whatever sicko got his rocks off taking girls and killing them for pleasure. Maybe he had a daughter the same age and that stoked his shame.

"So you just want me to try to find the bodies."

"If you can."

He straightened then and coated the request with a smile, trying to make it seem like this was an impromptu and casual request. As if he wasn't going to try and force me to help, or even threaten or guilt me into it if I dared refused. He was a man of facts and the law. Even through the easy grin I could feel the underlying irritation. He didn't think for a second I could find anything and it bit him in the ass to come here.

I untangled my feet from Wookie, got up, opened my fridge and pulled out a Coke. I raised a can in question to Agent Pierce but he politely shook his head. I figured him for the type who drank aged scotch, five-dollar coffee and juiced lemongrass. The thought made me smile. As I returned to the cracked vinyl booth and sipped my cola, Wookie repositioned his body to take possession of my feet while I ran a few calculations in my head.

"Three hundred eighty-five dollars."

He blinked in surprise. "That's an awfully specific number."

My Jeep needed two new tires and Gramps's birthday was next week. I'd saved most but not all I needed to get him a new recliner. The amount could've been higher but I tried not to profit too much off the dead. That didn't feel like it would be a good karma thing to do.

"Paid in cash and only half if I find nothing. My name stays out of the papers."

"I'll pick you up tomorrow morning," he said, getting to his feet.

"I work until noon and I'll meet you there after I'm done," I countered. "Just tell me where it's at."

"I can't tell you that."

Annoyance prickled inside me and I sputtered a raspberry through my lips, then grew embarrassed because it was a childish sound.

He got to his feet. "I'll pick you up at the gas station at twelve."

"Fine."

I gave a sharp nod, got to my feet and waited for him to do the same.

He left then and the moment his car turned and kicked up gravel as it pulled away I called Gramps to tell him all was good.

"You going to do work for him?" Gramps asked.

"Gonna try," I admitted.

I hung up and went through my stack of newspapers to look up everything I could on the three missing girls. After I read all I could in print I started up my old, slow laptop and did a search online. I'd followed the case, just like everybody else in the state. Hoping beyond hope that they'd be found alive but knowing deep inside that wishing for rainbows wouldn't stop a hurricane.

Thinking about those girls possibly dead and most probably under brutal circumstances caused my head to pound and my blood to cool. I flicked on my small TV and one sitcom flowed into another without me giving them any attention. My mind drifted to the dark place I called quicksand thoughts because struggling often just dragged me deeper. Once my head was in the dark place it was hard to pry it loose.

Somewhere around midnight I climbed into my bed and Wookie took to his. My head was still filled with vile thoughts but eventually I drifted off. Much later I heard the creak of the door open and the panting reception as my dog greeted someone he knew. Soon I heard the metal clink as a belt was unbuckled, followed by the unzip of blue jeans.

"Thought you had to work tonight?" I yawned and stretched under the covers but slid over to allow him room. My head still swam with black thoughts that had morphed into a horrid dream. I was incredibly relieved and grateful for a moment's distraction.

"I do have to work but not for an hour." Denny

breathed heavily as he climbed into bed, his warm breath faintly tainted from the cigarillos he liked. "I just want a little something to tide me over."

He reached up my T-shirt and cupped a cool hand on my breast. Moaning softly, I threaded my fingers into his thick black hair and pulled his lips to mine. He could feel my need and was more than happy to meet it. My urgency had nothing to do with the soft yearning for love and was more about a desire to quell the stench of putrid thoughts. I was fast asleep before Denny let himself out a half hour later.

THE DROOLY SLURP of Wookie's tongue across my face was my wake-up call at seven the next morning.

"Ugh, you are so-o-o gross."

I tried pulling the blankets over my face but he wasn't having any of that and began a tug-of-war with my comforter that ended with me naked on the sheets and him triumphantly dragging my bedding out of the room.

"Jesus. Fine. I'm up. I'm up."

I padded naked to the door and threw it open to let him outside to pee. The whoosh of cool spring air rushed into the room and it smelled of frost in sharp contrast to the mid-seventies temperature of the evening before. I shivered and hurried to fill the dog dishes with food and water, then tossed my blanket back on the bed. As soon as Wookie was inside I hit the shower while he gobbled his food. Twenty minutes later we were both climbing in my Jeep and headed the short drive up the road to see Gramps. We arrived to find him tugging his three-hundred-pound all-terrain vehicle over to the side of the house. I jumped out of my Jeep and went over to help him. Wookie followed to supervise.

"Jesus, you shouldn't be moving this thing by yourself."

I grabbed the opposite end of the bumper and helped him haul it the last few feet but, honestly, he was doing fine on his own. Hadn't even broken a sweat.

"It's not that heavy."

He dusted his hands on his pants and we headed inside the house. The weathered door creaked loudly as it swung open.

He kicked off his shoes and I brushed a kiss across the deep folds of his weathered cheek. Wookie's entire ass wiggled and waggled a hello and he received a scratch behind his ears.

"Haven't seen the ATV for a while. You going to get it working again?"

"Figured out it's the carburetor. Going to replace the pilot jet today. Just dragged it beside the house to make it easier to plug in my trouble light and see what's what. Once I get her going, gonna cruise around the property and see what's what."

Gramps was always walking around the dozen acres that were his own now and even beyond to the few dozen more that he'd sold over the years. It kept him fit and gave him something to do.

"Thought you enjoyed walking the property with Wookie? Your knee acting up?"

"Some," he admitted, giving the bad knee a hard rub with his palm. "But the rest of me is still strong as an ox."

That was a fact. His joints might ache some but the man had thick, ropy muscles in his arms and back like some kind of bodybuilder.

"You need me to get you more painkillers for your knee?"

"Picked up a new prescription yesterday," Gramps said. "I only take them when I need them."

"Hungry?"

"Not for what you're going to feed me," Gramps grumped. "I'm craving sausages and bacon fried until they're both golden and then potatoes stirred and browned in the drippings."

"And I can hear your arteries hardening at the idea." I fixed his breakfast and put it in front of him.

"Now that doesn't even look like bacon." He pointed to his plate and shook his head. "I know it's trying real hard to pretend to be a pig but that piece of flesh has never oinked."

"It's turkey bacon, Gramps, and it's better than nothing."

"I doubt that."

For all his bluster he ate the turkey bacon as well as the two poached eggs, multigrain toast and the banana I put in front of him. It all went into his mouth, at least the part that he didn't sneak under the table to Wookie.

"If he gets the poops it had better be here and not at my place," I warned. I glanced at my phone for the time. "Gotta run."

"Tell me more about your visitor last night. You said he was a cop?"

"Fed."

He raised his thick snowy eyebrows at that. "You don't say."

"He's getting me after work so I'm going to be gone longer today."

"Huh. So it's about them girls? The three?"

I nodded.

He pursed his lips together and frowned.

"I don't like you getting involved in that." He held up his hand to ward off an argument. "You're a big girl and you can handle yourself. I know. But I don't have to like it. You should take my gun."

He had an old handgun in his bedroom. He was always saying I should get one of my own but I never felt the need.

"No gun," I replied.

"What about one of those Tasers then? We'll get you one of those. They're easy to use."

"No. I'll be safe." To Wookie I said, "Keep an eye on him." I rubbed my dog's thick head before I headed out the door.

My vehicle bounced down the gravel ruts and onto the highway as I headed in to work. I rolled the windows down and breathed in the dank earth that was mildew and spring in the air and let it whip my hair until it was a tangled mass. It had rained long and hard most of the winter with some powerful sunny days of late, so everywhere you looked things were impossibly verdant and budding. My entire body itched for summer.

When I arrived at the filling station there was a line of Canadians already at the pumps. The station was a quarter mile from the border and people crossed over early just to save a few dollars on gas or run up to Costco for groceries. Mostly the job was a no-brainer. We only kept what I liked to call the redneck necessities in stock: pop, beer, smokes and potato chips. The store portion of the gas station had very little to maintain. I liked the easy quiet routine of it. Once, though, we had someone drive off with the nozzle still in their tank and it had been a big hullaballoo.

The FBI agent pulled up to the station fifteen minutes early and parked his fancy dark sedan alongside my rusty Jeep in the corner of the lot. It made me twitch when I thought about what lay ahead so I busied myself restocking the water bottles in the cooler. Suddenly a burst of femininity flew into the store. I had my back to the door but I smelled the oily bouquet of her cheap perfume and knew it was Katie before I even turned around.

"Julie Hall, is that you?"

She stood there, fists on her hips and a red-painted smile on her lips as bright as sunshine. I rushed at her and we grabbed each other in a giggly monster hug that was peppered with questions.

"When'd you get back in town?" I demanded.

"Just this morning."

"How long you staying?"

"Who knows?" Katie reached up and pulled my hair. "You still with that Indian boy?"

"Native American." I frowned and punched her in the shoulder. "You know that. Yes, Denny and I are still together. You still with whoever the hell was your last screw?"

"Of course not, Jules, that's why I'm back in the armpit of America!"

We laughed and hugged some more until she pulled back and pointed to the parking lot.

"Look! Mom even put new tires on my ride while I was gone."

Katie's metallic blue nineteen-seventy-two mustang was in the lot angle parked in two spaces.

"Fan-frigg'n-tastic!" I gushed.

We linked arms and giggled like it was high school all over again. Katie and I had been best friends forever and a day. Since my mom dropped me at my grandparents' farm when I was six and said she'd be back in a week that turned into never. Katie's feet were always on fire. When we were kids she'd spread her arms out wide and spin like a tornado until she was too dizzy to stand. Now she flew out of town for months at a time, blown by whatever cool breeze caught her attention. This last adventure was to travel with a band up to Vancouver, Canada. She was bad at keeping touch. No texts, emails or messages on Facebook but she always came back.

"God, I've missed you, Jules Baby." She smiled and tugged my hair.

Her own bottle blond locks were in a fancy French braid and she was wearing expensive knee-high boots and a too-tight sweater on top. She stood there waving a finger at me as she looked me over.

"Have you even had a single haircut since I've been gone?"

My hand went to my chestnut hair knowing it was still mussed from the drive up with the windows open. I tucked a long wisp of bang behind my ear.

"Of course not. I've been waiting on you."

She threw back her head and guffawed and snorted with unladylike laughter, and I joined in until we were breathless. We were just regaining our decorum from the giggles when Jonas arrived to replace me for my shift. He gave me a quick nod as a hello, pushed his glasses up his nose and gawked at Katie like he'd never seen anything as pretty before. Probably he hadn't.

"Well, first thing on the agenda is we go back to

your place and crack open a bottle of wine while I cut your hair."

My smile faltered.

"Are you still sober?" Her eyebrows went up when I nodded. "Good Lord, really? Huh. How about that." She shook her head in disbelief. "Well then, more for me just as soon as you're out of this hole." She nodded at Jonas. "Which I'm guessing is right now."

"I can't." I groaned. "I've got something I've gotta do." She caught my gaze as I glanced out the window.

"What kind of something?" She winked at me. "Or is that a some*one*? That one?" She pointed to Agent Pierce's black sedan. "You like them older and strait-laced now?" She leaned forward and poked a finger in my shoulder. "I hear that after forty it takes a lot more effort to get them to stand at attention."

I blushed.

"It's just…work."

She rolled her eyes.

"Fine." She pulled a phone out of her pocket and punched out a text to me. "This is my new number. Message me when you're done with your accountant there. We've got a *ton* of catching up to do."

She flounced out as quickly as she waltzed in, grabbing a bottle of beer from the cooler on her way out but not stopping to pay for it. I dug a bill out of my pocket and handed it to Jonas. He took it wordlessly and pushed his glasses up his nose again. I could tell he could care less if Katie took a beer. After Jonas worked his shift the trash can was always overflowing with chocolate bar wrappers. He liked to help himself to the candy se-lection. No skin off his nose if he ripped off the owner and no skin off mine if he bent the rules a little. Overall, I liked Jonas because he was easygoing and the few times I'd run into him outside of work he seemed fun.

When I stepped outside, a fat raindrop smacked my forehead and it was quickly followed by a dozen more. It might be upper sixties today but the rain felt like winter on my skin. I jogged across the lot, got my bag out of the trunk of my Jeep and tossed it into the back seat of the sedan. I climbed into the passenger seat just as the deluge hit.

"Ready?" he asked.

"Sure."

The rain came in torrents as he drove out of the lot and exited southbound onto the highway. Agent Pierce did not say a word as we traveled down the highway. Not a single syllable. About a half hour out I couldn't stand it any longer.

"How far we going?" I asked.

"La Conner."

His voice was clipped and he didn't look at me when he spoke, just kept his eyes on the road and his lips in a firm line. The car was immaculately kept, and I wondered if this was a company vehicle. Didn't seem like it could be his everyday car. Where were the fast-food wrappers and litter of coffee cups? If archeologists excavated the floor of my Jeep, they could track my every movement over the past couple years. Pierce's car didn't have so much as a gum wrapper or a wet ring in the cup holders. On the upper left corner of the windshield there was a red rectangular sticker with a bunch of numbers. FBI code for free parking? If we were headed to La Conner, we had another half hour to go. I put my headphones on and listened to a book on Audible as the wipers smacked angrily at the rain beating the windshield.

It poured until we left the I-5 at exit 230 and then it spit and spat until finally it stopped. The clouds begrudgingly parted and allowed a few rays of sun in, and I stopped listening to the book being recited in my ears. My palms began to sweat and I had an ache in my stomach that reminded me I should've grabbed something to eat.

For as far as I could see, the road was bordered by fields, some already bursting into color and others left dark and dormant. La Conner was a quaint town that attracted hundreds of thousands of people during the annual tulip festival. That gala would start next week and not a second too soon. The heads of thousands of tulips were poised to open and would remain so for only a couple weeks. Their petals were a flurry of garish color as if some would-be painter dumped boatloads of paint across acres and acres of dirt.

Agent Pierce did not take one of the tidy little roads off toward the colorful flowered fields. Instead, he slowed and took a dirt road that had mud fields and deep ditches on either side. The car dipped and bounced in the deep ruts toward a dilapidated weathered barn at the end of the road. It looked as though a well-tossed pebble could easily keel the entire thing over and that was where he brought the car to a stop.

"We're here," he announced briskly, turning the key in the ignition and kicking in the e-brake. He looked at me as if he didn't know what else to say. Finally he added, "The, um, body is supposed to be buried somewhere there."

He waved to the right and my eyes scanned the acres of dark wet earth plowed in rows but left fallow.

"Jesus," I muttered under my breath.

Second thoughts fled through my head but were replaced with empathy for the families wanting their girls home.

"Body?" I repeated. "So not bodies? You're thinking only one and not all three?"

He opened his mouth and then shut it again and replaced whatever he was going to say with a shrug.

"So that's how it's going to be, huh?" I gave him a rueful shake of my head. "You're fine to ask me questions and get me to work for you but you're going to treat me like a mushroom."

"Mushroom?"

"Keep me in the dark or feed me bullshit."

With a sigh I climbed out of the car. I stretched and cracked my neck as I looked out over the field. It was going to be a job and a half to stomp all over that oozy sludge. I opened the door to the back seat and unzipped my duffel bag. It was a good thing I had the forethought to pack my muck boots. They came mid-calf with ties on the inside so I could make them tight around my legs. I switched out my footwear as the agent stood there and watched. He shifted uncertainly from foot to foot, making me more nervous than I could stand. My guess was he had a lot riding on this, and everything about his posture said he did not believe it would end well. I wanted to reassure him. Give him a there-there-it'll-all-be-okay pat on the back.

Hell, I wanted someone to do the same for me.

Regardless of his obvious misgivings about the situation, I was still the one who'd be traipsing in that goopy mud for who knew how long. I just wanted to get it started and get it done. If there was a body buried beneath that mire, I'd find it. Then we'd both be on our way.

A glance at the sky showed thick cumulus clouds gathered in obsidian clusters. As much as I hoped the rain would hold off, I doubted I'd get my wish. I pulled off my cotton hoodie and replaced it with a nylon rain jacket. Last, I grabbed my dowsing rods.

The rods had been shiny brass at one stage but now they were colored with a dark patina. They were L-shaped and a foot long, then bent into a five-inch area to grip at the short end of the L. The minute I wrapped my fingers on the rods Agent Pierce's eyes were on me with a fierce focus that caused me to bite my lower lip. If he thought I'd wave the rods around and conjure up a body, he was in for a disappointing day. It was rarely so easy. When I met his gaze, it took a lot not to snap something mean and biting his way, but I turned and stomped into the field instead.

Arms out straight with only the slightest and lightest grasp of the rods, I began my walk. I tried not to think of the fact that a sixteen-year-old girl could be rotting beneath my feet. If she was here, I'd send her home. Her folks could hold a funeral and start the grieving. I didn't think about her though; instead, as I took slow, even steps, I imagined myself walking a beach, maybe Hawaii or Mexico, where the sand was soft and the sun kissed freckles across my nose. When the rain started I told myself it was the spray off the sea but the icy wind dampened my tropical fantasy. After fifteen minutes or so I'd walked to the end of the first row, then I turned and walked back down the next.

Agent Pierce's hard stare followed me and hardly faltered except when he occasionally got on his phone. I imagined him talking to his wife, or ex. Had he removed that ring from his finger willingly and with relief? I thought about those dark, worried eyes and thought no. He'd been in it for the long haul but she'd been tired of waiting around for him to come home at night while he was out chasing villains. He was all caught up in the act of being a hero. By the time I had rounded the third row I'd built an entire life around Garrett Pierce of the FBI. It wasn't as good as dreaming of a scorching beach but it was at least a distraction from the job at hand. I imagined him an orphan propelled into the life of an FBI agent in order to seek out revenge on whoever had murdered his parents. Probably too far-fetched. People were rarely that easy to figure out and maybe I'd watched too many made-for-TV movies but my imagination did kill time.

My legs grew weary of fighting the muck, and my arms were exhausted from holding up the rods. Even my head was tired of inventing scenarios around Agent Pierce or tropical getaways involving oiled-up cabana boys. I wanted to be home in my trailer under a pile of warm blankets and eating a grilled cheese sandwich. My stomach growled angrily at the thought.

It felt like I'd been out in the fields for hours and it may have been because Agent Pierce was a faded blur in the distance now. Another car had pulled up behind his, and two people joined him. My brain was tired but I attempted to build up a scenario about the two who stood next to Pierce. A man and a woman. A couple of coworkers here to berate him for hiring a water witch to find bodies? Nah. Nothing exciting about that. Maybe his ex and her lover? Come to confront him and demand the divorce he refused to grant?

I stopped for a second when one boot got sucked so tightly in the goop it took both my hands to yank it free. In the moment I wasn't moving I felt three pairs of eyes on me and three collectively held breaths. They were briefly hopeful. But it was going to be a disappointment. I could sense it as I rounded the final row. Would you hoist the dead weight of a young woman this far off the road and start digging her grave? It felt unlikely and wrong. I'd reached the end of the row and the dismay was heavy on my heart. Still, I worked the ditch and the area near the dilapidated barn, just to be sure. It was a half-hearted attempt at best. There wasn't a body here.

I walked through the ditch and held my head high as I approached Pierce. The couple who'd arrived earlier stood off to the side a few feet over. Maybe they really were coworkers ticked off that he'd hired a dowser. They certainly looked pissed about something. It sure as hell wasn't my fault the killer had given him the wrong information. My shoulders slumped. It might not be my error but I still felt horrible that the trip had been a bust, and the worst of it was that I knew he'd expected me to fail.

I straightened a little as I came up beside Agent Pierce.

"Sorry," I said, my words breathless with exhaustion.

He opened his mouth to say something in reply but suddenly the woman stormed up and screamed in my face.

"You're just as sick as that psycho killer!" she shrieked. "How dare you take advantage of our grief like this!"

Her hand came up and slapped me so hard across the face my ears rang and my vision momentarily blurred. Immediately Pierce and the other man restrained her but it was unnecessary. As quickly as it had exploded out of her, all fight was gone and she crumpled within herself. She sobbed and cried in big gulps and gasps and babbled incoherently as they took her away and buckled her into the passenger seat of their car. I shuffled off in the opposite direction toward Pierce's car. I climbed in, not bothering to remove my mud-caked boots or even put the rods back in my bag. My hand went to my blistering cheek. The imprint was raised and angry. It stung like I'd been scalded. I started to shake and couldn't stop. When Agent Pierce climbed into the driver's seat, I turned away so he couldn't see the hurt in my eyes.

"That shouldn't have happened," he said. "She wasn't to know about this or where we were. I'm sorry about that."

"She's one of the moms?" I tried to keep the quiver from my voice and failed miserably.

"Yes."

"Well then." I cleared my throat and buckled my seat belt with trembling, frozen hands. "I guess she's entitled. I'd probably do the exact same thing." My body felt like it was covered in ice. "Could you crank the heat?"

He did and turned on the seat warmer that made me feel like at least my ass was defrosted as he steered the car back the way we'd come. My throat was parched and my belly churned the acid around, making me feel nauseated. I wanted food but Pierce had gone just as long without eating and if he was going to be all hardass then I was too. Besides, I could ask him to stop so I could get something to eat but now my need to get away from him was greater than my desire for food. The rods lay on my lap and I rested my hand lightly on top when we cornered onto the main road. He accelerated as if he wanted to put an end to the afternoon as much as I did. We were now a quarter mile from the highway, speeding past a clutch of small houses close to the road. He slowed a little as we crossed a pothole-riddled bridge that covered a creek.

Then it happened.

The rods twitched sharply to the right.

"Stop the car!" I screamed.

Agent Pierce two-footed the brake and veered to the shoulder.

"You scared the heck out of me! Are you sick?"

But I didn't reply because I was already out of the vehicle, rods in my hands and arms extended. I made my way back a few yards to where the rods had reacted. The straight rods crossed over each other to make an X once I reached the bridge. When I continued on, they uncrossed again. I left the road and made my way down the embankment. Pierce ran to catch up and I could hear him breathing behind me. My feet slid the last few feet down the bank, the mud on my boots made them like grease on the wet grass. I stumbled and fell on my ass.

"Shoot." I felt the sopping damp as it soaked through my jeans.

Agent Pierce held his hand out to help me up but I ignored it and was on my way, focused on the tremble in the rods. They leaned right and I followed until I was almost beneath the dark underside of the bridge. The rods vibrated in my hands as they formed a near perfect X.

I did not want to look beneath the bridge. Still, I did.

There'd been no attempt to bury the little brunette whose naked form was twisted and broken. She had a wide white satin ribbon tied in a neat bow around her forearm like a demented wrist corsage. The swarming flies had probably feasted on her for days.

TWO

THE BUSINESS SIDE of death always took longer than expected. There was no quick procedure to scoop her up and put her in the wagon and haul her to the morgue. The uniformed scavengers had to arrive to search every blade of nearby grass for evidence. My stomach had stopped begging for food again but my mouth was cotton and my lips were cracked. I could do nothing but wait so I sat in the car while Agent Pierce directed the half-dozen people who showed up. It would be hours before that poor brunette would be moved from under the bridge.

At one point I got a text from Katie. She was itching to go out and party at the casino. I replied curtly that I couldn't go tonight. She sent me a frowning emoji in reply.

I took the time to put my running shoes and hoodie back on, then settled back into the passenger seat. I fell asleep after a few minutes. It was a stress crash and not because I felt finding a body was so relaxing I thought I'd snooze. When the driver's door opened I sat up quickly with a sharp intake of breath.

"Sorry that took so long. I'll drive you back now."

Twenty minutes down the highway he hooked his thumb toward a billboard advertising a diner at the next stop.

"I haven't eaten today. You?"

I shook my head.

"I think we've earned a bite."

There wasn't time to protest because he was on the exit ramp immediately, and a minute later we were walking inside the restaurant. It wasn't that busy and we slid into an orange vinyl booth far from the entrance. I looked out the window at the steady rain pelting the asphalt parking lot so hard the drops bounced a foot off the pavement. I wondered if the girl we found had died quick or if he'd dragged it out until she begged for death in the end. My hands shook and I closed my eyes against the vision of all those flies.

"What's the white ribbon for?" I asked.

Pierce had been staring long and hard at his phone and my question caused him to look up, startled as if he'd forgotten I was there. The waitress showed up then and brought us water and coffee and when I finished both within a minute she brought more. I ordered a grilled cheese and fries and he asked for a BLT with salad.

"Geez, I feel bad." He pointed at my glass of water, which was empty again. "I should've at least given you bottled water."

"I'm a big girl. I should've guessed this would go on for the entire afternoon. I usually plan things better and bring a snack and a bottle with me." My hands were still chilled and I wrapped them around the coffee mug.

"That's what you *usually* do, is it?" He shook his head slowly. "This is normal for you? A regular thing?"

I didn't reply. A woman a couple tables over had a glass of wine in front of her. My gaze followed her hand as it wrapped around the stem and lifted the glass to her lips. She took a large sip and swallowed. I licked my lips and forced my focus back to my own hands gripped tightly around my cup of coffee.

Our food arrived and I devoured everything on my plate. He ate slowly, methodically, and mostly watched me.

"I don't know why," Agent Pierce said.

It took me a while to figure out he was answering my question about the white ribbon.

"His modus operandi…his signature." He blew out a long breath. "There were white ribbons left at the scene where the girls were taken." He pointed a finger at me. "That is not for public knowledge."

Mister Serious looked like he'd crawl across the table and put me over his knee and give me a swift spanking if he thought I might reveal anything to the public. I was shocked when that brief vision appealed to me and got me a little hot and bothered. I needed a cold shower or large drink.

Pierce drank his coffee.

"There probably isn't an answer that would make any sense to us. The profilers…" He chuckled but it was a sarcastic, chilling sound. "They'll have a field day over that stupid ribbon."

His hands balled into tight fists for a few seconds. The waitress returned and refilled our coffees and waters.

"You're a thirsty bunch," she remarked.

Neither of us looked up or acknowledged her comment.

"So you get a lot of this kind of…work?" he asked.

"Well, it's not a weekly thing. That's for sure."

I drank this glass of water slowly. Briefly I imagined it was a fruity white wine and I felt a grappling need in my gut that I slammed down, then doused it by replacing the water with a sip of strong coffee.

"When people ask, I just feel bad saying no. Sometimes I have to, though. Like when that hiker went missing on Mount Baker. I don't like heights." I shrugged. "Besides, I knew they'd find him when the snow melted."

"How many?" he asked.

I sat on the question a minute before answering. "I haven't kept count. Maybe a dozen."

"A dozen?" His eyes were huge. "Holy smokes." He drilled his hand through his hair. "All in your small community?"

"Well, no. Word gets around."

The waitress took my plate and asked if I wanted dessert. I declined.

"And who hires you? Law enforcement?"

"A couple times," I admitted. "And some of the Native American tribes asked me over to confirm burial places." I smiled at his incredulous face. "It's not like people are just dropping dead all over Washington State. I'm not making a killing here. No pun intended."

Agent Pierce laughed then. It was a low and throaty sound that made me feel warm inside. He didn't look like he laughed much. If ever. A guy his age who'd been at this job awhile. He probably saw a lot of stuff. I thought of my own life and knew that horror had no real age.

After we ate I told him I was going to the washroom. He left a few bills on the table and said he'd meet me outside. When I stepped out of the restaurant, he was coming out of a bank next door, counting out bills. He met me at the car and once we were seated he handed me the money.

"Thanks."

I folded the bills and stuffed them into the pocket of my hoodie without counting. He hadn't bothered to get my payment in advance because he hadn't believed

I would do it. Part of me felt triumphant that I proved him wrong. That part was tamped down by the remorse for the poor brunette under the bridge and her mother who'd slapped me on the edge of the field.

When we reached the fill-up station he pulled his car alongside my Jeep. I unbuckled my seat belt and went to leave but he reached over and put a heavy hand on my leg. I froze.

"If I can get him to give me the location of the other two, would you help?"

It was painful to look at his face, all hard edges but with tired, beseeching eyes. I looked down at his hand on my leg willing him to move it before this got weird. Weirder.

"He didn't give you the whereabouts of this one either," I reminded him gently.

He removed his hand from my leg and I climbed hastily out of the car, hauled my bag from the back seat and jumped into my Jeep. I started it up but didn't put it in gear. I pretended to be playing with the radio; my shaky fingers turned dials while I waited until Agent Pierce drove out of the parking lot. Then I cranked the heat and took a moment to settle the tremor in my bones. Something about the way he'd asked, his hand hot and heavy on my thigh and the pleading in his eyes, made me uneasy.

The rain clouds had tumbled east on a blustery wind that caused my Jeep to shimmy on the highway. Gramps was in front of the TV watching the tail end of the news when I showed up, and Wookie was on the couch beside him. It was nearly seven.

"Can I fix you some dinner?"

"Nah, I made a sandwich."

I nonchalantly checked the sink. There was a small plate there with a few crumbs.

Wookie hopped off the sofa and stretched slowly. I paused to scratch the top of his head in greeting.

"Guess what? Katie's back."

Gramps glanced over at me and only nodded. He didn't like Katie. No, that wasn't quite accurate. He liked her well and good enough but just didn't like her hanging with me.

That girl is trouble with a capital T *that also stands for* tramp.

That's what Grandma always said, but then there weren't many people that Grandma liked. Me included. Gramps was kinder about Katie and just reminded me to choose my friends wisely.

"So you and Katie going out then?" Gramps asked.

"Not tonight. I'm tired."

Gramps's shoulders visibly relaxed. I sat on the arm of the sofa and kissed the top of his bare head. He gently patted my thigh in the exact same place Pierce had placed a hot hand.

"So, you found her then?" he asked. "One of the three?"

"Yeah."

My throat was suddenly clogged with emotion. Gramps took my small hand in his thick calloused one and gave it a quick squeeze before returning it to rest on top of the TV remote.

"It's not your job, you know," he said softly. "Just because you *can* do it, doesn't mean you have to."

"I know. I know." I got to my feet, not wanting to have this conversation because it made my own thoughts on the subject slippery. "C'mon, Wook."

When I slid my feet into my shoes, Gramps called,

"Oh yeah, Denny was at your place earlier. He stopped in here to ask where you were."

"What did you tell him?" I asked.

"I told him you were a grown-assed woman and you didn't answer to an old man like me."

I laughed on my way out the door. It was best Denny didn't know what I was up to. It would quickly become a thing. And not a good thing. Sort of a hissy fit stop-messing-with-the-devil thing.

The wind howled and blew a small branch Wookie's way. He hunted the stick, chomped it happily and carried it into the vehicle like a prize. When we got back to the trailer, the wind nearly ripped the door right out of my hands. The entire trailer vibrated from the breeze. Wookie carried his stick to his bed and gnawed it happily before he finally collapsed, exhausted as if he'd worked a hard day in the mines.

Denny had left me a note on the kitchen table. It was actually a sketch of me with a thought bubble that said, *I miss Denny.* The drawing was good. He had my hair blowing across my face like I was standing in a breeze and my eyes half-closed looking sultry. He always made me prettier than I could ever actually be. I put the picture on my fridge using a magnet from Pike's Place Market in Seattle.

Denny was talented. I wish he'd use his artistic ability for more but he lacked the drive to try. Or feared success on some level. He was probably on his way to work at the casino now but I sent him a text anyway saying I'd been out running errands for the day and was home now. The lie tripped off my fingers easily. Denny thought I was messing with the devil using divining rods. Not that he was particularly religious but he'd been raised by a father with a heavy moral hand when it came to such things.

"No different than using a Ouija board," Denny said to me time and time again.

It didn't feel like that to me. It felt like a gnawing ache, and if I knew there was somebody out there needing a body to bury it felt wrong to turn away.

Even though it was cool, the air inside the trailer was stuffy and smelled of dog and yesterday's soup. I stripped down to my bra and panties and, even though I shouldn't, I opened my laptop and dug up the articles I'd read about the three girls. Their pictures were everywhere. High school photos of them smiling brightly and innocently at the camera. It took only a couple clicks before I realized the girl I'd found today was the first to go missing. Luna Quinn. In the picture her brown hair was in a fancy updo and she'd carefully applied her makeup with a heavy hand around the eyes. She'd been missing for over a month. There'd been no update on the news yet to say she'd been found. I wondered why. My mind went to that white ribbon and to her twisted, naked form under the bridge, and I clenched my teeth.

Then, inadvertently, my hand went to my cheek. Her mom's slap across my face had been jarring. She was half-crazed with grief and I knew it was the knee-jerk reaction of someone who'd been living life on the edge of a razor for a month. It could've been worse. Some of the missing were never found and the hopeful left-behinds just kept on dreaming that they'd turn up somewhere with amnesia or something. That they'd walk through the door of their home one day acting as if they were perfectly fine and had just lost track of time in a fugue state somewhere. Maybe that was better than the reality. Maybe not.

I hoped Luna's mom found at least a tiny bit of comfort in having a body to bury.

"Rest in peace, Luna Quinn," I whispered.

After I turned off the computer I clicked on the TV. I didn't have many channels to choose from but sometimes I liked the box on just for the sound, a noisy distraction to help quiet the uneasiness in my head. Tonight it didn't give any relief. My mind was stuck in the quicksand. Movies and television in the 1980s loved to play up quicksand deaths for comical theatrics but the public eventually learned those deaths were not a common thing. But people were occasionally killed in quicksand-related deaths. Anyone pulled into the dark place of their own mind knew that a traumatic slideshow in your brain could kill you just as often. The pictures burst inside my head.

Tulip fields.

Boots in the mud.

Luna Quinn's body.

White ribbon.

Pierce's hand on my leg.

The snippets played over and over on a maniacal repeat playlist until my head ached. Previously a bottle of wine would've helped ease the soreness. Another would've obliterated the caring. That was no longer an option. I licked my lips and tried to think of something else. I started a game of Scrabble online but kept missing my turn because my mind wasn't in it. Whoever I was playing against called me a stupid ass and logged off. Scrabble people could be crazy as hell.

My thoughts kept drifting to the past, into the quicksand.

The first time I'd found a body I used just a switch of a willow branch carved into a divining rod. Gramps had handed it to me telling me a tale of how people used them to find water.

"They called them water witches," he'd said. "Not just anyone can do it. You have to be special."

He put the willow rod in my hands with a smile and told me to see if I could find some water. He was trying to keep me out of Grandma's way because she was in a mood. She was always in a mood and I was happy to stay away. I was twelve and skeptical but still intrigued enough by his story to walk the fields near and far holding out that forked stick.

When it finally twitched in my hands and nearly tugged me down an old abandoned well, I squealed with excitement. Then I lay flat on my belly and looked down that deep, gloomy space. The sun glinted off the pale white legs of a toddler who'd gone missing earlier that day. I ran all the way home screaming for Gramps. Breathlessly I told him what I found and where and how. Grandma listened with a firm set to her mouth and told me to stay put in the house with her while Gramps investigated my story. Once he'd left the house, she'd grabbed me hard by the arms and squeezed until I was on my knees and thought the bone in my upper arm would snap like a twig inside her fist.

"Did you do it? Did you push that baby down that hole?"

"No, no, no," I shouted over and over again but she kept squeezing tighter and tighter. I could tell she didn't believe me.

"What will people think?" she'd hissed. "You're stupid. Just like your mom. A dumb bunny just like her." She'd released my arm and clucked her tongue and whispered over and over. "Not a brain cell to spare between the two of you."

Abruptly, I brought my fist down so hard on the kitchen table that Wookie jumped up from his bed and barked.

"Wanna dance, boy?" I asked.

Throwing the door to the trailer open, I ran outside into the dark to the scrub of dried weeds and rocks that was my yard. The wind whipped my hair into my mouth as I tossed back my head and laughed. Stones and coarse weeds scraped my feet and I threw my hands out to the side and twirled around and around. The March wind pinked my skin, and Wookie woofed and jumped happily alongside. The dog didn't care how crazed it was that we danced and pirouetted nearly naked in a windstorm. Eventually I stubbed my toe on a rock, tripped over my own two feet, then landed hard on my ass. I sprawled out on my back, the weeds and rocks dug into my body, and the icy gale pummeled my skin. I looked up and took in deep gasps of the chilled air. Stars freckled the dark sky. Dust kicked up into my face and mixed with my tears as Wookie put his head on my bare stomach. We stayed like that in the dirt until the wind grew so cold that it felt like a burn.

Wookie's worried whimper roused me enough to go inside. Still dusty and dirty from the ground, I fell into bed and drifted into a fitful sleep. In the middle of the night my phone rang. I didn't recognize the incoming number but answered anyway with a mumbled half-asleep "Hello."

No reply came from the other end but I could hear background noise. A television maybe. The clink of ice cubes into a glass.

"Hello?" I repeated.

I sat up in bed and strained to listen. I could hear faint breathing before the call clicked off. I knew deep down in my bones it was Agent Pierce. After that it took hours before I drifted off again.

WHEN WOOKIE SLURPED my eyes awake the next morning, I was ravenous and ate two bowls of cereal before heading to Gramps's. I chopped up a few vegetables and threw them into the slow cooker with barley and frozen chicken thighs.

"By dinner it'll be ready," I told him.

"Because you won't be home for dinner," he said.

I tossed some garlic into the pot. "I'm going to be out late with Katie so I'll collect Wookie in the morning."

He nodded. "If you get into any trouble, you just call me."

"Don't worry." I went over and hugged him briefly. "There won't be any trouble. We're just going up to the casino for dinner and fun. I'm leaving right from work. In the meantime..." I patted his hand. "I want you to think about where you'd like to go for dinner next week on your birthday."

"I don't need anything special," he said but I heard the smile in his voice.

"Of course you do." I laughed and waved goodbye on my way out the door.

Grandma hadn't believed in making a big deal about birthdays. When I turned thirteen she handed me a wrapped gift for the first time ever. It was a dish towel and a sponge and she'd cackled with delight at my disappointment.

Every person alive has a birthday. Don't act like you're so special.

Gramps would still take me out for ice cream and sneak me a few dollars to buy myself something. Since Grandma died I always took him out for his birthday and let him eat whatever greasy heart-attack-inducing crap he wanted.

It was my eight-to-four shift and a Friday so the station would be busier than yesterday. I didn't mind busy. It kept my thoughts occupied. Jonas called my cell just as I was pulling into the lot.

"Hey, Julie, what's up?" he asked.

"I don't know." I rolled my eyes. "Why don't you tell me?" *And it sure as hell better not be you saying you can't come in for your shift at four because Katie will freak if I cancel on her.*

"I got a real bad toothache. It's killing me. Only time I can get into the dentist is this afternoon. Can you stay a bit later? Five at the latest?"

"You swear no later than five?"

"On my mother's grave."

"Your mother is still alive."

"Yeah, but I'll kill her if I have to keep listening to her nag about getting my ass to the dentist."

I laughed.

"Okay. Good luck with your tooth."

I disconnected the call and texted Katie that our evening would have to start at five. She was fine with it, said that would give her time for a manicure before I picked her up. I looked at my own nails as I walked inside the station. They were bitten short and riddled with hangnails. I wondered briefly about getting some of those fancy fake gel nails one day. Denny would think it was cool. He loved it when I got gussied up.

I'd texted Denny that Katie and I would be at his casino later but he hadn't replied. He didn't always check his phone or else he let the battery run down and didn't charge it. He liked Katie and he'd be happy knowing we'd be at the casino. The shift at the station went by fast. It didn't start off so great because somebody puked in the restroom and I had to clean it up, but the rest of the day was same old same old. When I glanced at my phone at ten to five I started to get antsy but Jonas walked in the door just a couple minutes later.

"Sorry," he said. He put a hand to his cheek and shook his head slowly. "It was abscessed and they had to pull it."

He opened his mouth to reveal a gaping hole where a bottom eye tooth used to be. I made a face.

"Are you sure you're okay to work?"

"Oh yeah, I'm good. I've got painkillers and antibiotics up the caboose so I'm really good."

He smiled then, revealing that bloody mess and I cringed.

"Maybe try not to smile at the customers too much."

He laughed like that was the funniest thing he ever heard. Then I tilted my head because I knew what was different about him besides the missing tooth.

"You're not wearing glasses."

"I've got my contacts in. I don't usually wear them to work but I already had them in so…" He shrugged.

"You look good without glasses."

"Because I look *bad* with them?" He smiled again and took his place behind the counter.

"No, because your glasses cover your face. You have a nice face."

It felt weird saying that but honestly I don't think I'd ever noticed anything about Jonas except those thick black glasses. He seemed pleased with the compliment.

WHENEVER I PULLED up to Katie's house it was a weird kind of painful déjà vu. The house looked exactly the same. Same dull gray stucco with white trim. Same crack in the concrete front steps. That unnerving feeling in my bones that Grandma would hate me being here. I knocked on the door and Katie's mom opened it.

"Hello, Julie!"

She hugged me tight and I was consumed in the familiar vapor of her perfume: Opium.

"You look good, Mrs. Cole."

She'd been doing her hair the identical color and cut for as long as I'd known her. She was a cookie-cutter version of her younger self. If that cookie had been left to dry out and get a ton of cracks in it. Mrs. Cole ran a beauty shop in town and Katie worked there too whenever she was around. I'd never known Mr. Cole because he'd been long gone and replaced by husband three or four by the time Katie and I met, but Katie's mom still insisted on being called Mrs. Cole. The house always smelled faintly of cooked cabbage which was odd because she didn't cook much. I glanced around and swore the porcelain figurines hadn't moved from their shelves and ledges over the years or been dusted. Mrs. Cole claimed that housework was a waste of her time and considerable attributes.

I found Katie in her room shimmying into a skin-tight red dress.

"You're not going like *that*, are you?" She looked with horror at me standing in front of her in blue jeans and a T-shirt.

"I'm not a complete idiot." I hoisted a backpack to prove it.

Although I didn't own anything as tight as Katie's dress, I could still get my act together and look nice when I tried and, for Katie's sake, I always tried. Before long I was in a black skirt and silver blouse with low heels.

"Let me do your makeup," Katie insisted.

"Not too much," I protested but I knew it was like talking to the wind.

"With your gorgeous eyes less is always more anyway," she told me.

She took me to the bathroom and sat me down on the toilet while she lined my eyes, rouged my cheeks and stroked on layer after layer of black mascara. Once she was done I glanced in the mirror and smiled.

"Not too shabby."

She'd actually listened and my face still looked like my own. I shooed her out of the bathroom so I could pee. The bathroom had a small window that looked out onto the street. After I was done I adjusted my skirt in the mirror and caught a glimpse out the pink-patterned curtains and frowned. I moved to the window and craned to see down the road. I could've sworn it was Agent Pierce's car that just drove by.

"Hurry up or we'll miss happy hour." Katie was banging on the bathroom door.

"Coming!"

We were halfway to the casino when Katie finally looked up from her phone and regarded me curiously.

"You going to tell me what climbed up your ass and died or you gonna make me guess?"

"What? Nothing." I flashed her a quick smile to prove it.

"I'm calling bullshit. Is it the drinking thing? Because, if you'd like, I won't touch a drop if that bothers you."

I almost burst out laughing at the thought of the look on Katie's face if I took her up on that offer.

"No, of course not. It's just been a while since I've been out. Probably since the last time you were here actually."

"Gawd, that long?" Katie sighed. "Well, you are long overdue then."

She reached over and cranked up the radio.

"Oh my God, remember this song?!" she shrieked.

It was Leona Lewis belting out "Bleeding Love." She cranked up the radio as loud as it could go even though that distorted the bass through my poor speakers. We sang along with abandon and screamed the words at the top of our lungs. When the song ended I lowered the volume.

"That brings back memories, don't it?" She poked me in the ribs. "I remember sleeping over at your place and then sneaking out your window to go and meet Tyler and Dustin. We smoked some weed and drank a couple beers out behind the high school and then your grandma pulled up and had a complete cow! I thought she was going to kill both of us. She drove me home and told my mom what we'd been up to."

"Your mom said, 'Why, that girl is going to be in *big* trouble,'" I quoted.

"Your grandma..." Katie let out a low whistle and

shook her head slowly. "She was the toughest crazy person I've ever met. Sorry, I know she's dead and all, but it's true."

I just nodded. I still had scarred grooves on my back from the metal-tipped whip Grandma used to beat me in the garden shed that night. Katie never knew about that, she just thought I'd been grounded since I didn't see her for a few weeks. When Katie did call, Grandma told her I got chicken pox but I needed to wait for the lashes to heal well enough so I could wear a shirt without them sticking to the fabric. Quicksand thoughts.

"What happened to make you come home?" I asked, wanting to talk about anything except Grandma.

"I like to party." She looked at me with a smile. "You know I do but it was getting to be too much. Every single night. The band wasn't getting gigs at the good places and, you know, it was such a drag hanging out in dive bars all the time without even any money to go out and do something. The last night the band got paid in cash." She opened her purse, pulled out a wad of bills and held it out to me.

"And you took it?" I gasped. "Won't they come after you?"

"Nick was in charge of getting the pay at the end of the night. He'd been going hard and strong with the coke, and when he was stumbling out of there, the roll fell out of his pocket so I picked it up. Next day all the band members were pissed at him because he couldn't find it. I hung around a few days and then told him I had to go back because my mom was sick."

She stashed the roll back in her purse and smiled triumphantly. Katie had always had big balls. Sometimes I wondered what would happen if I ever took what

I wanted the way she did instead of letting the world squeeze me so tight that I couldn't breathe.

Once we stepped inside the casino we were stopped almost immediately because Katie was carded by security. For some reason, she always looked like a teenager just trying hard to look older. Mostly that skill appealed to the wrong kind of men. She proudly whipped out her driver's license, then struck a pose while the guy glanced at the card and then back at Katie.

"Have fun, ladies," he said handing Katie back her license.

"Oh, hon, we certainly will," Katie assured him.

We walked a few steps and were swallowed up by a cloud of cigarette smoke and the strident chimes from the slot machines. We passed right through the tables and slots and zigzagged through the crowd to the bar on the other side of the expansive room. A blackboard outside boasted two-for-one drinks and free appies for another hour. The drinks were free if you sat at a slot machine but you couldn't chat up men that way. Katie scouted the area and beelined for the bar, cozying up next to a hipster with spiky blond hair and large black earplugs in stretched lobes. I hopped up next to her and ordered a Coke. Katie ordered a vodka and club soda.

"No wine?" I asked, almost relieved she did not choose my beverage of choice.

"Too many carbs. I'm a vodka soda girl now."

We shared spring rolls and chicken strips but mostly I ate them with glass after glass of cola and Katie laughed too loud and too long at spiky-hair guy's dumb jokes. When happy hour fell into full-price hour, I told her I was hitting the penny slots. She barely looked back at me as I left.

I perused the casino for Denny. He was a floater so he could be anywhere. I asked one of the other workers and he told me that Denny was emptying ashtrays on the casino floor. Though I tried, I wasn't able to find him so I sat down in front of a noisy machine and put in a twenty. Before long I was down forty dollars but a half hour later I was breaking even. Still no sign of Katie. I sent her a text telling her my approximate location and letting her know to send me a message if she needed rescuing from spiky-hair guy in the bar. She sent me a thumbs-up emoji in reply.

A strong bronze arm came around my neck and a voice whispered in my ear, "How's my errand girl doing?"

"Errand girl?" I smiled up at Denny.

"Yeah, you know, you texted that you were out running errands yesterday."

"Oh yeah. So you *do* read my texts," I chided. "That reminds me, it's Gramps's birthday next week and I found a recliner I'd like to get. Could we use your truck to pick it up?"

"Sure, babe." He leaned down and kissed me on the lips. "If I'd known you were furniture shopping I would've come along."

He hated shopping so it was his attempt at being funny. I hated implying that my day had been spent searching for recliners instead of bodies but it wasn't an outright lie. I had found a recliner for Gramps. I'd just found it the week before.

"You're looking good." He glanced over my body with a lusty grin. "Makes me think I should take you out more often."

He'd never taken me out anywhere that didn't have a drive-thru and I doubted that would change.

"The boss is all up my ass so I gotta keep moving." He picked up the overflowing ashtray next to my machine and dumped the contents into the can he carried. "I take it Katie is holding court in the bar like the queen she is?"

"Got that right."

"I'll pop over and say hi," he said. "Have fun tonight."

He was gone then and it was just me and my machine. I won a little and lost a little over the course of an hour but I was bored and getting a headache from all the lights and sounds and too much cola. I had a feeling I wasn't going to hit the jackpot tonight and neither would Katie. Unless you counted Katie's jackpot as a game of hide the salami later.

I went for a walk through the casino. I popped my head inside the bar and Katie was exactly where I'd left her with spiky-hair guy, except his hand had moved to her thigh and she had only half an ass on her bar stool as she leaned into him. I went to the washroom and then headed outside to get away from the smoke and lights for a while. The Jeep was parked a few rows back under one of the light stands. When I glanced over at it I caught sight of a black vehicle parked one spot over.

"What the hell…"

With annoyance punctuating my steps, I made my way to the black sedan and noted the red rectangular sticker with numbers on it located in the corner of the windshield.

Agent Pierce was here.

THREE

"Damn."

I squinted into the darkness and looked for his tall, lean shape but saw only clusters of people either coming or going. After a few minutes I was in the lot without the company of anyone except whoever might be watching from the security cameras that studded the parking lot and building poles. It was getting chilly and a damp breeze lifted my skirt and iced my thighs. I returned to the warmth of the casino and casually walked the perimeter of the expansive floor. It was amazing how many tall, slim, dark-haired guys there were but none were Agent Pierce. I poked my head into the bar where Katie was still making time with her guy. I saw one Pierce-looking guy across the floor near the exit and made a beeline for him. He'd have to answer for the fact that he was obviously following me. But when I reached the location where I thought I saw him by the exit, there was nobody there. As I turned I nearly slammed right into Jonas, who was entering the casino.

"Did you leave any money inside for me?" he asked, smiling and revealing the space of his missing tooth.

"Lots of money left," I said. "Seems like none of it wants to come home with me. Hope you get lucky tonight." Then I quickly added, "At the tables I mean."

He laughed, put his arm around my shoulders and gave me a friendly squeeze.

"If I win, I'll be taking you for dinner. Maybe even McDonald's if you're nice to me."

"Okay, Mr. Generous." I pulled out of his embrace. "I'm going to go check on Katie."

With a half wave to Jonas I wound my way back across the casino floor where I was nearly taken out by a very drunk woman twice my size. She was teetering on impossibly high heels and just as I drew near her arms windmilled comically. One thick hand grabbed hold of my shoulder while the other clamped onto a slot machine. I waited patiently for her to steady herself, allowing her pungent bouquet of wine and vomit to briefly invade my sinuses. It made me want a drink.

"Sorry," she mumbled and tilted off in another direction.

When I was rounding the last bank of slots a slight movement in my peripheral vision had me scanning the crowd. In that boisterous crowd I had the palpable feeling I was being watched. Suddenly I heard Katie's voice above the rest of the din and turned just as she rushed up to me.

"There you are!" she exclaimed. She linked her arm in mine and leaned in to whisper, "Can we spend the night at your place? Don't want to bring him back to mine, you know, 'cuz Mom's there."

Her words were slurred and her hot boozy breath tickled my ear.

"Sure. I don't mind." Not really anyway. "So you guys ready to go then?"

After Katie scooted off to the ladies' room, she returned with her fingers braided in her date's, and we left. The two giggled and guffawed as we went from the weighty noise of the casino to the airy din of the evening air dotted with drops of rain.

When we got to the Jeep the black sedan was gone. Part of me reasoned that black cars were a dime a dozen and the red sticker could be for anything and it probably wasn't Pierce's car. I was just being paranoid. My head explained it away while my gut knew it was a lie and I had a sickly feeling in my chest.

I played taxi with Katie and spiky-hair guy in the back seat mauling each other.

"Hey-y-y, don't do that," Katie squealed.

A few seconds later she tossed her heavy gold hoop earrings into the cup holder in my console up front.

"Keep those safe, Julie, they're my favorites but this guy is determined to chew them right off my ears."

I made a mental note to put Katie's earrings away someplace safe because I knew she'd forget them in the morning.

When we got to the trailer, they fell out of the Jeep and giggled like teenagers as they ran in the rain, burst into my home and stumbled into the spare room. The walls were thin and every groan and moan seeped into my ears and caused me to cringe. After a few minutes I grabbed a cup of water and went outside. The rain was only the occasional spit now as I lowered myself to sit on the old wooden steps. I drank my water and stared out into the night. Beyond the clutch of cedar trees down the road I could make out the glimmer of a light inside Gramps's house. I pulled out my phone and called.

"You waiting up for me?"

"Nah, just watching the TV," he replied, his voice low, gravelly and half-asleep. "Did you have fun?"

"Yes, but not too much fun." I paused. "You don't have to wait up. I'm not drinking."

"That chicken stuff you did in the Crock-Pot turned out real good," he said, not acknowledging my comment. "But it gave your dog the farts. I'm going to have to Febreze the hell out of the place for two days."

"Don't feed him table scraps, Gramps." I chuckled. "You'll spoil him and turn him into a beggar."

"You raise my great-grandson your way, and I'll raise him mine."

Wookie was the closest thing to a great-grandchild he was likely to get and we both knew it. After some small talk about the weather we said our goodnights and I watched his window in the distance until the light flicked off. I sat there, the cold of the steps seeping through my jeans and making my lower back ache. The sound of the headboard hammering the wall inside punctuated the night. I focused on the sway of the tall weeds on the edge of the acreage and let my thoughts drift. When my mind decided to recite all I knew about the missing girls, I got up and kicked gravel around the edge of the driveway.

The drizzle had stopped and the clouds parted as a cool wind skipped across my little corner of Whatcom County. As I stared into the starless pitch night, my thoughts went to the other two abducted girls and I wanted a glass of wine so bad I could taste the sour sting of it in the back of my throat.

THE NEXT MORNING the three of us went out to breakfast at Big Al's Diner and I let Katie catch the tab. In the harsh daylight Spiky Hair Guy looked like a tired old man playing dress-up and Katie looked bored. After breakfast, we dropped her date at a house up the road and I brought Katie home.

"I'm going to sleep until next week," she announced as she languidly crawled out of the Jeep. "I'll call ya."

I didn't have to work so I spent a few hours at Gramps's doing his laundry. We played a couple hands of twenty-one between loads and half-listened to CNN reveal the horrors of the world in the background. After a grilled cheese lunch I told Gramps I was going to get some groceries. I went into town and paid for the recliner I'd been eyeing for his birthday. The color was driftwood, another name for light brown. Not much different than the one he'd had since I was a kid but this one had a built-in cup holder, the fabric wasn't torn, and the reclining option actually worked. I told them someone would come by and pick it up in a few days then I texted Denny the store details, sent him a picture of it and asked if I could come along when he picked it up.

The grocery store had pork chops on sale and I brought them to Gramps's for dinner. I coated them in bread crumbs and fried them like Grandma used to except in olive oil instead of lard. Gramps had three and he talked excitedly about going to meet some of the boys for fishing the next day. I'd been worried his fishing friends would abandon him after the rush of consolatory visits after Grandma passed, but he seemed to see them more than ever. Growing up I'd been surprised he had friends. Nobody had ever come to the house that I knew of, not that Grandma would've approved of it anyway.

Before settling back inside my trailer, Wookie and I went for a long walk around the property. There were about a dozen acres left from the fifty Gramps originally owned and farmed. Row after row of red raspberries had bushed up from the ground and I'd picked them until my fingers bled. Gramps and Grandma hired out almost all the work until it was just more beneficial to sell the land to those who actually enjoyed working it. The remaining acres were waist-high weed-choked grasses where Wookie loved to hunt rodents. On the far corners of the twelve acres were sheds that used to house tools and maybe still did. I never got within a hundred yards of one if I could help it—there was nothing but soul-leaching pain within the weather-beaten timber.

Once inside the trailer, I turned on the TV and the news announced the discovery of Luna Quinn's body, contributing the find to "the hard work of our investigators." No mention was made about the location or the white ribbon. The feds were playing their cards close to their chests. At least Pierce had kept his promise and my name wasn't mentioned, although I had a feeling that was just as much to mind his own ego and protect the reputation of the FBI.

Wookie lavished me with love and kisses after my night away. That made it difficult to do anything but sit and think, since I was the prisoner of the hefty mutt, but I didn't mind having a relaxing day. As the hours slipped from day to evening I checked my phone a few times for a missed call or text from Katie, Denny or even Pierce, but nobody was focused my way.

The next morning I kept Wookie at home since Gramps was headed out to fish. I needed to be at the station by eight and, even though jogging was not my favorite thing, I took the dog for a long run to give him exercise before I left for work. The air was cool and we puffed out steam like dragons as our feet skipped along the winding road. I knew every ditch and every hump on that stretch of road that paralleled the I-5. We headed back after a couple miles and when we got back inside Wookie noisily slurped from his water bowl and left a slobbery trail back to his bed. I filled up his rubber treat toy with dog kibble and peanut butter before I made my way to the station for my shift.

My shift went until two o'clock and it was slow. I could pretty much tell how well the Canadian dollar was doing by the amount of business we had on any given day. I spent a lot of time listening to my book with one earbud in and the other free to listen for customers. Margie came in to relieve me, a surprise because she usually only worked really late or early shifts. She was the manager and she got to pick the schedule of this station and a few others.

"Jonas's in agony because of some tooth situation," she explained. "I'm going to work a double. Need the hours anyway so no biggie."

Jonas hadn't looked like he was in pain when I saw him at the casino, but it sure as hell wasn't my concern. I was just glad I hadn't been asked to pull a double shift. I changed my mind on that thought when I walked outside and found Agent Pierce leaning against the driver door of my Jeep.

"What do you want?" I could not even bother to hide my annoyance.

"Good afternoon to you too," he said. "Beautiful day we're having. Sun is shining. Birds are chirping. All is right in the world."

"Is it?" I folded my arms over my chest. "Is everything perfect in the world? It's all sunshine, lollipops and puppies today? Is that why you're here? To tell me how wonderful things are?"

His smile faltered and I felt bad.

"I thought we'd go for a drive," he said.

"Where and why?" I shifted my weight from one foot to the other.

An old man pulled up on the other side of my Jeep and eyed us curiously. Blaine was not a big town and locals knew each other either by name or by sight. Fortyish-year-old Agent Pierce in his designer jeans and shiny sedan did not look like he should be talking to the twenty-five-year-old girl who worked the gas station.

"Ya okay?" the old man asked.

"I'm good. Just having a word with my uncle," I quipped.

The old guy looked skeptical but headed inside to buy the pack of smokes he got every day at this time. Pierce opened the passenger door of his car and motioned for me to get inside. I was tempted to refuse but I was also curious. Maybe they'd found the other two girls. I climbed into the passenger seat and noted not a trace of dried mud on the floor mat from our trip the other day.

He's hunting a killer and takes time to get his vehicle detailed?

Pierce climbed into the driver's seat and turned to face me.

"I was thinking that we could drive near suspected locations just to see if you—" he struggled for the words "—feel anything with your..."

"My what?" I blinked at him innocently, wanting him to say the name.

"Those divining rods."

"It doesn't work like that."

"It did last time."

"That was a fluke." I pushed my hair out of my eyes.

"Last time I had the rods in my lap and we literally drove over top of the bridge where her body was. I have to be pretty close for them to work."

"So we should try that again. You with the rods in your lap and me driving over bridges and—"

"So the killer you've got in custody just clammed up, I guess? He's not giving you any idea where the other two could be? Is that it?"

He didn't reply.

"Is it because he never wanted us to find Luna Quinn?"

"I can't really talk about—"

"So we're just going to drive over every frickin' bridge in Washington?" It was a ridiculous idea. "There are probably hundreds. Maybe thousands. It's a stupid idea."

"I'll pay you for your time."

That pissed me off. Like I was some prostitute out for hire who'd accept his money and do his bidding.

"I don't have time to just drive all over the place like that. It's dumb."

"Don't you see? It's all I've got!"

His fists pounded against his steering wheel. The force of his anger was a hot surge that caused me to flinch and shift my weight closer to the door. Then I looked at him, his back hunched and defeated. I relaxed.

"My rods are at home. I'll meet you there."

He followed me all the way, close to my bumper and not a single mile an hour over or under what I drove as if afraid I'd take off. What would he do if I had? Would he put pedal to the metal and chase me down the I-5? When I pulled up to the trailer, he parked directly behind me and waited in his car while I grabbed the rods.

I didn't bother to take my bag with boots and gear. This trip didn't feel like it warranted that level of confidence. I let Wookie out for a minute and he promptly peed against the agent's tires.

When we were on the road, rods on my lap and off to God knows where, I finally asked him.

"Have you been following me?"

He glanced at me and opened his mouth as if to vehemently deny it then instead simply winked. The look was so absurdly out of character I laughed.

"For God's sake, why?"

"Just in case…" He nodded to my lap.

My mouth opened and closed a couple times wordlessly until I blurted, "In case I stumbled across another body?"

The idea was so ludicrous that it smacked of foolish desperation. I wanted to rant about the laughable nature of his assumption but then I remembered what was at stake. There was a glimmer of empathy under my skin when I realized how heavy his responsibility was to find the abducted girls.

"For the record," I said, taking a deep breath. "If I *do* just happen to trip over the other two, I promise to call you."

"I appreciate that."

We both seemed to relax and enjoy the ride. Well, enjoy it as much as you possibly can when your goal is to find the dead. I plugged my earbuds in and listened to my book while the divining rods remained inert in my lap.

Agent Pierce probably had a reason for crisscrossing over certain areas and towns, pulling U-turns and doubling back in what appeared to be innocuous locations but he never offered an explanation and I didn't ask. From what I knew, the towns we drove through were not near the locations where the girls were abducted. However, we'd found Luna Quinn far from her hometown so maybe he had no clue and only a hope and a prayer. There'd been times when those two things had kept me from losing my mind so I wouldn't judge.

After a couple hours we stopped for coffee and pie and to use the restroom in a town so small that the coffee shop seemed to be the entire village and the smattering of people inside the whole population.

"You ever think of moving away?" he asked me from behind a thick white ceramic cup. "Heading off to the big city?"

I put my own mug down. As I considered the question the waitress delivered our pie, apple for him and lemon meringue for me.

"I did move away. Right after high school I moved to Portland, then Seattle and Tacoma." I dug into the pie and placed a bite full in my mouth. The tart of the lemon balanced perfectly with the sweet meringue on my tongue. "I'd come home only for holidays."

And even then, seeing Gramps had hurt my heart and listening to Grandma had been venom for my soul.

"You moved back after your grandmother died." He took a bite of his apple pie.

I nodded. "Gramps is pretty self-sufficient but, still, I wanted to be close to him. He's not getting any younger."

"But you didn't want to be close to your grandmother."

"She was…" I sipped my coffee, then shoveled another forkful of pie into my mouth while I struggled for the word. After I swallowed I said, "She was difficult."

His eyes met mine and they bruised as he tentatively poked around in that abscessed part of me.

"You ever think about going back to your wife?" I countered, wanting to match cut with cut.

"No. She died a few years ago."

Damn.

"I'm so sorry." The fork was midway to my mouth and I placed it back down on the plate and reached my hand to briefly touch his. "I shouldn't've asked. I just saw the white space where a wedding band used to be and thought, you know, that you're divorced or separated."

"It took me a while to take off the ring," he admitted.

We ate our pie in silence for a few minutes. I tried to chew and swallow nonchalantly but inside I cringed for being presumptive. I wanted to ask how she died and how long they'd been married and whether they had kids but I just swallowed my questions with the lemon and crust. We didn't speak for the rest of the time in the diner and, when we resumed our journey, our words were few. He slowed and looked at the rods in my lap at every small bridge that lay over every single creek bed. Jesus, how many brooks, rivers and streams were there in Washington? The answer seemed to be: a lot.

Even though it was probably a million to one shot we'd find any bodies this way, I found myself also wishing the rods would twitch. But nothing.

"How did you find me?" I asked him eventually, more out of boredom than really caring.

"Well, I was going over missing children in Washington State. Your name appeared in two reports saying you found the bodies. Not how you found them, just that you had. That seemed like an unlikely statistic. Most people will go their entire lives without finding a body."

"Aren't they lucky," I murmured.

"I stopped in to visit one of the families since the mom had moved to Seattle and her address was close to my office. She said when her little girl went missing they'd heard through the friend of a friend about your, um, abilities. They hired you to find their little girl who was presumed drowned in the Nooksack River."

"Oh. Mrs. Buchanan. Nice family. At least she was nice. Her husband was a bit pissed that she was spending money on me. Geez, that was a long time ago. I was only…"

"Sixteen," he finished.

Same age as Luna Quinn, I thought and closed my eyes against the image of the white ribbon.

"Yes, well, Mrs. Buchanan described exactly how you did it walking with the rods. She said the river had been dragged numerous times but they never found her daughter but you went out in a kayak—"

"That was my first time ever in a kayak. I really liked it. I thought it would be tough to keep steady but it's really not as hard as it looks. Maybe I was just lucky 'cause the river was calm, but it was kind of cool and—"

"There was talk that she'd been abducted and thrown in the river."

"Really? No, everyone 'round here always said how she liked to swim in the river even though she wasn't a strong swimmer. The river was just too strong for her that day." I paused. "I like to kayak."

Why the hell was I was rambling about being in a frickin' kayak? I let it go.

"I like kayaking too."

His voice was wistful and faraway for a second, and I wondered if that was something he had done with his wife but didn't dare ask.

"Anyway, Mrs. Buchanan said a friend paddled and you held the rods out and about a mile downstream from where everyone had been searching, you found her daughter caught up in a fallen tree on the shore."

The mom had hugged me and thanked me over and over. She'd been so nice and had bragged to all who would listen about how I'd given them their daughter to lay to rest. When word got back to Grandma the price I paid made me stop dowsing until I moved out after graduation. She said she was going to beat that devil out of me. I almost died when she tried.

The quicksand tugged and pulled.

"I'm just going to listen to a book for a while." I plugged my headphones into my ears and turned away before he could answer.

I listened to three complete chapters and was tired of driving around. As we drove out the east side of the town of Sedro-Woolley, I was going to ask him to call it a day but then Pierce abruptly pulled the car to the shoulder. I yanked out my earbuds and turned to look at him. He had his phone to his ear and was talking in a clipped monosyllable tone. Flipping open the center console between us, he tugged out a notebook and a pen and began scrawling notes in rapid cursive. When he ended the call, he looked at me and flashed a quick smile.

"We've got a tip." He made a U-turn in the middle of Highway Twenty. "Know where Acme is?"

"I think so, maybe fifteen or twenty miles north of here."

"Yup."

"What kind of tip?" I asked warily.

"The kind where you're going to need those things."

He nodded to the rods in my lap and I covered them protectively with my hand.

From my estimation it should've taken about twenty minutes to reach Acme but Pierce was on a mission and his foot was heavy on the accelerator as we rocketed north on Highway Nine. We arrived in Acme but he just blew on through and veered northeast on Mosquito Lake Road and kept driving. He slowed when we reached a truss bridge over the Middle Fork Nooksack River.

"Ready?" he asked me.

I nodded but my throat was dry and I felt an ache in my bones.

He took the road over the bridge at a crawl. His eyes were on my lap and I remained motionless, both wanting to help him and not wanting to face another body. After we crossed he turned the car around and crossed again. Even slower this time. When nothing happened he pulled to the shoulder and looked at me.

"Is there something you need to do?" he asked.

"Like what?"

"Like… I don't know." He shrugged his shoulders up to his ears. "Let's get out and walk around."

"Okay."

The truss bridge was behind us a few feet. He started walking along the road to cross the bridge and then he looked at me.

"Coming?"

I took a few steps and stopped.

"I don't like bridges. The kind like this…you know…high ones." I swallowed.

He walked back until he was standing directly in front of me.

"We just drove across the bridge twice. It's strong enough for a car. It's not going to collapse under your hundred pounds."

"One-twenty," I corrected but my feet didn't move.

"How about if you walk right down the center of both lanes? Not on the sides. I'll stay right beside you. Traffic is light and we'd probably cross a dozen times before another car came along." He talked calmly but, when I didn't reply, impatience lifted off him like steam. "Give it a try."

"Okay."

But it didn't feel okay at all. It felt like I was going to throw up and wet my pants and, quite possibly, both of those things at the same time.

The bridge was about three hundred feet long and maybe sixteen feet wide. The metal triangular truss structure did not look weak or dilapidated in any way so I understood that my reluctance could be seen as silly. But fear is a monster with two heads and just because you can distract one set of teeth doesn't mean the other won't bite you in the ass.

I thrust out my arms with the rods straight and hoped that the tremble in my fingers would not be misinterpreted as a body indicator by the eager Agent Pierce. One foot in front of another was easy enough. Agent Pierce walked backward in front of me; I'm sure he felt it would offer me reassurance.

Look at me, the big strong FBI agent, walking on this bridge. If I can do it, you can do it.

There was no way to explain that the panic and trepidation was inside my head and not beneath my feet. *Quicksand.*

Mid-span on the bridge I picked up the pace. A slight breeze played with my hair. At any moment it could become a gust so powerful it would shove me unwittingly over the edge.

"Not much farther," Agent Pierce coaxed.

Not far? It was far enough that the earth could heave and propel me to the side railings and long fingers of despair could pull me to climb the sides.

"You're doing great."

Leave me alone.

Seriously.

I fought the urge to bolt past him and leave the rods in the dust as I ran.

There was maybe fifteen feet left on the bridge deck. We'd walked over the support column piers holding the bridge up. No longer over the river but suspended up on the sloped bank. The rods shimmied slightly. Another step. They twitched and swung right.

I heard Pierce's intake of breath as I took another step and they swung sharp to my right. I kept walking straight and they resumed their straight position.

"Go back," he said. "Don't you have to follow where they point? Step back."

Oh God.

I sucked air in through my teeth and did as he asked. Two then three steps backward and the arms of the rods swung right again. I shuffled over in that direction with trepidation.

"I can't."

"Just a little farther. Then I'll go beneath."

My feet skidded over the pavement in small side baby steps, the rods tugging that way, my head screaming not to follow. When I froze in place he walked over to the railing. He leaned and peered over the sides like I could never do in a million years and with a dozen Xanax. That close to the edge and the yearning to die and throw myself over would be too much. Even now it felt like the suck of a powerful vacuum pulling me to that edge.

Quicksand.

While he leaned over the railing completely oblivious to the vortex that could propel him to his doom, I sat down on the pavement and curled into a tight ball.

Abruptly there was the strident blast of a car horn and I was dragged out of the way in time for a pickup to careen over the bridge. The driver slowed enough to show me his middle finger. Pierce carried me off the bridge then crouched beside me on the dirt. I could not stop shaking.

"It's okay." He awkwardly wrapped his arms around my shoulders in a gawky bear hug.

I did not even know that tears flowed down my face until I saw the wet imprint on the shoulder of his shirt. Appalled by my own weakness and by his close proximity I shoved him back. Too hard and too abrupt.

"I'm good." I cleared my throat. "Sorry…sorry."

I let out a long breath, glanced at him and then had to turn away. I could not meet his gaze, which was concerned and empathetic but also really confused by my complete lack of control and crumbling.

He jogged back to the middle of the bridge where I dropped my rods, then returned them to me without saying a word before he scooted down the embankment. After a minute I walked farther away from the bridge and followed the shoulder a few yards where it veered into the trees. I leaned against a tall cedar and dragged air deep into my lungs. The rough bark scratched my shoulder blades as I pressed up against the tree. I looked in the direction where the agent had disappeared. I'd been expecting him to come up immediately and declare he'd found her stuffed under the bridge just like the other but ten minutes went by without a word. When at least twenty minutes had passed, I thought he must be examining the scene. A pine-scented breeze rustled the trees overhead. I zipped up my hoodie and waited. The rods were in my back pocket and I pulled them out because I wanted to park my ass on a nearby rock. Once the rods were back in my hands, though, they twitched.

"Oh shut up," I told them.

I took a step and they moved with force, not pointing toward the underside of the bridge at all but along the riverbank on the left. There was an easy slope cleared in the brush probably by fisherman anxious to catch a big one. I followed and the rods brought me to the edge of the rushing water and then toward an outcropping. Smoothly the batons in my hands crossed over into a perfect X formation.

The water was choked with tall weeds and smooth rocks.

Cupping my hands into a megaphone I pointed my body in the direction of the bridge and yelled, "Agent Pierce!"

I decided to wait for him to come. There was no need to go wading into those weeds. But even as I told myself to wait and heard his footsteps as they crunched in brush not far away, I still couldn't stop myself from taking a few steps closer.

The white ribbon on her wrist was caught on a branch tangled in the weeds, or maybe she'd been intentionally moored. Her hair was a corn-yellow fern as it swayed in the rippled waves. Unseeing eyes opened in infinite surprise stared up at the sky.

FOUR

PIERCE CAUGHT ME just before I fell in the water. Don't know why I felt faint because I'd seen bodies far more bloated and distorted than this one. Perhaps it was the bridge trauma, which made me weepy even an hour later.

I sat on the ground nearby while Pierce talked on his phone and described the scene. Then he jogged back over the bridge and brought the car closer so I could sit inside.

"I'm sorry." I felt feeble, weak and ashamed.

"Whatever for?" He leaned on the open passenger door, looking down at me.

"The bridge thing…walking on your crime scene." I waved my hand at him. "Take your pick."

"Are you kidding me, Julie?" He placed a hand on my shoulder. "You are the reason we found her and Luna Quinn. She hasn't been in the river long so there could be evidence that hasn't washed away. Thanks to you." He gave my shoulder a squeeze before releasing it. "We actually collected evidence off of Luna Quinn and whatever we find here could help catch this psychopath."

He closed the door then and I watched him walk away. It was probably the kindest thing anyone had ever said to me regarding finding bodies. I let that adulation warm me a little as he disappeared down the path to stand sentry over the body. Soon all those involved in the death trade arrived in droves wearing uniforms and coveralls, carrying notebooks, cameras and specialized equipment. This was going to take a while.

Before Pierce returned to the car I'd used my phone to search up the blonde girl in the water. Iris Bell was seventeen with a promising future in the sciences according to teachers. She was "the best person in the world" according to her friends. If I'd been murdered at seventeen there wouldn't have been anyone besides Katie to brag about me. There still wasn't.

I sent Katie a text asking if she wanted to come over and cut my hair later. She loved nothing more than sitting me down and making me over.

She texted me back immediately: Awesome! I'll bring wine!

Then she added: For me. No wine for you.

And added a winky emoji.

I messaged her that I was out for a couple hours but would let her know when I was back home. Her reply was a simple K.

It made me feel better to have something to look forward to besides the awkward ride home with Agent Pierce. Katie would be a nice distraction. I didn't want to be alone to brood about Iris Bell and her white ribbon.

Agent Pierce was in a jovial mood when he climbed back behind the wheel of his car. Apparently finding bodies did not have the same morose effect on his personality. He gushed on about how he felt they were getting closer to finding the killer. He also said it would be good to give Iris Bell's family closure.

Yeah. I'm sure it'll make their day to find out that their daughter was floating in the Nooksack. I bet they'll throw a frickin' party.

"This kind of asshole, well, he just keeps killing. He

won't stop at three." Pierce started up the car. "The more evidence we get, the quicker we'll nail his ass."

We were quiet as he turned the car around, crossed the truss bridge and then put miles between us and Iris Bell. Eventually we were back on the I-5 and making our way north. The road stretched out in front of us and death was far in the rearview mirror. I stared out the window in silence and watched the fields roll by.

"I owe you an apology," Pierce announced suddenly.

I turned and blinked at him as I thought I'd missed something.

"The bridge," he said.

"Oh. That." I turned away as embarrassment heated my cheeks. "Don't worry about it. I'm just weird about high bridges."

"You told me you didn't like heights and I pushed you so, yeah, I'm sorry. That was cruel."

"It's okay," I murmured and kept my face turned to look out the window.

"The medical examiner thinks she's been in the water less than twenty-four hours. We're getting closer to finding this guy. I can feel it. The preliminary report is back on Luna Quinn. Asphyxiation. Strangled. No sign of sexual assault."

I chewed on that comment quite a while and turned it over and over inside my head. It wasn't until he exited the highway and drove past Gramps's place that it occurred to me.

"Hold on," I said, sitting up straight. "She was in the water less than twenty-four hours?"

He looked at me and nodded. "Give or take a few."

"She hadn't been dead that long. I mean, I've seen

them when they've been dead a while and she looked...
there wasn't much..."

He frowned and nodded.

"Yes, he's keeping them alive a while before killing
them. He grabbed her on the fifth of the month. Three
weeks ago. At least that gives us hope we can catch him
before he kills again."

"What the hell?!" I punched him hard in the arm.

"Hey!" He looked at me like I'd lost my mind.

"You told me you had someone in custody!" I
screamed. How dare he manipulate me like this! "You
led me to believe we were looking for bodies because of
stuff he told you. This guy is still out there!"

"No, wait a second," he said in a reasonable tone.
"We've had a few people in to be interviewed and—"

"You lied to me."

"I didn't lie, I just—"

"You lied."

We were only a few yards from my place. If I hadn't
been so caught up in Agent Pierce's betrayal I would've
noticed Denny's pickup earlier. Now Pierce pulled up
alongside Denny's truck.

"Oh, no." I blew out a long breath. "This isn't going
to go so well. You should probably just go."

As soon as Pierce stopped the car, I hopped out.

"Hi, Denny."

I smiled brightly and walked over to where he was
sitting on my steps. I tried to kiss him but he turned
his head.

"Who's that?"

Agent Pierce climbed out of his vehicle and walked
toward us, and Wookie started barking inside the trailer.

"Denny, this is Agent Pierce. He's an FBI agent."

"Am I supposed to be impressed?" Denny asked sullenly as he got to his feet. "That's where you've been all day? Hanging out with some damn FBI agent?"

"She was doing me a favor—" Pierce began.

"I was not talking to you," Denny snarled at Pierce.

"Just go," I said to Pierce.

"I think I'd better stay."

"What the hell, Julie? You off doing your wacky voodoo thing? Sneaking around behind my back so you can conjure up some bullshit witchcraft to find dead people? Is that what you're doing?"

"It's not bullshi—"

"It is!"

He screamed right up in my face, and before I knew it Agent Pierce had Denny on the ground and had his knee pressing into the middle of Denny's back.

"Let him up!" I hollered. "For God's sake, Pierce, stop that!"

Pierce helped Denny up and stood between us.

"I think you'd better leave unless you can talk to Julie with respect," Pierce told him.

"Yeah, go to hell." Denny spat at Pierce and a blob of spittle landed mid-chest. Then he stomped over to his truck, climbed inside and fishtailed out of my driveway, kicking up a cloud of gravel all the way back to the highway.

"Jesus." I covered my face with shaking hands and tried to regain control. After a few seconds I looked at Pierce. "You need to go."

"Hey, I wasn't going to just stand here and watch the guy put his hands on you."

"He would never do that!" I cried. "He was just pissed

about the dowsing. He doesn't like it. There is no way he'd hurt me. Not ever."

"I'm sorry then." He cleared his throat. "I just assumed that maybe that was the reason why…" He let his voice trail off.

"Why what?" I demanded.

"Why you're so damn skittish, like a dog that's been kicked too often."

His words slammed into my chest and crushed me.

"Just go. Please."

Tears smeared my cheeks and the words came out on a strangled sob and I hated myself for letting him see me cry.

I went inside my trailer, sank to the floor and listened to the sound of Pierce's vehicle heading back toward the highway. I sat on the floor and let Wookie lick my face as I bawled.

My phone chimed a text after a few minutes, and I hoped it was Denny but it was Katie.

Are you home yet?

I replied: Sorry. I have to cancel. Maybe tomorrow.

Katie: Oh come ON!

She sent me an angry-faced emoji.

Although Katie was the queen of the last-minute cancellation she did not like to have it done to her. She was pissed.

I turned the phone on silent then opened the door to let Wookie out. He sniffed and peed on every rock and weed within a dozen yards of the trailer. Once he was back inside I locked the door and, even though it wasn't even seven o'clock, climbed into bed and pulled the covers over my head. Wookie usually preferred his own bed but seemed to suspect my thoughts were in a dark place. He climbed into bed with me and pressed his sizable body against mine. I dozed but my head was filled with sticky, quicksand dreams.

When I woke up it was nearly ten. I glanced at my phone and winced. Over a dozen furious texts from Katie demanding an explanation. The last one was a couple hours ago and, after that, she appeared to have given up. I decided to go straight to her house and talk to her in person. I stopped at the store and bought her a bottle of cheap red wine and some chocolate ice cream. When I arrived at Katie's, Denny's truck was parked out front.

"Great. Just great," I muttered.

No doubt he drove right over here to tell Katie all about how I did him wrong with my occult black magic.

Mrs. Cole's car was gone so I pulled in the driveway behind Denny's truck. When I climbed out of my car I could hear the heavy bass of some death metal song pounding from inside the house. I went up to the front door and knocked. The music was loud and there was no way they'd hear me even with a jackhammer. They were probably drinking and talking about their mutual disappointment in me. The bell had been broken since I was ten so I didn't even bother to try it. I stood on tip-toe and ran my fingertips along the top of the doorframe until I found the spare key. When I opened the door, the first thing I saw was Katie's phone in a docking station blasting out tunes through the speakers. The bass was so loud my teeth vibrated.

"Katie!"

Nobody was in the living room or kitchen. I stuck the ice cream in the freezer, left the wine on the counter and headed down the hall. There were garbled sounds from inside Katie's room so I opened the bedroom door. Katie was bent over the desk where the two of us used to sit and do homework together. Her skirt was hiked up and Denny was doing her hard and fast from behind. There was an empty bottle of vodka on the floor. Nobody even noticed me until I flicked on the lights.

There was a quick scramble while they both attempted to right their clothes and called after me but I turned and ran out of the house. A scream caught inside my throat did not release until I was two blocks away. Then I couldn't stop screaming. Half an hour later I was at home with a bottle of wine. There'd been a second bottle but I'd unscrewed the cap and drank that one on my way home. My phone rang and rang, and eventually stopped ringing because I threw it out the front door and let it be swallowed by the night. Wookie lay in his bed where he watched me with wary, sad eyes.

In the morning even Wookie's slobber couldn't rouse me but my own bladder finally did. I flung the door to the trailer wide-open for the dog to go out, then went to use the bathroom myself. I filled Wookie's bowls and attempted to call him to come back inside but my tongue was thick and cracked dry and my voice was hoarse. The whisper that left my lips came up from the deepest level of my sour gut.

Wookie lumbered back inside and when I went to close the door I spotted my phone facedown near the front tire of my Jeep. I walked out in bare feet, sucking in ice-cold air when a sharp rock bit into the bottom of my foot. The phone was dead and the glass was cracked but it worked once I plugged it in. Texts rolled in from Katie and I ignored them all. None were from Denny.

I called the gas station and told them I was too sick to come in. Then I called Gramps.

"I've caught a bug so I won't be coming around," I told him with a cracked whisper. "I don't want you to catch what I've got."

I could hear the judgment slick and oily across the line as he offered to come and take care of me. I hung up without a reply, then got in a hot shower and let the slow dribbled water pressure in my cramped stall wash away the shame. After the shower, I loaded Wookie in the Jeep and went to the store for more wine. I bought six bottles and would've bought more but didn't want to make two trips to the car.

Two-hundred-three days ago I'd received the call from Gramps that Grandma was gone. I'd packed up my life in the big city and come back here. I'd left the booze behind. Now it hugged me tight like a long-lost friend, and I sighed back into that embrace, feeling almost grateful.

By midafternoon I was well into my second bottle. Gramps came by with a sack of peanut butter sandwiches. He wordlessly tossed them onto the kitchen table, then snatched my car keys from the counter and stuffed them into the pocket of his jacket.

"Take the dog with you," I said when he turned to leave. My words were slurred and I didn't care. "Go, Wookie. Get the hell out of here."

Gramps opened the door then looked over his shoulder at me.

"You've done good since you've been back. This is just a small setback. Get it outta your system and then start again."

He headed out the door then, Wookie happily lumbering along beside him. My head space had been stuck in the quicksand for hours and I'd given in to the pull of thoughts better left buried. I stumbled out the door and onto the steps spoiling for a fight.

"Why didn't you stop her?" I screamed so hard it burned my throat, and I could feel the veins bulging in my neck. "Why the hell didn't you ever try?"

He paused mid-step and I thought for a second he would turn around and give me an answer to that long overdue question, but he just climbed into his old Taurus station wagon with Wookie and was gone.

Eventually the wine I bought was gone and I'd lost track of time. A couple of days might have passed but I wasn't sure. All I knew was that I did not want to get sober and think about Katie, Denny or Agent Pierce. Or Grandma. Even though every cell inside my befuddled, inebriated brain was zeroed in on them. I thought about walking the few miles into town but then I remembered I had the spare keys for Gramps's Taurus in the kitchen junk drawer. It was a quarter-mile walk to his house from mine but I'd walked much farther for a drink before. The car was parked in the back and I knew I could get to the store and have the car back before Gramps even noticed the car was missing.

I was on my way back from the liquor store when the state trooper pulled me over. He said my grandfather had called the vehicle in as stolen. What the hell! I thought I'd sobered up enough after the brisk walk in the cool air to Gramps's place but I still blew over the limit on the breathalyzer. After being processed and officially arrested for driving under the influence, I just sat in a cell feeling sorry for myself. This was a new low. I'd always been good about not driving once I'd been drinking. There were a few ways I justified my behavior, and their names bounced around inside my head burning a white-hot searing pain in the pit of my stomach.

Hours later, my mood somewhat assuaged and repentant because the liquor had left my system, I was left feeling hollow and contrite with shame. I was told I was being let out and that someone was waiting for me. I expected Gramps and was prepared with all the apologetic phrases I'd practiced inside my aching head. It wasn't Gramps. It was Agent Pierce. I took one look at him and wanted to vomit with humiliation.

"I went by your place to talk to you and your grandfather said you...could use some help," he said.

I looked over his shoulder instead of directly in his face. He turned and headed out the building and I followed him to his car.

"He's wrong," I said to his back. "I'm fine. I don't need help. Don't get me wrong, though, I appreciate the ride."

Pierce held the passenger door open and waited while I buckled up.

"So this is what happened because you had a fight with your boyfriend? You just implode?" He angrily slammed my door shut then walked around and climbed behind the wheel.

"It's really none of your goddam business, Agent," I told him.

My head was a siren but I resented the implication I was a teenager acting out because of some boy. I buckled my seat belt and turned away. My sour breath steamed up the passenger window.

"What the hell were you thinking?" he yelled. "You could've killed someone. You could've killed yourself." He shook his head with disgust.

I waited until he was on the highway and then released a heavy sigh.

"You're right," I sullenly admitted. "I never drive if I've been drinking. I don't know what I was thinking. I guess I was thinking about how I just caught my boyfriend doing it with my best friend."

"That's rough," he said after a minute. "But no excuse."

"Yeah, well, it's partially your fault, you know? You insisted I go out and find that Iris girl's body. If I hadn't been out with you, this wouldn't have happened between me and Denny."

"I'm not an expert," he drawled. "But any man who screws your best friend isn't much of a catch, and any friend who goes along isn't a friend either. Also, I'm guessing any relationship where the guy makes you deny a part of yourself has got to be doomed anyway."

His logic stung like acid mostly because it was true. I licked my lips and wished for more wine. Emotion burned my eyes and I bit the inside of my cheeks to keep it from overwhelming me.

"It wasn't perfect," I whispered. Then I cleared my throat and added, "But it was mine. Katie and Denny were all I had besides Gramps."

When we pulled up to my trailer, I climbed out as he reached into the back seat and took out a grocery bag.

"What's that?"

"I'm making you dinner."

"Um. No. You are sure as hell *not* making me anything." I made shooing motions with my hands. "Thanks for the ride. Now go."

He ignored me and followed me to the door. When I opened it he was prepared to step inside and I blocked it.

"You don't take no very well, do you?"

"You failed to notice your grandfather's Taurus parked back at his place when we drove by. Know how it got there? I had someone deliver it back to him."

"Well, um, thanks. I appreciate it but—"

"And your DUI will disappear. Not so much as a suspension of your driver's license. The Bureau has that kind of power. We did that because you are an asset, Julie. We need you on this case. I need you."

I frowned as that sank in. "Look, I don't know what to say but—"

"What you can say is thank you."

He pushed past me, put the bag of groceries on the counter and began emptying the contents.

"Get in the shower and clean yourself up," he ordered. "While I put together a gourmet meal the likes of which you've never tasted."

"You've got a box of pasta and a jar of sauce," I pointed out, a smile creeping across my face. "I think you might be stretching things to call it gourmet."

"And a bag of salad," he added.

When I didn't move he looked me in the eye.

"When was the last time you ate?"

I glanced over at the table where the bag of sandwiches Gramps brought over days ago still sat untouched. The burning in my gut did not crave food. My body was bone weary and achy and I could smell the stench off my own skin. Wordlessly I gave in and headed for the shower. If my hot water tank wasn't so impossibly small I probably would have stayed in there for an hour but it ran cold after a few minutes. I brushed my teeth and gagged when the toothbrush got near my back molars. I quickly slipped out of the washroom with a towel around my body and went next door to my bedroom where I found clean sweatpants and a sweatshirt to put on.

Pierce was ladling sauce onto the pasta when I came back to the kitchen. I poured myself a glass of water and drank it empty. Then I refilled it and got a glass for Pierce and brought both to the table and sat down.

"Thank you," I said. "For the DUI thing. It would be hard to get to work without being able to drive."

Panicked, I looked around for my phone. Did I even have a job? I got up and disconnected it from the charger. There were still a dozen unread texts from Katie and there was one this morning from Jonas asking if I'd be making my shift tomorrow. He had plans and didn't want to work another double. I looked back on the calendar on my phone and saw I'd lost nearly forty-eight hours and almost missed Gramps's birthday. Jesus. I hit reply and told Jonas I'd be there tomorrow.

Pierce was right about one thing. That bagged salad and jarred sauce on spaghetti was probably the best meal I'd had in a long time. I was ravenous and finished everything. The meal calmed the pain in my head but I was mortified beyond belief.

"Thanks for the food and for getting me out," I said quietly.

He handed me a small stack of money.

"What's this for?" I asked.

"Iris Bell. You didn't say how much so I just got you three-hundred-eighty-five again. Figured it was your going rate."

It felt wrong to take money for that after all he did. I pushed the money back toward him.

"You did more than enough to pay me back for that," I said. "Thanks but no thanks for the money."

"You performed a service and I'm paying you." He pushed the money back to my side. "But you still owe me. i'm going to need you to help me out."

This had been my fear. My gaze went to the kitchen counter where I'd tossed my dowsing rods without care. It hurt to even look at them.

"I hate to say no after you helped me out here but—"

"No isn't an option, Julie, and I'm sorry about that. You've got a lot of stuff going on so I wish it could be a no but it can't. This is bigger than both of us. It sure as hell is a lot bigger than your stupid boyfriend and the fact that you want to bury yourself inside a bottle. Another girl went missing yesterday and I have a loose tip on Kari Burke."

Another girl? That hurt my heart. I couldn't look him in the eye so I looked down at my plate smeared red with sauce.

"I might be able to find bodies but you are the one that needs to catch this guy and make it stop."

"I'm trying. I feel like we're close. We had traces of evidence on Iris Bell. Possibly the killer's DNA. That's huge."

He reached across the table and covered my hand with his. It was meant to be reassuring but it felt wrong. Sexual. I pulled my hand away and quickly agreed to help under one condition. When I said what that condition was he only smiled.

The next morning Agent Pierce helped me remove the seats from my old Jeep and then we stopped by the furniture store to get the recliner. It was heavy as hell but we managed to squeeze it into the back of my Jeep and then used bungee cords to tie down the hatch. Gramps had tears in his eyes when he saw it.

"I'm so-o-o sorry," I whispered in his ear as I caught him in a swift hug. Then I sang out loudly, "Happy birthday to you-u-u!"

Agent Pierce stood there awkwardly after he positioned the chair in the living room. Wookie insisted on sniffing his crotch and no matter how many times Pierce pushed his head away, the dog was not giving up until he got a good sniff.

"I'm sorry to leave you stuck with the hound again," I told Gramps. "A few hours maybe and then you'll need to put on a clean sweater so I can take you out to dinner."

"I'll put my dancing shoes on," Gramps said.

He plopped himself down in his new chair and grabbed the handle. The footrest flung up with a loud bang that caused Wookie to scatter.

"Thanks for helping with that," I told Pierce as we left Gramps's place and climbed into his car.

"No problem. It's nice that you do something special for his birthday. Now that your grandmother's gone, I'm sure he's lonely."

Was it possible that he actually missed her? I'd often wondered. Maybe she was good to him when I wasn't around to see it. Kind even. It seemed like an almost impossible thing that she could be a different person. Growing up I had no recollection of the two of them interacting romantically at all or even uttering words beyond those necessary when sharing the same space. Then again, I'd been so intent on her in relation to me, I'd not exactly been in tune to them as a couple.

"The new missing girl was older this time," I remarked.

I'd briefly listened to the news. Sue Torres had been snatched on her way home from her job at McDonald's.

"Yes. Nineteen. That doesn't necessarily mean that he's changing his MO. When you look at her picture she looks about the same age as the others."

He exited the I-5 and took a road lined mostly with tall cedars and long private drives. The more well-to-do farmers lived this way. You could guess that from the prettily painted mailboxes clustered every so often and the long paved drives. Even when our land had been leased at a hefty price to those wanting to coax raspberries from the soil, we'd never had the kind of money that would lend itself to anything extra or fancy like a paved driveway. We drove through one town after another, and I had the rods in my lap and was hoping for a bridge-free day.

For the first time Pierce broke the silence of one of our drives by turning on the radio. He tuned into a classic rock station playing music definitely more in his realm than mine. He even hummed along as the fields went by as if he was strangely happy. I didn't know quite what to make of it.

"Did you ever try and find your mother?" he asked.

The question was so out of left field it took me a minute to process both the question and my answer.

"Um, well, I used to dream that she'd just show up one day," I admitted. "I had this fantasy where she'd come get me at school. Of course she'd be in a limo because she'd become a world-famous actress and only left me with my grandparents while she was seeking fame and fortune." I forced a laugh at my own naiveté and found myself blushing. I added more seriously, "When I was young I'd go to the library. I could use their computers to search but I didn't have any luck finding her."

"She tossed you out of her car like a hamburger wrapper," Grandma hissed. *"Why the hell do you care where she is? She doesn't want you. Neither do we, but guess what? We're stuck with you!"*

"When I got older I realized she knew where I was if she wanted to find me and I was probably better off without her in my life."

Sometimes I wondered if Grandma had treated my mom the same way growing up. That hurt me the most because then she knew exactly what my life would be like and she still never looked back.

"That's a very mature mindset but it must've been really hard."

We were beyond rows of cedars now and farm fields went by my window. Pierce slowed the car to a crawl to let a hesitant squirrel cross the road, and just as he began to accelerate again the squirrel doubled back and he slammed on the brakes to avoid hitting it.

"Why the hell do they do that?" Pierce called out in frustration.

"Fear can make you do crazy stuff," I whispered.

He looked at me and our gaze held for a split second before I put my headphones in my ears.

"What book are you listening to?" he asked.

"How do you know it's a book?" I pulled out one earbud so I could hear him.

"I can make out the tone of someone speaking but I can't hear any music."

Damn cheap headphones.

"It's a self-help book," I said sheepishly with the shrug of one shoulder.

"Huh. I've read a ton of those. I'm actually somewhat of an expert I think."

"No way." I turned in my seat to look at him to see if he was pulling my leg. His face looked both abashed and serious. "Which ones?" I challenged.

"Um... *The Happiness Project, The Secret, Feeling Good*..." He rolled his eyes. "Those are just a few from the past few months. Oh and don't let me forget all the ones on handling grief and moving on with your life."

It was very weird to think of him reading self-help books when he looked like he had his life completely together. Certainly more together than I ever had but then he'd had a wife and she died. Maybe it had been true love, the forever kind you see in movies and read about in books.

"Did the books help?"

He considered that for a while and finally he nodded slowly.

"You know what? Sure." He glanced over at me. "I'd say they helped but not in the way you'd think."

"What do you mean?"

"Well, when you read the books they give you an idea about how to fix yourself and your life. Some of the ideas you think, okay, sure, I can do that but others you know won't ever work for your own situation. I couldn't bring myself to write long essays about my feelings and stuff like that. It just wasn't me. But, in the end, even though I didn't try many of the exercises they tell you to do, whenever I was hit with a really low day, I'd think back to something I'd read and it made me feel better somehow. Maybe because I knew others had suffered before me. Hell, so many people had gone through it there was a book out there just about my situation. I guess misery loves company. Made me feel like if others could handle it, so could I." He laughed then. "Sounds crazy."

It didn't sound crazy to me. I'd been listening to the same book over and over for months and had not tried any of the suggestions. It hadn't healed me but I felt like it had softened the jagged edges a little because there were a few passages that spoke to that damaged part of me.

"Maybe we're all a little crazy. I like self-help books because it makes it feel like I'm learning how not to give up."

My face grew hot and red and I tried to cover it up with a light chuckle but he looked at me like I'd just said something wise or profound and that made me feel stronger inside. After that, I didn't put the earbuds in because it seemed like he wanted to talk and it made me curious.

"I've been researching what you do," he announced after a bit.

"You have?"

"Yes. The dowsing thing. Well, not just what you do but other kinds as well." He glanced over at me. "Have you heard of pendulum dowsing?"

"Yes."

"It's when you dangle a weighted object from a string or chain or something and—"

"Yeah, I know."

"And sometimes people who are intuitive, like yourself, can ask yes or no questions of the object and—"

"I know what it is!" I shouted.

Pierce glanced at me curiously because of my outburst.

"I mean," I said quickly, "I've tried it before and it doesn't work for me. Sorry."

"Fair enough." He nodded and gave me a quick smile.

Ugh. Now my head was sinking into syrupy quick-sand thoughts that made my stomach roll. Desperate to change the topic and talk about something…anything… else, I blurted, "So do you have kids?"

"Damn, I think I missed the turn."

Pierce cursed under his breath and pulled the car over to the shoulder. He tapped on his phone a minute before turning around and heading back the way we came.

"Dakota Creek." He looked at me. "Do you know it?"

"From here? I don't think it's too far." I pointed straight ahead. "You're going to want to turn left at Sunrise Road and I think it's right there."

Dakota Creek. Great. More water. Probably more bridges. My stomach turned and I clenched my hands into fists, willing myself to remain calm. And he hadn't answered my question about kids. Now I didn't know if that was because he wasn't willing to talk about it, or he didn't hear me. Either way, I couldn't exactly ask again. No matter how curious I was.

"So this is Kari Burke we're looking for, right? The one that went missing after Luna Quinn and Iris Bell?" I wondered out loud. "What kind of tip do you get that tells you almost where the body is but not exactly?"

"The kind I can't talk to you about, Julie. Honestly I wish I could." He gave me an apologetic half-smile.

I rolled my eyes.

"The FBI must have a ton of profilers all over this, right? I mean, you said so before. Why do they think the guy puts girls under bridges or near creeks and rivers?"

"I'm sure the profilers would say a lot of mumbo jumbo about it. Maybe his mother bathed him too roughly." He sneered. "I think it's because water washes away evidence. It's spring. The creeks and rivers are moving fast because the snow cap is melting."

It made sense but it didn't.

"Luna Quinn was stuffed *under* the bridge. She didn't even get wet."

He licked his lips before answering. "My personal opinion? Something or somebody scared him off before he could get her in the water."

He took the corner on Sunrise and slowed as the road crossed over the creek. Not even really a bridge so much as a hump in the road with guardrails. My kind of bridge. We both glanced at the rods in my lap. Nothing. Pierce drove a few yards ahead and pulled into a short dirt drive that crossed over a ditch and led into a field. The short gravel road was the kind farmers used to get their equipment on the fields. He turned off the ignition and climbed out of the vehicle.

In the car it was warm; the spring sun was trying its damnedest to encourage plants to grow and we'd been in an aquarium atmosphere because the car windows angled the sun's rays on us. Once I stepped outside, though, the cold March breeze bit my cheeks and stung my eyes. I zipped my light hoodie up to my chin but it wasn't much protection from an icy blast blowing in from Canada on forty-degree temperatures.

Pierce rubbed his hands together to create some warmth. "Man, it's cold." He was wearing a lightweight nylon jacket that didn't look much warmer than what I had on.

"So-o-o cold," I agreed.

With a tug I yanked my hood up and pulled the drawstrings tight under my chin, then stuck out the dowsing rods and started to walk. The sooner this was done, the quicker I'd be back inside the warm car. The rods occasionally jiggled and trembled but whenever Pierce grew rigid with attention I had to point out it was just the wind. With no hints from the rods other than the occasional wobble caused by the breeze, I followed my gut and our history and made my way along the creek bed first on one side of the road and then on the other.

Pierce was so close I could hear his anxious breathing over the wind in the weeds and he kept staring intently at the rods. Agitation lifted off him in waves. It felt like I was letting him down by not finding a body.

"Nothing?" Pierce asked me after we'd been stomping around in the cold forever.

"No." I tucked the rods under my armpits and blew hot breath into my hands. "Maybe this is a good thing. She could, you know, still be alive."

His reply was just to stare at me expectantly with his arms folded tight against his chest. I was tempted to hand the rods over and tell him to give it a shot. But, with a reluctant sigh, I walked on. Time passed and we were both irritated and frustrated after over an hour of nothing but numb fingers and faces.

"Just a few minutes more and maybe a little closer to the water," he suggested. "If nothing comes up, we'll call it a day."

He stepped through the tall weeds along the rushing water. I followed a few steps behind, arms outstretched, willing the rods to move and yet simultaneously terrified that they would.

"Watch your step here, it's a little rocky."

It was a fine warning but the words reached me too late. I tripped over a rock the size of a basketball that was obscured behind a choke of wheatgrass. My arms were still stretched out in front of me with the rods in my hands when I landed gracelessly in the glacial creek up to my waist. One of the rods flung out of my hand but I splashed around and grabbed it again just as Agent Pierce hauled me up by my armpits.

"F-f-freezing."

The mountain runoff that had been snow a month earlier quickly soaked my clothes and pasted against my frigid skin.

"Christ, your hoodie and shirt are soaked right through. Take them off."

I just stood there violently shaking. He moved as if to help me and I backed away.

"Quick! You need to take them off or you'll get hypothermia!" He pulled off his own windbreaker and held it around me. "Take them off and wear my jacket."

My fingers numbly fumbled with the zipper of the hoodie, but my hands shook so hard I couldn't work the simple mechanics. Swiftly Pierce came up behind me and yanked the hoodie up over my head and my T-shirt with it. I wanted to be mortified but I was too cold. At least my back was to him and my soaking bra was still on.

I heard his sudden intake of breath and a mumbled curse as he tugged the jacket down to cover my back, and I was immediately ashamed and mortified by what he'd seen but too frozen to process those emotions. With a quick motion I reached up inside the jacket and unsnapped my soaking bra and pulled it through the sleeve. The waistband of my jeans was also wet but there was no way in hell I was taking those off. I couldn't stop shaking.

He gathered my wet clothes in a ball, picked up the

rods I dropped, then rushed me back up to the car with an arm securely around my waist. He started up the vehicle, cranked the heat and my seat warmer. Leaving the engine running, he got out, popped the trunk and returned with a large sweatshirt.

"I keep my gym clothes in a bag in the trunk. They're a little rank but better than nothing." He tossed the navy sweatshirt at me. "It'll definitely be more comfortable than a nylon jacket with nothing underneath."

"I-I'm okay." I exhaled loudly against my chattering teeth. "God, I c-can't believe I'm so clumsy."

"That was my fault. You had your arms out and you were concentrating. I should've warned you."

"You d-did."

"Just put on the damn sweatshirt and I'll take you home." His voice was angry as he turned his body away from me. "Tell me when you're done."

I wanted to protest but the nylon jacket was flimsy and as uncomfortable as crisp chilled plastic wrap against my skin. Even though the sweatshirt was large enough to fit two of me, it would be more comfortable. Turning my own body sideways I unzipped the jacket, slipped it off and quickly slid the sweatshirt over my head. It was faded and worn and smelled faintly of him. Once I had it on, I slipped the nylon jacket over it.

"I'm done. Th-thanks." I buckled up my seat belt. "I'm sorry we didn't find anything and then I f-fell and—"

"Not your fault."

His words were clipped. He was definitely pissed off and wouldn't even look at me as he accelerated out of the area. I put in my earbuds and turned away. Half an hour later he pulled up to my trailer.

"I'll just go inside and change and then I'll bring out your sweatshirt and jacket," I said.

"How long were you together with that Denny guy?"

"What? Why?" I looked at him wondering what the hell that had to do with anything.

"How long, damn it?!"

He slammed the palm of his hand on the dash, and I nearly jumped out of my skin. I flung the car door open and my feet ate up the gravel drive. He was behind me and stopped me with a hand on my shoulder that made me flinch.

He sighed.

"Sorry. How long, Julie?" he asked, quieter this time, his voice pleading.

"I don't know…" I stared at him with uncertainty and dragged a hand through my hair. "Like maybe six months or something." I dug my keys out of my purse. "What's that got to do with anything?"

"So then it wasn't him." He rubbed the back of his neck and his face scrunched up in concentration.

"It wasn't him that what?"

But as soon as the words left my mouth I knew. He'd seen my back when he ripped off my T-shirt and hoodie. He'd seen the ugly raised scars that crisscrossed my back and knew enough about the healing process on this type of disfigurement to know that the marks were older than six months.

"Who then? Who did that to you?"

"It doesn't matter." My face got hot and I felt myself blush as I headed for the trailer and stabbed my key in the lock. He was right behind me.

"What do you mean it doesn't matter?" His voice was incredulous as he followed me inside.

I turned in my small kitchen to face him with a straight backbone and as much confidence in my voice as humanly possibly when dealing with such massive humiliation.

"Listen, Agent, I appreciate your concern but this is *really* none of your business. It's old news. Seriously."

"Old news," he parroted and licked his lips. "Tell me someone did time for that, Julie. Someone went to jail, right?"

"You should go."

But he didn't budge so he stayed in the kitchen and I headed to my bedroom without answering. I stripped out of his huge sweatshirt and jacket. Then I took off my damp jeans and reappeared a few seconds later wearing my thick old terrycloth housecoat and fluffy slippers. There he sat at my kitchen table with his head in his hands. I balled up the shirt and jacket and tossed both. They landed on the table in front of him.

"Tell me the truth." He turned slowly to look me in the eye. His voice was cooled steel. "I feel like I need to kill someone for that. I need to know."

"Jesus," I muttered. "Let it go."

The barely contained rage in his voice made me uneasy. Why did he care? What did it matter? Goddammit, I wish he'd never seen those old scars! When Denny had noticed the deep grooves and marks, of course he'd asked about them. I'd told him that they were from an accident when I was younger. He'd left it. Never even asked what kind of accident. Thank God.

I grabbed a Coke from the fridge and leaned casually against the counter as I snapped the can open. I wanted to give Pierce the same line about it being an accident but he knew it wasn't. In his line of work he'd seen marks on people and knew when something was intentional.

"She's dead, okay? So it doesn't even matter. Please don't make this a big deal." I took a couple of gulps from my Coke. The cold burned my throat. "Oh no, don't look at me like that," I pleaded.

He looked away but not before I caught the look of horror laced with pity that painted the color of his face as realization dawned.

"Your grandmother."

There was a palpable shift in the air of the room. We'd become, if not friends, then a bizarre kind of coworkers. Today in the car it hadn't even felt weird being in his passenger seat as we talked about self-help books. The axis of that now shifted. I was now a victim and an object of pity to be talked to like a toddler and treated with kid gloves. Pierce just sat there at my table shaking his head with a mixture of sadness and disgust. It humiliated me to watch him try to wrap his head around the idea that my grandmother had permanently disfigured my body. Hot shame boiled in my belly. I felt like I was standing there naked while he judged me, and I pulled the belt of my robe tighter.

"Okay, I'm going to have to get ready to take Gramps out for his birthday dinner so-o-o…" I looked at him and then at the door.

"Oh. Yeah. Sure."

He got up and walked the short distance to the door and stuffed his feet back into his shoes. He had his hand on the door handle when he abruptly turned around and strode the couple steps back toward me, his face pulled taut with determination. I flinched when he wrapped his long arms around me and hugged me so hard and so tight against his chest that I could not even lift my arms from my sides. I just stood there as he squeezed me against his body, my face buried against him and his chin on the top of my head. Then, just as suddenly, he released me and walked out of the trailer.

He didn't have to say a word for me to know that it was goodbye.

FIVE

I HEARD HIS CAR kick up the gravel as he drove off.

"Damn."

Forcefully, I rubbed my eyes with the heel of my palms and choked back a ball of regret that was lumped in my throat. He'd left his sweater and jacket on the kitchen table. I gathered them up and stuffed them into an overflowing closet. Then I cleared my throat and called Gramps.

"Are ya hungry?" I asked with forced enthusiasm.

"Starved," he assured me.

"Good. I'll be there in half an hour."

The two of us didn't go out to eat often so I took extra care to put on a dress and some makeup even though we were only going to the buffet inside the Bellingham mall.

"You look spiffy," he said when I walked into his house.

"Well, not as gussied up as you." I whistled in admiration at his wrinkled button-down shirt and khakis. "I don't know if those pants are such a wise decision though. You might want to wear your sweatpants on account of I know how much you're going to eat."

Wookie could sense the happiness so he jumped and barked playfully at us.

"I'm entitled to eat like a pig," Gramps rubbed his belly. "Wookie and I took a mile-long walk today."

"Really?"

"Well, he mostly chased rabbits and I followed him but, yeah, it was at least a mile. We circled the property."

My mind tilted to the sheds that backed onto the acreage. It was an area I steadfastly avoided. Quicksand thoughts slipped in and threatened to stay.

"It was a cold day for a walk," I said quickly.

"Sure was. I had to wear my parka but my ears still froze. That wind felt like the Canadian Rockies for sure."

Memory of falling into the icy creek earlier caused me to break out in goose bumps. Gramps talked about how spring was going to turn into summer before long and then we'd be complaining about the heat. I smiled, nodded distractedly and scratched Wookie's hard skull in the area between his ears.

"Let's go. I'm starved."

The words were mine but, truthfully, hunger wasn't my motivator. I just wanted off the property for a short period of time at least.

We climbed in my Jeep and drove to the Bellingham mall. The buffet restaurant was about half filled and we were seated in a worn booth near the food. Gramps went back to refill his plate three times and I laughed when every single time he moaned in ecstasy at simple things like fried chicken and mac 'n' cheese as if these luxuries had been denied him for years.

"I can't eat another bite," he announced, pushing his last plate away.

"What about dessert?"

"I can't move. I unbuckled my belt fifteen minutes ago. My drawers will fall on the ground if I get up and I'm too full to bend over and pick them up. Nobody here needs that kind of after-dinner show."

"Should've worn your sweatpants." I snorted with laughter.

I got up and fetched us each a warm chocolate brownie with soft-serve ice cream. After I put it in front of him, I stabbed his with a small candle and made him wait while I asked people around us for a lighter. Once it was lit, the entire restaurant joined in to sing "Happy birthday." Gramps beamed.

He managed to keep his pants held up until I delivered him home. He immediately changed into a worn T-shirt and sweats, then happily settled onto his new recliner. Wookie placed his large head on Gramps's lap and looked up at him with adoration...or with hope there'd been some bacon smuggled home from the restaurant.

I took a seat on the couch and turned on the TV.

"You're too good to me." Gramps yawned and stretched and offered me a languid half-smile.

"Everyone deserves a good meal on their birthday." I smiled back.

We watched an old movie but he fell asleep halfway through, leaving me to feel uneasy listening to the creaks and groans of the old house. A few months after Grandma died, Gramps went away on a fishing trip. He'd been making noises about putting away Grandma's things but hadn't been able to get the job done. Katie and I used the time he was away to pack up all Grandma's stuff. We brought it to Goodwill, leaving only a few small keepsakes inside a curio cabinet in Gramps's bedroom. We bought a ton of paint and painted the entire inside, changing it from the dingy eggshell color it had always been into soft grays and bright white trim. I ran out of money when it came time to replace the drapes but Katie thought it was going too far anyway to change absolutely everything. Still, I replaced the bristly brown front door mat with a pale blue one with yellow daisies that actually said Welcome and made you feel like it meant it.

Even with all those cosmetic changes, as I sat now in the house where I grew up, the new paint did nothing to keep the weight of the air from pressing heavily on my throat. It was why I lived in the old trailer down the road rather than here with Gramps. If the house burned to ash and was rebuilt entirely new on this same spot, I still wouldn't be able to stay the night. The very ground here was tainted, quite literally, with my blood.

With quicksand thoughts threatening to drown out the memories of a happy birthday, I kissed Gramps on the top of his sleeping head, gathered up Wookie and brought the dog back to the trailer. It wasn't very late and I wasn't sleepy. I played tug-of-war with him for a few minutes with his braided rope but once Wookie won he took the toy back to his bed.

I looked at my phone and decided, against my own judgment, to read Katie's numerous texts that were sent the night I caught her with Denny and into the next day. The messages were exactly what I expected.

The first few were apologies and *I'm sorries.*

Then they were excuses: We'd been drinking and it just kinda happened.

The last ones were angry: You and Den broke up. If you didn't want anyone else to be with him you should've stayed together.

I deleted all the messages and blocked her number. The craving for wine was a gnawing spasm of need in my gut that felt like a dragon wanting to be fed. I made a pot of ginger tea to busy my hands and mouth and choked it down, half-scalding my lips and tongue. Hours drifted by before I headed for bed and fought the bad quicksand dreams.

On my way into work the next day the radio was sharing breaking news that the body of Iris Bell was found. It was followed by clips of the sheriff's voice pleading with people who may know something about the new missing girl or any of the other girls to please come forward. I turned the radio off and thought about Agent Pierce. I wondered what would happen to him if girls kept going missing and the guy was never caught. Maybe he'd lose his job or get demoted to some kind of paper-pushing position or sent into the basement to work in the mailroom. Then again, could be they'd just let the case file sit while it gathered a fine layer of dust, and assign Pierce to a newer serial killer. One with less of a propensity for bridges, white ribbons and water that washed away evidence.

When I walked into the station, it was dead. The Canadian dollar had been dropping, making it less cost effective to cross the border only for gas. I cleaned the restroom and wiped down all the shelves but even that didn't eat up much of my time. A flamboyant fiftyish woman wearing dangly four-leaf-clover earrings walked into the store just after one o'clock. She bought a couple of energy drinks and asked if I knew the best route to get to the Nooksack River Casino. Even though most people had GPSs these days, we still kept a stock of road maps. I pulled one out and traced the route with my finger.

"The Mount Baker Highway has construction so it'll be slow going through that way, but if you go left on Everson and right on Smith, you'll end up back on Mount Baker before you get to the casino and you'll miss all that mess."

She thanked me and bought the map to take with her.

Looking at the map made me think, and since things were slow, my mind had a lot of wandering it could do. The casino I directed that woman to was located in Deming. The town where Iris Bell was snatched from. I pulled out another map, smoothed it over the counter and grabbed a pen. I placed Xs over the towns that the missing girls were from. Then I drew Os around the spots we'd found Iris and Luna and I drew a question mark on the spot where I'd fallen in the creek because Agent Pierce had a tip about that area. I wished I could have a rocket-launching epiphany after looking at the map. I wanted to be able to call up Pierce and say, "I figured it out! I know where the girls are being kept and where the rest of the bodies are." But there was no epiphany. Looking at the Xs and Os just gave me a cramp in my gut.

After folding up the map I tucked it into my purse to look at later.

"Planning a big holiday?" Jonas asked.

He'd walked into the store without me even noticing.

"You know me," I joked. "Never miss a reason to travel. Except, I was hoping to go to Paris or Madrid instead of local."

"This time of year I think about Mexico," he admitted. "Hot beaches and sizzling señoritas, ooh la la."

I laughed politely and then regarded his face.

"Still doing the contacts instead of glasses?" I grabbed my jacket off the chair behind the counter. "Is that because I said you were good-looking without them?" I winked awkwardly.

"Exactly. I thought to myself, what the hell am I doing looking awful with thick glasses when I can get compliments from Julie?" He pointed a finger at me. "So you're all better now, right? Margie said you had the flu. Let me know if I've gotta wipe down all your cooties from the area." He waved his hand to indicate the counter and cash register.

"I am positively cootie free."

But as I said that I wondered if he'd consider my close proximity to dead bodies to be contrary to that statement.

He came behind the counter to take my place as I stepped out. There was a moment when he paused in the passing as our bodies slid against each other and it made my nerves ping.

"Maybe now that I'm no longer the geek with the thick glasses and you're germ free, we can go out for a coffee sometime."

The suggestion was put with a casual don't-care-if-you-say-yes-or-no air, but it felt weighty none the less.

"Well, sure, we could do that," I said with a quick nod. Then I told him I had to run, gave him a wave and headed out the door.

I wasn't particularly attracted to Jonas with or without glasses but I was a little short on friends these days. It was probably a good idea for my personal sanity to keep the option of a coffee date with Jonas wide-open.

Before work I'd put a small roast in Gramps's slow cooker along with a handful of potatoes and carrots. When I walked in his house it smelled homey and delicious. Wookie had taken up residence on the kitchen floor directly in front of the counter that held the roast.

"Somebody is hoping for a taste," Gramps said.

"That somebody is me," I said with a smile.

After I'd sliced and divided the roast and veggies, there was still enough for Gramps to have leftovers tomorrow. I brought our full plates to the table and we dug in.

"So Katie came by for a visit today." Gramps skewered a hunk of potato with his fork. "That was interesting."

A frown tugged at my mouth before I could replace it with a neutral stare.

"Yeah? What did she want?" I asked around a mouthful of roast that now tasted like sawdust in my dry mouth.

"It seems she thought it was time she took Wookie back."

My heart pounded painfully. I put down my fork and felt tears sting my eyes.

I looked back down at my plate and began slicing off another hunk of meat. "So what did you tell her?"

"I said that the dog was no longer hers since she dropped Wookie off for you to take care of five years ago."

"I'm guessing she didn't see it that way." I chewed my lower lip with worry. "And I guess you figured out that we had a fight."

"All I know is that I told her if she tried to come around here and take Wookie, I was going to get my shotgun and shoot her for trespassing."

There was an uneasy feeling in my skin. Part of me had been hoping that this was all a bad dream or, at the very least, Katie would be running over to apologize for banging Denny and begging to do my hair and go out dancing. If she wanted Wookie back she was severing ties and she was white-hot mad. Katie wasn't used to being told no.

"I'm sure that didn't make her too happy." I smiled.

"Thanks, Gramps. I've become kind of attached to Wookie."

"Me too." As he said that I pretended not to see him slide a sliver of roast beef under the table.

"I guess now's as good a time as any to tell you that Denny and I aren't together anymore either."

He nodded. "I figured. He was the one who drove Katie here."

Ouch.

"I guess betrayal comes from friends and not enemies," I said on a sad sigh.

"It cuts deeper that way for sure."

He was right. Knowing Denny had driven Katie to take Wookie was like a fine razor cut that stung in the instant but then much later, back at my own trailer, it throbbed painfully like a pulsing wound.

It was hard to get my mind out of the quicksand. I'd lost my best friend, boyfriend and even Agent Pierce in just a few days. The yearning for booze was a relentless, lusty hunger. That small voice in the back of my head said I could handle it. That voice was the best infomercial convincer in the world: *Not only can you have a drink but you can have two, yes, two bottles of wine and it won't hurt at all. As a matter of fact, if you act today—right now—we'll throw in a lot less guilt and blackouts and even erase some of that guilt, but only if you act right now.*

My inner voice was a pathological liar but that didn't mean I could ignore it. I had three cups of different kinds of herbal tea and ate a bowl of popcorn just to have something to do with my hands and my mouth. Boredom was not my friend. Then I remembered the map inside my purse.

With the methodical determination of a wife looking for proof of a cheating husband, I went over the road map and compared it to all the information I had on the missing girls and those we found. When plotted on the map the only thing I could see was that all had been taken from Northwest Washington and, unless Agent Pierce could find this guy, they would probably all die here.

On the map it looked like a small patch of the state but it was almost five thousand square miles. Way too much area to be traipsing around with my little rods doing the corpse-searching-mambo to find bodies.

Or was it? It wasn't like my days were packed full of places to see, friends to coffee, or people to screw. I was actually friend and screw-free.

Tapping a pen on top of the map, I thought about it. It wouldn't hurt to do a little driving during the day. I didn't need Agent Pierce to wander aimlessly in my Jeep with the rods on my lap. If I marked out the roads that went over rivers and creeks, that certainly narrowed down the routes considerably, probably reduced the streets from a thousand to five hundred even.

Not that I actually wanted to find a dead girl. Of course if he was holding on to these girls for weeks and then killing them right before he dumped their bodies, it would be so much better if he could just be found and the girls saved. But if they were already dead, they needed finding. I looked at their faces on my laptop screen and sighed. Why couldn't I have a psychic power to see the killer? Finding bodies using rods suddenly felt really stupid. But ridiculous or not, it was the only thing I had to occupy my brain.

Idle hands might be the devil's workshop but boredom

was an alcoholic's nemesis. My kryptonite. The Volde-mort to my Potter. I needed to be busy.

When I went to sleep that night it was with a plan weaving inside my head. My strategy was to work my shift from eight to two o'clock the next day and then spend a few hours in a different area of Dakota Creek than I'd fallen into when I was with Pierce. It might not be a perfect plan but it was, at least, a strategy to keep me from diving back into a bottle of cheap merlot.

Unfortunately, the world had other plans. I was woken by the sounds of my phone ringing and Wookie barking simultaneously. I hushed the dog but he refused to quiet so I grabbed the phone and stuck a finger in my other ear so I could hear.

"Hello?"

"We're letting you go," said Margie. "We've had to hire security just so customers can get to the pumps."

"Wha—?" I glanced at my phone. It was six in the morning. "What are you talking about?"

"The reporters are everywhere. I told them you no longer work here so half left but that still leaves more than I wanna deal with. Sorry, Julie, but we just can't handle this kind of thing."

She disconnected and Wookie was going crazy. I put my hand on his head and gave him a stern warning to shut the hell up. He stopped his rapid-fire barking but continued to growl.

While I tried to wrap my brain around why I'd just been fired I grabbed my housecoat and walked into the kitchen. My phone rang again.

"Gramps? Are you okay?"

"Don't answer your door. There's gotta be a hundred of them!"

"Of what?" I walked to the window and peered through the drapes. My stomach dropped. "Holy smokes."

There were dozens of news vans and, Gramps was right, probably a hundred people in my driveway.

"Sweet Jesus," I muttered under my breath.

Abruptly a reporter noticed my face staring between the parted drapes and rushed forward. I snapped the drapes shut and stepped back. I remembered Gramps was still on the phone when I heard him rambling in my ear.

"It's all over the news," he said. "Someone told them you were out with the FBI and that you were able to find two of the missing girls."

"No-o-o!"

This was my worst nightmare come true.

"Have they come to your door too?" I asked.

"Yeah but I told them I was calling the sheriff. They're trespassing. Forget the sheriff, I'm getting my rifle."

"Don't do anything stupid," I warned. "I'm calling Agent Pierce."

I went into the bedroom and paced as I dialed his number. It went straight to voice mail.

"You said you'd keep my name out of the papers! Now I'm surrounded by reporters. I don't know what to do." I meant to sound angry but the last bit came out on a whimper.

"Okay, okay, okay…" I blew out a breath and tried to calm myself down. "This is not a zombie apocalypse. There isn't a pitchfork in sight as far as I can tell. It's only newspeople and they only want a story," I told myself. "It'll be okay."

My cell phone rang in my hand and I answered it, hoping it would be Pierce.

"Julie Hall, can you confirm that your supernatural black magic is what helped the FBI find Luna Quinn and Iris Bell?"

I hastily disconnected then stared at my phone in disbelief. Immediately, it rang again and I ignored it.

Supernatural black magic? I ran my fingers through my hair. That was the kind of thing Denny would say but I couldn't imagine him calling up news stations just to ruin my life.

"Katie," I murmured.

Hell hath no fury like a Katie scorned.

She was the only one who'd be this vindictive and pissed off. She told them what I did, where I lived, where I worked and gave out my cell number.

A text came in and it was from Agent Pierce: Hang tight.

"What the hell does that mean?" I cried and tossed the phone to the kitchen table.

I went into my small living room, sat on the couch and pulled Wookie's massive body onto my lap. His eyes were wild and his body shook with tension as he growled deep in his throat. Every once in a while he'd lick his lips and look at me nervously. If I let him out he could scare the reporters away but there was also a good chance he'd bite at least one, which could lead to a lawsuit and also cause him to be put down.

"It'll be okay," I whispered and kissed the top of his large head.

There was a bang and my door shuddered. Wookie ran to the door snapping, snarling and barking.

"Bed," I told him, reaching for my shotgun.

He kept on barking when another bang was heard. Someone was throwing rocks at my house. It was a small old trailer that had its own dents and wear but nobody was going to trash what was mine.

"Bed, Wookie," I ordered a second time.

He reluctantly went to his corner, sat and just looked at me. I tightened the belt on my robe and stepped outside with my gun.

The mob rushed forward.

"Can you tell us where the other girls are?" shouted one reporter.

"How long have you been working with the FBI?" came from another.

"Are you a good witch or a bad witch?" yelled a particularly stupid woman with a death wish.

I pumped the shotgun and brought it to my shoulder. The crowd took a step back and grew quiet.

"You are trespassing on private land. I'm going to count to ten and if I don't see your taillights I'm going to start shooting." My voice was loud and clear but my hands shook like Chihuahuas in heat in a room full of horny Saint Bernards.

"If you could just give us a second of your time..." a persistent reporter called out. "We just want to know—"

"One," I called and aimed the shotgun at him.

Nobody moved.

"Two." My voice was louder this time and I was reaching deep inside for some inner strength.

A few of the crowd began walking backward to their vehicles.

"Three." I walked forward down one step.

"Four," I yelled and steadied my aim.

By the time I got to six all but a couple were inside their vehicles and reluctantly leaving in a swirl of dust down my drive.

"Seven."

I pointed the gun directly at one of the remaining few who had a camera focused on my face and a cocky grin.

"Do you really feel that lucky?" I channeled my inner Dirty Harry but felt more like a skittish Pee-wee Herman. To add to my misery I felt the belt of my robe begin to slip.

"Eight!" I screamed with more gusto than I felt.

I was at the bottom of my steps now and I was tempted to fire off a shot just over his head but before I could totally lose my mind I heard sirens and could see a marked car racing down my drive with flashing lights. Grudgingly the photographer lowered his camera and those remaining got in their cars just as the local law pulled up.

When the officer got out of his car, I lowered my gun and engaged the safety. He followed me inside.

"Stay," I told Wookie.

"You're to pack a bag and come with me," the officer said.

I tightened the belt of my robe as I turned and placed fisted hands on my hips. "I'm not going anywhere."

"That wasn't a question." He spoke through gritted teeth and thrust out his square jaw. "Gather your things." The cop was my age or maybe a few years older so he couldn't have been on the force long. He looked like he had something to prove and wasn't above bullying me into following his orders.

"Where exactly am I going?"

"You're going where I'm told to bring you," he said.

"Far as I can tell, this is still a free country and this is still my property so…" I sat down at my kitchen table like I had all day.

We stared at each other for a few seconds and finally he appeared to rethink his bossy tactic.

"I'm told I'm bringing you somewhere safe. FBI orders I'm guessing because we don't have the manpower locally to protect you from reporters. I have my orders."

He looked around my small trailer with disdain.

"The FBI isn't paying as well as I thought," he remarked.

It rankled but I let it slide because obviously Agent Pierce had sent him and, at the moment, this was all I had.

"What about my dog?"

"I was told to bring you and only you."

I went into my bedroom and loaded up a small bag and then I called Gramps and told him what was happening.

"Go with him and just call me when you get to where you're going," Gramps replied. "Leave the mutt with me. We've got rabbits to hunt."

"But, Gramps, the reporters will be back. They'll probably harass you. We can put Wookie in a kennel and you can come with me."

"I'm not leaving my house and that's final, young lady," Gramps said. "Bring your big sack of dog food and treats when you come. We'll be fine."

With a grunt of agreement I disconnected. At Mr. Bossy's insistence, I dressed quickly in jeans and a T-shirt and pulled a sweatshirt over top. Since I didn't know how long I'd be gone, I grabbed my gym bag and tossed in a few changes of clothes, some toiletries, a jacket, my boots and, of course, my rods. I stuffed my laptop and phone charger on top of all the clothes and then grabbed my map and a secret stash of gummy bears.

The officer took the heavy bag and put it in his trunk while I hefted about twenty-five pounds of dog food and did the same. I snapped a leash on Wookie just in case he spied a wayward reporter on our way to the car and decided he wanted to snack on an ankle. We drove up the bumpy gravel road half a mile to Gramps's place, and Wookie happily bounded out of the car and up to the door.

The cop stayed leaning against the hood of his car while I hauled Wookie and his dog food inside the house.

For Wookie this was just like any other day his mamma would be going to work and he'd be hanging with Gramps, but for me it had an uneasiness about it.

"I don't like it." I looked through Gramps's drapes at the cop waiting for me. "I'm leaving my house just because Katie couldn't keep her stupid mouth shut. I'm sure she's the one who called the newspeople."

"Katie?" Gramps thought about it a beat and nodded. "Guess that makes sense. She always had a mean streak."

"I don't want to go. What about you and Wookie?"

"Now don't you be worrying about us. We can take care of ourselves. Maybe we'll take a fishing trip."

Gramps pulled me into a hug. He wasn't one for physical displays of affection and the brief embrace brought a lump to my throat.

"Besides, Agent Pierce called and said he was going to have a big temporary fence put up across the driveway to at least keep them reporters off the yard."

"He called you?"

"He sure did." Gramps made shooing motions. "Now go. Be safe and do what you were meant to do. Let your bright light shine, little girl."

I buried my face in his neck as I returned to hug him tighter.

"I don't have a light, Gramps. I don't." I sniffed. "I'm just a big weirdo with some stupid metal sticks."

He pulled me away and with a firm grasp of my arms he gave me a sharp shake.

"We both know you are definitely not made of sugar and spice and all things nice. You are tough as nails and smart as a whip. Nobody gets you down. Got it?" He turned away from me and headed toward his bedroom. As he walked away he mumbled, "Go get 'em, sweetheart. Help them catch the bad guy."

Outside, I stopped for a second and cracked my knuckles and gave myself a little pep talk, then walked toward the car. The officer stood there with the back door held open and a let's-get-this-over-with look in his eyes. Once he gunned the accelerator, quite literally leaving my home in the dust, I settled back into the seat and tried to get a grip. Gramps was wrong. I wasn't tough as nails. I was a jelly sandwich on soft white bread. With maybe a little tenacious green mold on the crust. As we angled off the drive and encountered all the reporters waiting, I sank low in the seat and covered my face with my hands.

When some of the news vans were determined to follow us down the highway, the officer put on his lights and sirens and put pedal to the metal until they were a distant memory. I caught the crooked smile on his face in the rearview mirror. It was difficult to ignore that my predicament had probably made his day; possibly his year.

After almost forty-five minutes heading south on the I-5, he took an exit near Burlington and wove through side streets before stopping in front of a two-level motor inn with outside corridors. Wordlessly he got out, popped the trunk, retrieved my bag and then opened my door, tossing me a faded navy Mariners ball cap and a pair of wide-framed dark sunglasses.

"Put those on," he said. "Tuck your hair up under the hat."

It seemed like overkill. I couldn't see a news reporter anywhere. As a matter of fact, there wasn't a single other person in the weed-choked asphalt lot. Just a half-dozen older cars and a woman pushing a cleaning cart filled with dirty laundry. Still, I did as I was told with the hat and glasses and he walked me up to the second floor and opened the door to a dimly lit room. After tossing my bag on the bed he held out his hand.

"I'm to take your cell phone."

"What? Why?"

"In case anybody is tracking it and also to make it less tempting to answer all the reporters who'll be calling." He handed me an old flip phone. "You can use this one in the meantime to stay in touch with your grandfather. I imagine the feds will contact you on that too."

I'd turned my phone off when it wouldn't stop ringing and now I begrudgingly dug it out of my pocket and turned it over.

He turned to leave and then said, "Oh yeah. You're not to leave here or tell anyone where you are. Including friends and family. You keep the drapes closed and sit tight until someone calls you on that." He pointed to the old phone in my hand.

"How am I supposed to eat if I can't leave?"

"Someone is supposed to drop by a bag of groceries later."

He tossed the room key on the bed next to my bag and was gone.

First thing I did was call Gramps. It went to the machine first but as soon as he heard my voice he picked up.

"I'm at some motel," I told him. "Not the Ritz that's for sure. This is the phone I'll be using. I don't even know the number."

"When was the last time you were in a hotel? Treat it like a holiday," he said brightly. "Sleep, watch television… relax."

I looked around the depressing room with the old-fashioned décor and chuckled softly.

"Sure. I'll do that." I laughed. "I guess things could be worse. You okay? Anyone bothering you?"

"Nobody's come onto the property since they parked a cruiser at the end of our drive. The phone's been a bit nuts but I'm just letting 'em all go to the machine. Wookie and I are planning a fishing trip if the weather holds so don't worry if you can't get hold of me."

We said our goodbyes and I checked out my new hovel away from home. The last hotel I'd stayed at was years ago. I'd woken up after a bender next to a man I didn't know. It was not exactly a spa day in paradise. This room was depressing and old. The furniture, carpet and drapes were brown and green and circa nineteen-seventy but at least it was clean. Although the purple flowered bedspread was the only thing not green or gold in the room, I stripped it off the bed and tossed it in a corner. I'd heard hotel bedspreads weren't regularly washed. I collapsed onto the center of the saggy queen-sized bed and sighed. There was a small white refrigerator and microwave in the corner. Even the small bathroom had brown linoleum and a beigey sink and toilet. I turned every light on and still the room was dark so I pulled off the lampshades to give the bulbs a chance. It helped only a bit.

It felt like I'd been stuck in the room forever but in reality it had been maybe fifteen minutes. Finally, I just clicked on the television. I switched to a news channel and the first thing I saw was my own face. There I was standing on the steps of my run-down trailer in a housecoat that threatened to part and reveal all that God gave me while I yelled and waved a shotgun around. I looked positively depraved.

Beneath the clip of me yelling was the headline: Psychic Witch Helps FBI.

If the picture of me in the housecoat wasn't enough, they showed other shots of me: school pictures where I had hollow eyes and stringy, unwashed hair and also my employee ID from a place I'd worked years ago when I was still regularly swimming in a lake of chardonnay.

A serial killer on the loose was big news, but add to that some crazed girl with supposed psychic powers and the story exploded. I watched report after report on every channel I could find. It sickened me but I couldn't bring myself to turn it off. Every time I tried to think of something else, that something was always Denny with Katie followed up with a powerful yearning for some cheap boxed wine.

After a while a knock sounded at the door. I looked through the peephole and saw a woman of about forty in a tidy suit holding two grocery bags. The officer had mentioned someone coming by with groceries so I opened the door.

"Rule number one," the woman said as she pushed her way inside. "Do *not* open the door." She held up federal identification but it disappeared back in her pocket before I caught her name. "You only open it if you receive a text or phone call in advance."

"Okay, but nobody texted or called and yet here you are."

"That's because—" she grabbed the Do Not Disturb sign, opened the door and stuck it on the outside "—the newbies never listen."

She strode inside and clicked off the TV.

"Watching that stuff won't do you any good." Then she looked me up and down and shook her head. "So you're Garrett's little secret, huh? His little psychic Annie Oakley?"

I felt myself turn crimson. "Um, I didn't get your name?"

"Jill. I'm your keeper."

"My…?"

"Your keeper. I'll be checking in with you to make sure you're holding up okay and you'll contact me if there are any issues." She looked me firmly in the eye. "To be clear, there will *not* be any issues unless you break the rules like rule number one, opening the door, and rule number two, leaving this room." She pointed to the phone I'd been given. "My phone number is already programmed in that phone. From now on I'll text you before I come by. Rule number three is no contact with anyone besides me, and we're letting you also contact your grandfather once a day."

"But what about Agent Pierce? I thought—"

"Don't worry your pretty little head about him. He's off chasing bad guys. I'm guessing if he needs you for any, um, whatever it is you do, he'll call you up. He has this new number."

"Okay, but I don't have his number so I can't just call him."

"Right. You can't. If there are any issues, you call me. If I feel he needs to know, I'll give him a ring."

"Okay." I licked my lips nervously. "But I was told they're putting up a fence to keep reporters off my property so why can't I just be home?"

"The Bureau doesn't want to take any chances about you revealing things about the case that you might know and, besides, you're much safer here because of all the death threats."

"Death threats?"

"Sure, honey, your very existence has lit a fire under every screwball and nutcase in the entire Pacific Northwest." She waved her hand in the direction of the television. "Or haven't you figured that out by now?"

"Oh." I lowered myself onto the edge of the bed and let that sink in. "But my grandfather and my dog—"

"We've got people watching them." She turned away, grabbed the grocery sack and began to empty it on the small corner table. There was a lot of instant and microwavable food, some feminine hygiene items, a loaf of bread and a small jar each of peanut butter and jam. Lastly, she held up a box of hair dye.

"You ever been blonde before?"

"No." My hand went protectively to the top of my head.

"Well, you're in for a treat."

She opened the box and snapped on rubber gloves. An hour later my hair was "natural ash blond" according to the box. I thought we were done, but then Jill pulled out some scissors and started cutting. She snipped off about eight inches until my hair was cut into a wispy bob. When I looked in the mirror I almost didn't recognize myself.

"Holy smokes."

"You're lucky it was me," she remarked. "I actually took a few classes in hairdressing before joining the Bureau. If you'd had one of the other agents watching you there's a chance your head would look like it's been hacked at with a weed-whacker."

"Oh. Thank you" is what I said but I didn't feel thankful at all. "If I'm not leaving here until things are good, then why the new hair?"

"We have no idea how long you'll be here. And in case we need you to help find a body on-site, we don't want you easily recognizable." She then added, "Oh yeah, there's also these."

She tossed me an eyeglass case. I opened it up to see rectangular glasses with blue plastic frames.

"They're nonprescription," she said. "Put them on."

I did and they were a little tight and pinched my temples. She grabbed the Mariners ball cap and put it on my new blond head.

"Your own grandfather wouldn't recognize you."

I glanced at my reflection. She was right. I'd been erased. My eyes briefly burned with emotion.

"So are these the things you use?" She walked over and picked up my dowsing rods, which were sticking out of my bag.

I didn't want her touching them but I just nodded wordlessly.

"You know, I had an aunt that did dowsing." She put the rods back in my bag.

"You did?"

"Yup. Well, not like you. Not for bodies or even for

water. She did pendulum dowsing. Are you familiar with that?"

I nodded and Jill smiled at me like we were buddies now since we'd found a common thread. Jesus, I hoped she didn't want to paint our nails, giggle about boys or sing "Kumbaya."

"Yeah, my aunt used to take her wedding ring and dangle it by a long thread and then we'd ask yes or no questions. If it swung in a circle the answer was yes and if it went back and forth the answer was no."

My thoughts got all sticky and dark. At Katie's four-teenth birthday sleepover she brought out a long chain with a crystal so that everyone could take turns asking the crystal yes or no questions. The questions were sup-posed to be secret but, of course, the girls all shared af-terward the question that they'd asked and, predictably, the questions were all boy related. Did he like me? Will he ask me out? Will he kiss me?

When it was my turn I politely declined. Katie tried to insist and pouted when I wouldn't give in but even-tually let it go. I'd been afraid that the crystal might show me something far worse than a boyfriend who didn't like me.

"I did some checking and, you know, Albert Ein-stein was into dowsing. He thought it had to do with electromagnetism. He said just as birds migrate by fol-lowing a magnetic field, dowsers go after energy that isn't seen and—"

"Yeah, I know!" I didn't mean to shout. I coughed and cleared my throat and then added quietly, "I've done a little research on the subject myself over the years."

"I bet you have." Jill narrowed her eyes and regarded me coolly. "Well, I guess that's it for now." She glanced at her phone. "I've gotta run. You have my number if you need me. Before I leave, repeat the rules back to me."

God, seriously?

"Rule number one, don't open the door unless you text first. Rule number two, don't leave the room. Rule number three, I can only contact you or my grandfather." I reined in my sarcastic tone with a ton of effort using the years I'd had at mastering a blank face and tone, courtesy of my grandmother.

"You got it, kiddo. Now, lock the dead bolt when I'm gone."

As soon as she left I locked the door and exhaled loudly. I didn't know what to do with myself. It had only been a few hours but I missed Gramps and Wookie and having a job to go to. I looked through the groceries and ate an apple and a muffin that was more like cake. The people in the next room had young children and I listened to them bouncing on the bed and laughing. They were maybe five and seven years old. It made me smile. I listened to the dad chase them around the room pretending to be a monster and then the mom gently admonished him for disturbing others in the motel. It felt good and normal. Eventually they went out and I turned the TV back on to the news and saw the footage with my crazy ass outside the trailer with my shotgun.

"I'm never going to live that one down," I mumbled. "I'm going to be a short-haired blonde for the rest of my life." I snagged another cakelike muffin. "And if I gain fifty pounds that'll help the disguise."

They replayed the same crazy-me clip over and over.

Things got kind of interesting when the news station interviewed someone from the university who legitimized dowsing. She talked about the history of dowsing

for water and mentioned how it's been called witching
and divining as well but even now it was considered a
reasonable way for farmers to look for wells. She also
said that in the late nineteen-sixties the marines used
divining to find tunnels in Vietnam and in the eighties
the Norwegian army used dowsers to find dozens of sol-
diers buried in an avalanche. I hadn't known about that
and I found myself becoming very still as I listened. She
mentioned the different kind of dowsing using L-rods
like mine and then even brought up pendulum dowsing where people ask yes or no questions. When asked
if she'd heard of dowsing to find bodies she admitted
she hadn't heard of it being used in this way before but
confirmed that dowsing had been used to locate unmarked graves.

"So there!" I fist-pumped the air and shouted at the
television, feeling vindicated.

After the news I dug out the map and my laptop and
brought them to the small desk-like table in the corner.
I'd given up life as I knew it for these missing and dead
girls. I wanted to feel like I knew the case inside and
out. I put the names on the map:

Iris Bell taken from Maple Falls.

Luna Quinn gone from Arlington.

Kari Burke from the town of Alger.

Sue Torres missing from Burlington.

After I put their names on top of their town I reviewed
the spots where Iris and Luna were found. Then I stared
hard as if expecting that my low-tech gas-station-map
approach could possibly compete with the FBI's investigative techniques. When I was riding around with Agent
Pierce I'd felt like I was doing something worthwhile.
He made me feel important. Now he'd pawned me off

on Jill to be taken care of in a cheap motel. I tossed the map aside in frustration.

Next to the motel phone was a card indicating that Wi-Fi was free. I started up my laptop and was impressed because things loaded quickly. The first thing I did was go on social media. I'd signed up for Facebook because Katie had insisted it would be a cool and fun way to keep in touch when she wasn't in town. Mostly that meant that I would "like" the pictures she posted online but have no real interaction with her at all. Now when I looked at my page it was riddled with hateful messages. Random strangers called me a satanic witch who should be burned at the stake. People who knew me said much worse things. I fumbled through the settings and finally learned how to delete my profile. Too bad the delete button didn't work as easily in my head.

The television in the room got pay-per-view. I figured the FBI was paying the tab for the room and decided that, even if they balked at the cost of a show, I'd just pay them back. I chose a romantic comedy, which was silly in its simplicity but made me almost smile and nearly forget about the crazy show that was my current situation and the fact that I'd kill for a bottle of wine. The movie coated my brain with thoughts of happily-ever-afters, making it much easier to drift off to sleep.

A couple hours into my sleep there was a crash in the room next door followed by the mom shrieking at the kids to settle down and then the skin-on-skin reverberation of a slap when someone disobeyed. I winced at the sound and my hand shook as I reached for my cell phone so I could put my headphones in my ears. Then I realized I still had the earbuds but my phone was with Jill. The kid who'd been slapped was wailing loudly.

This wasn't a bad thing. Kids who were beat regularly didn't cry like that. With an exasperated sigh I clicked on the TV to a music station and let Top 40 drown out the noise. When I woke up the next morning I felt like I'd fought dragons all night.

The room had a two-cup drip coffeemaker that made pouches of the worst coffee possible. I made a pot and brought a cup to the corner desk, where I cracked open my laptop.

After viewing the news websites I was relieved to see there'd been a cop killed in Seattle and that bumped me off the top five stories. Not happy about a cop killing, just thrilled I was no longer the center of attention. However, a serial killer on the loose in the Pacific Northwest was not the kind of story that would go away.

Since the laptop was open I decided to open my email. "Wow!"

My spam filter caught most of the emails I ever got. Rarely did anyone ever send me any kind of actual mail that wasn't selling me something. Now there were over two hundred messages in my inbox. It was seven o'clock in the morning and I had nothing but time. I refilled my mug with coffee and ate another of the cakelike muffins in Jill's supply. Then I cracked my knuckles and sat down to go through my mail.

Since I figured there'd be hours to do this, I began to separate the emails as I read them and move them to different folders. I made a folder for the crazies and another for the requests for interviews. The majority of the messages could be moved into one of those two files. The third folder I made was dowsing-related requests. People wrote me for help finding lost relatives and some of those messages were from far away. A mom in Australia offered to pay for my travel to help locate the remains of her son. There was a man who wanted help finding the body of his dad who was an Alzheimer's patient who'd wandered into a Colorado forest the year before. Some offered me huge sums of money. Others said they couldn't afford to pay at all. I felt like I should reply to each and every one but I didn't know how or what to say so I just moved their messages into a folder marked Jobs.

Halfway through the couple hundred emails there was one I recognized. It was Jonas from work:

Hey there, I tried texting and calling but never got a reply. I'm thinking either A) you lost your phone or B) there are so many crazies calling you stopped checking your phone or C) you just hate me. If it's C then you don't have to reply. I just wanted to say I heard about all the stuff and wow and holy cow you should've told me about that dowsing stuff if it's true. I don't know if it's true because you never mentioned it and I try not to believe everything I see on the news. Anyway, I'd still like to go for coffee or something sometime if your answer isn't C. By the way, I know you love how good I look in my glasses. I'm attaching a picture of my new ones. Chill, Jonas.

The attached picture was a silly shot of him wearing goofy nose glasses that had a mustache and made him look like Groucho Marx. I burst out laughing and replied immediately:

Thanks for emailing and not giving up on getting hold of me! The reason is a cross between A and B and definitely not C. I would love to go for coffee sometime when things get less crazy. Hugs, Julie.

It was the best moment of a few lousy days. After I hit Send I went back to sorting the other messages. After a while I got up from the chair and stretched. The sun was streaming through a crack in the brown drapes. I opened them a smidgen wider and peered out into the parking lot. There were only a handful of cars. I wished that I had my Jeep so I could hop in and take off. Of course that would be breaking rule number two and Jill would have an absolute bovine. Then again for all I knew she might not ever come by again. She never said for sure and, for all I knew, this could all be over by tomorrow.

I opened the phone she provided and looked through the contacts. Hers and Gramps were the only ones listed. When I called Gramps he was out of breath. He and Wookie had been out chasing rabbits.

"He caught one, Julie," Grams said excitedly. "He caught it in his mouth and ran back to show me and then you know what he did?"

"What?" I asked.

"He just dropped it at my feet and watched it run away!" Gramps howled with laughter and I joined him.

"I guess he is not the great hunter you like to pretend he is," I said.

"That's a fact. So what's happening with you today?"

"Nothing. A lot of nothing. I'm going to go crazy if I stay in this room much longer." I ran my fingers through my hair and was reminded of how little hair I had left. "Are the reporters still bothering you?"

"Not much. They put up one of those temporary fences at the end of our driveway. It's a pain in the ass to move it if I want to drive out but you've put so much food in my freezer I don't think I'll need anything for a while."

"Have you heard from Agent Pierce again?" I asked, holding my breath and hoping there'd be a yes, but he said that he hadn't heard from him since yesterday morning when he'd promised to send reinforcements.

"You wouldn't happen to have his phone number written down there anywhere, would you?"

"I might have taken it down here somewhere. Hold on."

He put the phone down. I could visualize him shuffling around the kitchen where he always had a collection of junk mail, notes and flotsam. I worried my lip with my teeth while I waited for him to come back.

"Found it," he announced and rattled off the number.

I jotted it down on the back of a receipt at the bottom of my purse and told Gramps to feel free to call me if he needed anything.

"Your number doesn't come up on call display. What is it?" he asked.

I had to admit I didn't know and then I just gave him Jill's number and told him to contact her or Pierce if there was an emergency and, meantime, I'd call as often as I could.

After I hung up I stared at that piece of paper and memorized Pierce's number. Twice I started to send him a text and then stopped. Jill had said he would contact me if he needed me.

"Ugh."

I blew out a breath and pushed the phone away. If I had a way of getting around and if I knew when Jill was coming, I'd sneak off for a few hours just to clear my head. Grabbing the phone again I fired off a text.

Jill, do you plan on coming by?

She replied almost instantly: Yes. Is there a problem?

I considered my reply and then typed: It's noisy here at night. Could you bring earplugs?

She replied saying she would be here soon and not to open the door until she texted that she was on the other side.

It was almost an hour later when I saw a shadow pass by the crack in the drapes and then the phone chimed with a text saying to open the door.

"Earplugs, huh?" She tossed me a package of them as she walked in the door. "Most people ask for a ton of other stuff like junk food or pizza or clothes, and you ask for earplugs."

Damn. I should've asked for pizza and maybe socks.

"Thanks," I said, holding up the earplugs.

"I brought you some more junk food and fruit." She put down a bag and I thanked her again.

"How goes the, you know, case?"

"It's puttering along." She shrugged and looked around the room. "We'll catch him. It's just a matter of time before he screws up."

"Hopefully soon before another girl dies," I said.

"That would be good," she admitted.

She stood there in the doorway looking around and then stepped over to close the drapes so that even that tiny sliver of light would not shine through.

"I know you're probably going stir-crazy here so I appreciate your patience." She looked at her phone and frowned. "Jesus, they expect me to drive down to Olympia now." She rolled her eyes.

"I was in Olympia once. It's pretty there."

"Yeah, but I'll be in the inside of a motel like this." She pointed a finger at me. "Nothing to do with this case though." She put her phone back in her pocket and her hand on the door. "Gotta run. If you think of anything else you need, let me know. I might make it back later today or I might not."

"Okay," I said.

Then she hastily added, "But don't leave here, though, no matter what. I mean that. If I get tied up I might just send another agent to check on you so you'd better be around."

I nodded but I could tell she was just bluffing. She didn't want me leaving but I doubted she'd send anyone else. The second she was gone I went to the window and watched through the drapes as her car peeled out of the lot. Then I opened my laptop and checked to see how long the drive was from here to Olympia. Almost two hours so it would be at least four before she could make it there and then back. I closed the laptop and heard the roll of the laundry cart going by outside my room. I jumped up and opened the door a crack.

"You want your room cleaned?" the lady asked.

"No, but maybe I could just have more coffee?"

She grabbed a couple of pouches of the horrible coffee and handed them over.

"And more of those little shampoos and soaps?"

She handed me a fistful of toiletries and I thanked her.

"Do you know if there's a car rental place nearby?" I asked.

"In town I'm sure." She pointed down the highway in the direction of the town a couple miles away. "Also, the guy who runs the garage next door." She hooked her thumb to indicate a business on the other side of the parking lot. "His name is Sid. Sometimes he has old cars he will loan you for twenty bucks for a day."

"Really? Thanks so much," I replied and meant it.

In a whirl I showered and dressed. I pulled on my blue-framed glasses and ball cap and, after a swift look right and left down the outside corridor, left the motel room. The air was cool but the sun felt glorious on the back of my neck as I jogged across the lot.

When I walked into the garage office, a heavyset man with *Sid* embroidered across filthy mechanic coveralls gave me a cursory glance.

"Yeah?"

"I was wondering if you had a car I could borrow."

"Twenty a day. I've got one left if you can drive a stick. Otherwise you're outta luck."

"Yeah, I can," I said.

He wiped meaty palms across his stomach and pulled out a piece of paper.

"Write down your name, address, phone number and driver's license number."

I hesitated and then filled out the form under my seldom used name, Delma Arsenault, and gave my home address and Gramps's phone number because I didn't want him calling my old cell since Jill had that. He took the paper back and asked for a credit card.

"I thought I'd just pay you cash."

"You sure will pay me cash, darlin', but the credit card is in case you don't bring it back."

Opening my wallet I found my Visa and handed it to him hoping he wouldn't notice it wasn't in the same name as I'd written on the form. If he did see the difference, he didn't mention it. He handed back the card and asked for the money.

He stuck the twenty in the pocket of his coveralls and reached in a drawer for some keys.

"Garage closes at six. Have it back by then or I have to charge you another day." He handed me the keys. "It's the green Camry out back. Fill up the tank before you bring it back."

The Camry was late nineties, jade green with some old front-end damage but it ran just fine. I got on the highway and headed north. With lack of a better plan I figured I'd drive an hour north and return to Dakota Creek where we'd had no luck finding the body of Kari Burke. My purse was on the passenger seat and my dowsing rods fit snugly inside. I blasted the radio and sang along, glad to be free of the confines of that small motel room and enjoying the bit of rebel freedom. The feeling was short-lived when I exited the highway and tried to head in the direction where Pierce and I had stopped. There was a barrier up and a flag person directing people down a detour.

I pulled off to the shoulder, climbed out and lowered the brim of my ball cap to cover a lot of my face and shield my eyes from the sun.

"You can't go that way," the flag person told me. "You gotta take Enterprise farther on or turn onto Delta Line Road."

"How come it's closed?"

I could just make out a cluster of vehicles in the distance. Dark sedans that made me wonder if Agent Pierce was there.

"Who knows?" She shrugged and then walked over

to me. "I think they're looking for one of those girls. You know, the missing ones."

"Oh really." I lowered my face. "They find one?"

"I doubt it because they've been at it for two days now. They brought out the dogs and everything."

"Well, damn, I was hoping to do some fishing in Dakota Creek."

"Yeah, well that's not the best spot anyway. You wanna go back that way." She pointed back the way I came, then leaned in and whispered even though there was nobody else around, "Take Custer north and you'll see an old red barn on your right. Once you see that, you're close to where the South Fork of Dakota Creek meets up with the North Fork. That's where you'll find the sweet spot. Right there on the muddy banks."

I thanked her and climbed back into the Camry. As I turned around I reached inside my purse, took out my rods and lay them on my lap. I turned onto Custer and started looking for the red barn she mentioned. I kept telling myself there was a reason there was a crowd of sedans at the other location of Dakota Creek. Pierce had said he'd received a tip about that area. Then again, I remembered him also receiving information about Luna Quinn and I stomped all over that field for half the day and then we'd found her body in a different area on our way back.

The red barn cropped up on my right just as the flag person said and I slowed. The road was narrow with no shoulder where I could safely stop, but I rounded a bend and there was a wide pull-out. I grabbed my rods and phone then locked my purse in the trunk and started walking.

From where I parked there was a path leading into

the bush and you could hear rushing water. It was as good a place as any to start. I glanced at the time on the phone and realized to be safe I shouldn't stay out here more than an hour in order to make it back, return the car and high-tail it back up to my room in case Jill did decide to return promptly after her drive to Olympia.

The path was smooth and barely muddy since we'd had a couple dry days. I asked myself if I was carrying a dead body would this be too far to come. The path was downhill and not at all treacherous. You could drag a heavy load down this way and you'd be invisible from the road. The air was so crisp it stung my nose a little when I breathed in deep the scent of cedar and the musty smell of a nearby dogwood tree. I kept my rods out front but they didn't flinch or tremble.

After a half hour, I gave up on the area and walked back to the car. I wish I'd thought to bring a water bottle and a snack but I'd stop at a store if I found one. I'd only driven another hundred yards when I realized I was in a ritzy residential neighborhood. No wonder I didn't find a body where I'd been, it was a high-traffic location. I pulled over at a small corner store and grabbed some chips and a Coke. When I climbed back in the car, I pulled out my map.

"Think. Think."

The old map didn't include the new development but I traced my finger along the expanse of Dakota Creek as I sipped the Coke. A vague sickly memory tickled the back of my mind. After her birthday party Katie had given me the chain and the crystal. She said it was junk and I could have it. The next morning before school Grandma walked into my room and caught me with the crystal poised over a piece of paper that said *yes* on one side and *no* on the other. She was furious about my "witching ways" and slammed me against the wall and tugged the chain around my neck. It would've strangled me but it was cheap and broke, which infuriated her even more. Over and over she slammed my head into the wall until Gramps walked in and quietly told Grandma he was taking me fishing. It was the only time he'd ever interfered in one of her rages. We'd made our way to Dakota Creek and I watched him reel in salmon. I would clap and laugh with glee whenever he caught another. He'd tried to show me how to cast but my arm hurt. After a while he took a look at my wrist and sighed. It was broken. We went to the small local hospital and Gramps told them I tripped while fishing. He wouldn't look me in the eye afterward and wouldn't sign my cast.

I closed my eyes and thought about that location. He'd called it his secret fishing spot. It was under an old trestle bridge and near a gravel pit. The phone they gave me did not allow me to do a search. I walked back inside the corner store and asked the old guy working there if there was still an old trestle bridge nearby.

"The bridge is still there but the road doesn't go over it anymore," he said.

"Oh." I sighed. "I was just going for a drive and remembered it was an old fishing spot where my grandpa took me."

"I know the spot well." He gave me a gap-toothed grin. "Caught a huge steelhead there one time. You follow the road back to the highway about a quarter mile and you'll see the turnoff for the old road. It's got a concrete barrier there now but after the block, the old road still leads to that bridge."

I thanked him and walked back to my car. I opened

the bag of salty chips and nibbled as I drove with the rods resting on my lap. I didn't have my hopes up about that area. It was ten years ago and with all the construction there was a good chance I'd miss it even if I knew where to look. Plus, if the road was no longer accessible it wouldn't exactly be the easiest way to bring a body, even if you were a messed-up killer hell-bent on tossing a ribbon-clad girl over a bridge. I shuddered at the thought.

Almost immediately I saw a sign showing the road back to the interstate. Only a quarter mile later the new road I was on carried on straight while parallel you could see an older road swallowed by trees. The road I was on passed a briefly forested area and curved over a small bridge. The rods twitched in my lap and I slammed on my brakes. A pickup truck driver behind me leaned on his horn and accelerated around my car as I pulled off to the side.

Licking my lips, I looked over my shoulder and slowly backed up over the bridge. Again, the rods twitched to the right. A few yards before the bridge I'd completely missed the pull out with the concrete barriers just like the guy in the store said. The bush was thick around the area, and if the rods hadn't twitched I would've continued on by. Now I backed into that drive until the bumper of the Camry touched the concrete barrier.

My hands shook a little as I picked up the rods and climbed out of the car.

"You got this," I told myself.

I stepped around the three-foot-high concrete barrier and headed down what used to be the old road. Only a few feet in and the old road curved just enough that I was hidden from view of anyone passing by. Hundred-foot cedar trees rustled in the slight breeze, and my rods vibrated with unleashed energy as if pulling me forward. The old road went up the trellis bridge but there was a chain fence in front of the entrance and a huge white sign with red lettering stating Bridge Closed.

I got up to the bridge and the rods urged me forward. I tried edging left and right but they always pulled me back to the bridge entrance. There was a break in the fence to walk through and enter the bridge deck. I stepped through the fence and started to sweat. My feet shuffled forward a few steps but my legs felt like rubber.

"It's just an old bridge. It won't collapse," I told myself but my feet were like lead and wouldn't bring me farther.

The Coke and chips in my stomach churned and threatened to come up when I forced myself to go farther.

"Just a few steps," I muttered. "Just enough to prove she's here."

I thought of the killer. What would be the point of him carrying her onto the bridge deck? Just to toss her in the water? I wiped the sweat from my face with my hand as I thought about that. If she'd gone over, the swift-flowing creek would've carried her to my right. I backed up onto the safety of brush area before the bridge and I ignored the urge of the rods to continue and, instead, turned my body sideways to squeeze between a tight crop of trees and shuffle down the right embankment.

There she was, lying bent and broken facedown and naked on a boulder in the middle of the creek. Water rushed forcefully on either side of her right hand, trailing a white ribbon in its wake.

SIX

WITH SHAKY HANDS I pulled out my phone and punched in Agent Pierce's number. The call went right to voice mail.

"Damn!"

I started to text and heard the unmistakable sound of someone walking in the nearby brush. I ran back to the car as fast as I could and, once there, my fingers fumbled with the keys as I panicked to open the car. When I finally got in the driver's seat I locked the doors and my breath came in ragged gasps as I looked in my rear-view mirror. My throat was parched with alarm. I could feel someone's eyes on me.

Awkward fingers fumbled with the phone as I texted: I found Kari Burke.

I hit Send and tried to take a calming breath but it came out on a strangled sob.

Immediately the phone rang in my hand.

"Where the hell are you?" Pierce barked.

I directed him as best I could. Everything in me wanted to drive far and fast away from this place but I sat and waited. His sedan came screeching up less than ten minutes later. My legs were wobbly as I climbed out of the car to greet him.

"What the hell?"

He stopped short as he looked me over and I realized the difference. I pulled the cap and glasses off and tossed them onto the driver's seat.

"Where?" he demanded.

I pointed.

"There's an old bridge down there and she's..." I swallowed thickly. "She's under the bridge on a rock."

He went to leave and I grabbed his arm.

"Don't," I pleaded. "I heard someone. Maybe you should wait for help."

"It's okay," he said, his voice calm but his eyes sharp. "Wait for me in your car. Lock the doors."

He pulled a revolver from a shoulder strap under his jacket and continued on toward the bridge. I chewed my thumbnail nervously as I stared intently in my rear-view mirror.

"Come on, Pierce," I moaned.

It felt like he was gone forever but it was maybe five minutes. When I saw him coming up the old road behind I sighed in relief and climbed back out of the car.

"I'm sorry... I'm sorry." I covered my face with my hands. My entire body was trembling. "I know you didn't want me to help you anymore but I just couldn't stay in that room and I thought it couldn't hurt to at least try."

Pierce put firm hands on my shoulders.

"It'll be okay," he said awkwardly.

To his horror I began shaking uncontrollably. He wrapped me into a hug.

"Sh-h-h," he whispered into my hair. "You did a very stupid thing coming out here by yourself but it turned out okay."

I couldn't speak. Could hardly even breathe. After a few moments I stopped shaking and managed to swallow my emotion enough to regain some of my composure.

He held me out at arm's length then and ruffled my hair.

"You don't look half-bad as a blonde."

I tried to laugh but it came out as a trembling strangled sound.

"It was Jill. The dye, the glasses, the hat."

"I figured."

He called for the investigators to come, and once they arrived I told him I was going to head back to the motel.

"Oh no, no, no," he laughed. "There's no use in sticking you back there."

"Okay." I nodded. "I still have a bag there and my laptop. I'll return the car and then check out and go back home."

"You're not going home either. We'll figure out something but, right now, you need to wait for me right here," he said and firmly pushed me back inside the Camry to wait.

"Maybe I should tell Jill," I remarked.

"Trust me," he chuckled softly. "She already knows and she's not at all happy about all the rules you broke. My ears are still burning."

"Oh."

After a while a different agent approached the car. He said Pierce was going to be tied up here for hours. He introduced himself as Agent Spence and I had no idea if that was his first or last name and didn't really care. My head hurt and whenever I closed my eyes I saw Kari Burke's body.

"I've been instructed to drive your car back to wherever you got it and have you pack up at the motel," Spence told me.

"I can drive," I said.

"That's a no. You've experienced a trauma here."

He held his hand out and I felt immense relief when I handed him the keys and walked around to climb into the passenger seat. It was a good thing I wasn't driving. My hands were still shaky. Once we were back on the interstate he glanced over at the cup holder that held the empty cola can and crumpled bag of chips.

"Was that your lunch? Because I was told to feed you if you hadn't been fed."

Like I was a toddler or something. I rolled my eyes.

"I'm fine. There's food at the motel that Agent Jill brought."

"Agent Jill, huh. She's a real pip, that one." He laughed and I guess I was supposed to laugh along but I didn't.

We traveled along in silence except for Agent Spence's incessant whistling. We were a couple of miles from the motel exit when I caught him making the sign of the cross as he nodded toward an overpass.

"That's the spot," he said.

"What spot?"

"You know, the spot where Agent Pierce's wife and kid died. Right there." We were under it now and he was pointing up.

"What happened?" I asked quietly.

"Drunk driver." He shook his head. "So one minute you've got a wife of ten years and a five-year-old boy and then *bam* it's gone."

"Oh wow," I muttered, rubbing the back of my neck.

"Wow is right," Agent Spence said. "Everyone thought he was going to lose it. We figured all the counseling in the world wasn't going to make him right in the head after that, but he did all the things you're supposed to do. He took time off. Let the relatives take care of him a while. Did all the intensive psychotherapy stuff they make you do these days, and when he came back he was good as new." Then he sort of cringed. "Maybe not good as new. Don't think you can ever be, you know, normal after that kind of stuff happens to you."

"When did it happen?" I asked.

"Four years ago. Maybe five."

He'd had a five-year-old son. Wow. I closed my eyes and tried to imagine that level of pain and grief and couldn't even touch it. Then I remembered how I'd asked Pierce about his ex-wife and him saying she died and he'd just managed to remove the ring not long ago. Sheesh. No wonder he was so…serious. And then he bailed me out of a DUI. That must've just rocked his world. I cringed in shame.

We exited the highway and I told Agent Spence where to drive the car. I realized that I hadn't stopped to fill the tank so when I dropped off the keys I gave Sid an extra ten bucks.

Agent Spence walked me back to the motel and came inside the room.

"You don't have to stay," I told him.

"Oh I *definitely* have to stay." He laughed. "I was told not to take my eyes off you for a second because you are sneaky."

Jesus.

So he sat on the chair and ate the last muffin and I made instant oatmeal in the microwave inside a coffee cup and ate it with a stir stick.

"That's very creative," Agent Spence said, pointing to my oatmeal mug.

I ate my oatmeal in silence. When I was done I washed out the mug and made us some coffee. Agent Spence added three packages of fake sugar to his claiming he needed the caffeine boost but hated the taste.

"How long do you think Kari Burke was on that rock?" I asked.

Spence just shrugged.

"The medical examiner will give us an idea, I guess. I didn't even get to see the body. There's a protocol with these kinds of things. Pierce, he's numero uno on this case so, of course, he'd be there until the ME arrives and then there are other agents who help Pierce on the scene."

"And you aren't one of those?"

"Well, sure, but I'm more surveillance. Checking the area. There are only so many people they want tracking through a crime scene."

I guess that made sense. The room felt smaller with him in it and if I was being moved to another location, I just wanted to be gone. Spence was playing a game on his cell phone so I opened my laptop and continued with sorting all the new emails that arrived. The crazies and threats were still outnumbering any kind of support about a hundred to one.

On the bright side there was another email from Jonas: Guess where I am? The attached picture was him behind the counter at the gas station making a funny face. He said the number of reporters hanging around hoping for a glimpse of the dowsing girl had died down. He also said he was working all my old shifts and trying to save enough money to replace the tooth he had yanked. I replied with a goofy message to him not to eat more chocolate bars than he sold or he'd end up with more missing teeth.

Damn. I missed that stupid job.

Sitting back on the bed I tried to clear my mind and relax but every time I blinked I saw Kari Burke's naked, broken body draped over the rock.

"I'm having a shower."

Hoisting my bag that contained my change of clothes I headed for the bathroom. I needed to wash away the vision of Kari Burke inside my head and I ran the shower as hot as I could stand it. The motel had more hot water than my trailer but not enough for any kind of a mind cleanse. When I finally climbed out, the small room was sweltering and steamy. I dried off with the scratchy towels and dressed in new jeans and a long-sleeve T-shirt. Because there wasn't much hair on my head I just dragged my fingers through instead of bothering with a brush. I sat on the closed toilet for a while with my head in my hands. There was an anguished clawing need in my belly for wine to obliterate it all. It wouldn't take much. Just a bottle or two.

When I stepped out of the bathroom my fingers were still pruned.

"I was beginning to wonder if you'd drowned in there."

It was Pierce, and Spence was gone.

"Where's Agent Spence?"

"Out doing agent stuff."

"Oh. How'd it go over at…the bridge?"

He was in the lone chair and I sat on the edge of the bed. His face was drawn and weary. Deep grooves cut around his eyes, aging him.

"It went well, I guess." He blew out a long slow breath. "I want to make this stop. We need to catch this guy. It feels like I'm just one step behind him."

The three original girls were now all dead. Sue Torres had been taken just a few days ago.

"Maybe there's time now. It's possible he'll hang on

to Sue Torres as long as the others and that'll give you more time."

He shook his head.

"He's speeding things up. He hung on to Luna Quinn and Iris Bell just over three weeks. Kari Burke was only two." He rubbed the back of his neck. "Sue Torres is on borrowed time."

He got to his feet then and nodded to me.

"Pack up. We're going."

"Where?"

He didn't reply, just motioned for me to get moving.

My clothes were already in the duffel but I slid my laptop and map into the bag and then went to the bathroom and got all the little shampoos and soaps. Pierce stopped me when I started to pack up the small amount of food.

"You don't have to bring all that." He waved at the instant noodles, oatmeal, granola bars and remaining apple.

"But if I leave it, that's such a waste." I ignored him and stuffed it in my bag and then slipped my shoes on.

"Where are we going?" I asked again as we headed out the door.

"Far away from this dump," he replied, taking my bag from my hands and carrying it himself.

When I climbed into the passenger seat of his car I was surprised to see empty coffee cups strewn on the floor, and an apple core in the cup holder.

"Sorry about the mess," he said as he buckled up.

"It actually makes me a little glad. I was beginning to think you weren't human."

He laughed in a low throaty way that came from a place of debilitating fatigue. And maybe a dash of grief.

He'd lost his wife and son and yet here he was. Back to catching the bad guys.

We made our way south toward Seattle. The interstate traffic became thicker as we neared the city. He took the Mercer Street exit, angled onto Fairview then took a right on Virginia. At least if they put me up in a hotel in downtown Seattle there'd be more to do. Not necessarily good things though. A week after graduation I was living a block away from here schlepping drinks at a dive bar and sharing a two-bedroom apartment with a slobby roommate who kept trying to climb into bed with me when I was drunk. I put a lock on my door and, if I was coherent enough to remember, I also moved my small dresser in front of the door before I crashed for the night. That was seven years ago and felt like yesterday.

Agent Pierce drove into the parking garage of a tall condo tower and then parked.

"I guess this is it," I remarked.

Definitely not the cheapo motel I'd been expecting. Maybe a private FBI place where they kept witnesses. That kind of thing.

He got out of the car, popped the trunk and retrieved my bag. We rode up to the thirtieth floor in silence and then walked to the end of the hall where he pulled out keys and opened the door. The apartment was nice but littered with debris; boxes were piled high in what could've been a dining room but there was no table. The small kitchen had light-colored cabinets and stainless steel appliances that looked like they'd never been touched.

"Is this *your* place?"

"Home sweet home." He didn't sound proud of it.

I followed him down a short hall and he opened the door. "This'll be your room for the foreseeable future."

He tossed my bag onto a small bed against the wall. The room looked like it was supposed to be an office but there was only a twin bed and a desk and nothing else.

"There's a bathroom down the hall." He stifled a yawn with the back of his hand. "Help yourself to whatever you need. I'm going to close my eyes for an hour. I've been up for days."

He disappeared into a room down the hall and I just stood there feeling awkward. It was after seven and all I'd had to eat for hours was that oatmeal in a mug. I didn't dare go through his cupboards. I grabbed the remaining apple from my bag and a granola bar and took them into the living room along with my laptop and the map. I sat down on the beige microfiber couch and held my laptop on my lap. The coffee table in front of the sofa was covered six inches deep in paperwork—files, newspapers, notes and pictures of dead girls.

Putting the laptop down next to me I began stacking the papers into a neat pile. With the exception of pictures of the missing girls, none of the other paperwork seemed to relate to this case but I didn't want to snoop through his stacks of notes to see. I put the pictures of the missing girls facedown on top of the pile and pushed the entire stack to one end of the table. Once I cleared a space, I moved the laptop onto the table and while it started up I ate my apple and granola bar. I found the trash bin under the sink in the kitchen and disposed of my apple core and bar wrapper, balancing it precariously on top of an overflowing trashcan.

The laptop was ready to go except for one thing. I

didn't know Pierce's Wi-Fi password and couldn't access the internet. Damn. I stared at the flat-screen TV over the fireplace that was covered in a fine layer of dust. I didn't want to chance turning it on in case it woke him so I just sat there with my hands in my lap looking around. Being in his apartment made me edgy. All those boxes stacked in the dining room were covered in dust too. He hadn't just moved in. He'd been here a while, escaping wherever he'd lived with his wife and son. I felt like the worst kind of snooping intruder.

Closing the laptop, I opened my road map and looked it over. Two hours later Pierce was still sleeping and I was still looking over the map with eyes that stung with fatigue. It was after ten when a distinct chime sounded from my room down the hall. I frowned and walked swiftly to find the cell phone buried at the bottom of my purse.

It was a message from Jill: Open the door.

I hesitated. She had to know I was no longer at the motel, right?

Another message followed: Yes, this door. Garrett's door.

I walked to the door, looked through the peep hole and saw Jill's smiling face so I opened it.

"You are one cunning little sneak, aren't you?" She bustled past me carrying two grocery bags and a large pizza.

"I-I'm sorry," I stammered as I locked the door behind her and followed her into the kitchen. "I know I was supposed to stay in the room and that may have got you into trouble because you were supposed to be watching me."

"Oh my dear, I *was* watching you." She pointed to

the phone in my hand. "You don't really think the Bureau would give you a phone that wasn't equipped with a tracking device, do you?"

I stared at the phone in my hand and she shook her head and laughed.

"Once I saw you were on the move and where you were headed, I thought you were making your way directly to the site Garrett and the others were looking for that girl so I didn't hurry. I didn't know that you were headed to a different area nearby and by the time I figured it out…" She shrugged. "Oh well, what's done is done and it worked out awesome, right? One more dead girl found and checked off the list."

I cringed at her flippant description. Finding Kari Burke's destroyed body was a tick on a horrific to-do list?

Jill put the pizza box down on the granite counter and started emptying her grocery bags. She opened the fridge and removed three beer bottles and replaced them with a sack of oranges and a package of sandwich meat. Then pulled out a few cans of soup and a loaf of bread from her sack and left them on the counter. "Where's our boy?"

"Um. Sleeping."

"Guess he's earned it," she said over her shoulder.

She opened and closed random cupboards that held nothing but a few plates and cups and she stopped when she got to a supply of liquor. One by one she bagged a couple bottles of wine, the three beers she pulled from the fridge, and a half-empty bottle of whiskey. When I realized *why* she was cleaning out Pierce's liquor supply, a blanket of shame washed over me.

"So the rules here are the same as at the motel, not that you listened…" She offered me an eye roll. "No leaving here unless you're with Garrett or me. No opening the door unless you get a text first from either of us. Oh and here's a new one…" She leaned in close and I could smell spearmint gum on her breath as she whispered, "No climbing into Garrett's bed. I know he's got that whole sexy, rakish thing going on and those serious tortured-soul eyes, but he's off your bucket list, got it? He's what? Twenty-five years older than you? Besides the ick factor involved, it would be a big no-no for you to contaminate our investigation by trying to screw him."

"I-I-I…" I stammered, my jaw gaping as a rush of heat probably turned me into a giant tomato. "I wouldn't even, you know…"

I snapped my mouth shut and swallowed in mortified silence then turned around to come face-to-face with Pierce.

"Well, good morning, Garrett," Jill quipped. "Just taking care of biz."

"Right. Thanks. You can go now," he replied coolly.

"Sure." She gathered up the sacks of liquor bottles and they clanked noisily together as she walked to the door. "The pizza's still hot so dig in. Your favorite."

He thanked her again and locked the door behind her as she left.

"Sorry about that," he said with a frown. "Jill can be a bit…"

"Of an elitist twit?" I offered. "Yeah, I get that."

He laughed loudly and shook his head then grabbed the pizza box and two bottles of water and brought them to the couch.

"C'mon." He opened the box of pizza and grabbed a slice. "You must be as hungry as I am."

The smell of melted cheese and meat wafted over to me, and my stomach growled in reply but there was no denying it felt weird being in his apartment.

"That's okay. I should probably just leave you to… um…you have work to do and stuff so…" I didn't know what to say. "I should probably just go to bed."

"Sit. Eat."

He patted the cushion next to him on the couch and I walked over and dutifully sat.

"Have you ever had pizza from Serious Pie before?"

I shook my head and he lifted out a section of the strangely oval pizza with the puffed blackened edges and handed it to me.

"Sweet fennel sausage, roasted peppers and provolone," he said. "It's as close to heaven as you can get."

It was definitely the fanciest-sounding pizza I'd ever tried and, after I gingerly took a bite, I nodded.

"Really good."

"Good?" He looked at me with mock horror as he devoured his second slice. "I know I probably spoiled you with my gourmet spaghetti but you have to admit that it's a helluva lot better than 'good.'"

I laughed around a second bite.

"Delicious."

"That's closer." He grabbed his third slice and took a bite. "I was beginning to wonder if all the excitement had caused you to lose your taste buds."

The pizza and his casual conversation helped assuage the embarrassment and horror of my conversation with Jill.

"So you never tried Serious Pie even a few years ago when you lived just a little ways from here?"

"No." I looked at him sideways. "You know where I used to live?"

"Yeah, sure, I checked you out thoroughly before I visited you and dragged you into this messed-up situation." He drank from his water bottle and reached for a fourth slice of pizza. "Of course I couldn't find out everything based on just searches and talking to random people. Even the Bureau has its limitations on what we can uncover." He paused before taking a bite of the pizza poised at his mouth. "By the way, I'm sorry about what happened with the reporters. It wasn't me and I don't think it was anyone at the Bureau, but I'm sorry just the same."

"Thanks. I think it was Katie," I admitted and let out a sigh. "It was really crazy."

"Scary as hell, I'm sure."

We ate in silence until the rest of the pizza was gone. I got up with the box and dumped it into a recycle box in his kitchen. When I got back he had my map sprawled out on the coffee table.

"Been doing your own research, have you?" he asked.

"Kind of," I admitted sheepishly as I sat back down on the sofa. "I know you've got all kinds of technical tools and profilers and dozens of agents so it's not like anything I come up with could help. I guess I just wanted to see if anything came to me."

"Don't knock what you've accomplished so far. Who knows how long it would've taken us to find these girls without you." He tapped the map with his finger. "And did it? Did anything come to you tonight?"

"Not really." I shrugged a single shoulder.

"Know why I had you brought here instead of keep you in a motel?"

"No idea." And that was the truth.

"After today I realized you are a valuable tool in this investigation and all we've done is try to hold you back with rules. I want you to work with me on this. I want to know your thoughts, no matter how crazy you might think they are. Tell me what you know, Julie."

And so I talked. He put his feet up on the coffee table and leaned back with his fingers locked behind his head and his eyes closed as he listened.

"Every girl has been found about a half hour from the place she was taken. They've been found in or near water and bridges," I began.

I pointed out other obvious things we knew about the girls, listing what was already common knowledge about the individual victims: where they worked, went to school and lived and their obvious physical attributes. I expected him to rush me or interrupt or ask me to skip the part we already know but he let me ramble, and I could put on a long-winded gabfest if encouraged.

"They each had part-time jobs but I'm guessing none of these girls knew each other or that would've been too big a detail to keep quiet. It would've been all over social media for sure." I took a long drink from my water bottle then added, "There's a casino almost within walking distance of where every girl was abducted and—"

"Is that true?" He sat up then and looked at me sharply.

"Yes, but it probably doesn't mean much because there's gotta be, like, forty casinos in Washington State. You can't swing a cat without hitting one."

"There's something you're not telling me." His eyes were shrewd and I just shook my head. "Then it's a good thing we're not swinging cats here," he joked. He pointed to my laptop. "Can we use yours or do you want me to get mine from my room?"

"Help yourself. I didn't know your Wi-Fi password."

He logged my computer into his internet and then Google searched the casino locations.

"Fifty. There are fifty casinos in the state and, you're right, there was one within a mile of each girl's abducted location." He patted me on the leg. "Good job."

"It probably means nothing."

"Investigative work is like wading through a lake filled with shit to find a diamond."

He dug out his phone and made a call so I got up to give him space. I opened the sliding doors and walked onto the balcony. I heard him talking to someone on the other end of the line asking for lists of employees at the casinos near the abduction sites and a list of suppliers that delivered to all three.

The concrete balcony froze my stocking-clad feet. I put my arms on the icy metal railing and leaned forward to check out the view thirty floors below. Strange enough, a balcony never elicited the same fear in me as a bridge.

A breeze kicked up and coiled around my bare neck. Just like that, the quicksand sucked me in. I closed my eyes and remembered another night of cold. Locked out of the house by Grandma for some infraction or another. Temperature had dipped to freezing and she locked me in the garden shed wearing nothing but thin pajamas. I was only about eleven at the time.

At first I piled the bags of soil and mulch around me to keep warm but it only helped for a while. In the corner of the shed there'd been a bucket of rusted gardening tools and some old fishing lures. Somehow I figured out that I could pop the cover off the plate on the double dead bolt so that the screws were visible and, using an old metal trowel, I began to turn the screws holding the dead bolt on the door. The screws were rusted on tight and it took me forever. I had to keep stopping to warm my fingers under my armpits or blow on them to get the feeling back but finally it worked. When I got back to the house everyone was asleep and I slid my bedroom window open and crawled inside. I slept in the closet until the sun came up and then dressed and ran off to school. When I returned home after school, whatever had crawled up Grandma's backside had subsided and no mention was made of my escape or subsequent return.

A siren on the streets below snapped me out of my memory. An ambulance whizzed down the street and, once it was gone, the city noises resumed the normal clamor. I found it funny that all those people below just went on about their lives. They'd heard about a serial killer in Washington taking teen girls but it didn't affect their everyday meanderings. It probably just made good watercooler talk.

I didn't hear Pierce come up behind me until he spoke.

"It's freezing out here. Do you want me to grab a sweater?"

"No."

But even as I said the words I thought again of Grandma and shivered visibly so he grabbed the fleece throw off the back of the couch and put it around my shoulders.

I thanked him even though he had no way of knowing the shiver had more to do with PTSD than the icy breeze blowing in off the Pacific.

Silently Pierce stood there next to me and we stared out at the world below. The wind picked up and I reveled in its bite. I felt like I'd been slogging through a tepid swamp for years. I wanted the cold to clear my head and wake me up.

"What are you thinking about?"

He stood next to me, our shoulders pressed together, and it felt wrong to just brush him off so I told him the truth.

"How most people will go their entire lives without knowing how much evil there is in the world."

"Because it doesn't touch them."

"Evil touches everyone. Most people just sleepwalk right past it," I murmured.

I've always known how to lighten the mood in a room.

We walked back inside and I excused myself for bed. I knew what I had to do. I brought my laptop and map to my room, then went into the bathroom where I examined the sink faucet. Thankfully it wasn't a more modern kind. I unscrewed the end piece and brought the small cylinder to my room, where I popped out the filter, leaving me with a piece of chrome in the shape of a heavy ring. I took it to my room and fished the long string out of my hoodie and tied the end of the string to the metal ring.

I sat cross-legged on the floor with the ring dangling off the string, waited for it to become still, and then I quieted my mind as best I could.

"Show me your yes," I whispered.

Slowly the pendulum began to swing left to right, east to west, in a deliberate sway. I stopped the movement with my free hand and waited for it to become motionless.

"Show me your no," I whispered.

The ring swung north away from me and then south toward me, back and forth, back and forth, gaining momentum with every sway.

"Thank you," I said and stilled it with my hand.

Then I got out the map.

SEVEN

FOR HOURS I tried pendulum dowsing but could not get beyond yes or no. Whenever I asked a question regarding the map I got zero response. It would remain motionless and my hopes were dashed. Not that I thought I would magically be shown where the killer was hiding the last victim, Sue Torres, but, admittedly, there'd been a spark of hope there. After all, I was facing the demons that good ol' Grandma had nearly beaten out of me. I wanted a reward.

I fell into a fitful quicksand sleep and dreamt of dark times. I fought so many battles in my sleep that when the sun came up, I pulled the covers over my head and slept some more.

When I finally woke up it was after nine and there was a text from Pierce: Gone out. Stay here. The alarm is set and will go off if you leave.

"Damn you," I groaned.

After a quick shower I called Gramps. He let me talk to Wookie but I don't think the dog missed me nearly as much as I missed him. Gramps sounded chipper and I think he liked the challenge and celebrity that came with a flock of reporters constantly trying to talk to him. He regaled me with stories of how he'd only gone to get gas and a loaf of bread, and two of the reporters had followed him even into the store.

"But I held firm," he said. "They're not getting any-thing out of me. Not even a 'no comment.'"

"Good for you." I smiled. He was treating this like an adventure or a challenge but, still, I missed my low-key gas-jockey life.

He went on to say that his hot-water tank decided to die and he'd had to go into town for a new one and in-stalled it himself.

"I hope you got help hauling that inside the house. Those things are damn heavy."

"I'm not exactly a flyweight." He laughed.

That might be true but he wasn't young and there was bound to come a day when lifting hundred-pound tanks like it was nothing would become a problem for his aging body.

After the call I went into the kitchen and there was a note propped up against a Starbucks coffee cup telling me the latte was for me and I could microwave it to heat it up. I'd tried an instant latte mix before and found it too sweet and chemical for my tastes so I was prepared to hate it. After I heated it a few seconds and took a sip I reluctantly admitted it was probably the best coffee I ever had. Huh. Before you knew it I'd be trying to juice lemongrass.

I dragged the map out to the coffee table and my pendulum dowsing string as well as the ring from the faucet too.

If you poke the devil you'll get jabbed back.

I shook my head of Grandma's voice then began a computer search. After watching a few videos on You-Tube I tried again. Maybe my head wasn't in the right place or perhaps my questions were improperly worded. Or maybe I needed to summon a demon, an angel or the spirit of famous psychic Jeane Dixon. Didn't seem to matter what I tried, the answer was the same. Nothing. Zilch.

"Argh! This is so-o-o frustrating," I called out to the empty apartment.

There was a website listing professional dowsers that I didn't even know existed. One woman's bio stated that her area of expertise was pendulum dowsing. Her email was given so I decided to send her a few questions. Maybe she'd answer or maybe my questions would sit in cyberspace forever. Nothing ventured, nothing gained, right?

Afterward, I went through my emails and was happy to see another from Jonas with yet another picture. This one was a selfie taken at the casino where I'd seen him that night when I was out with Katie.

I tried to win myself some new teeth and maybe even a haircut but I was only up by ten bucks at the end of the night.

I replied telling him he'd have far better luck making money at the gas station than he would at those casinos.

Almost immediately he emailed back asking if I felt like Skyping so we could chat in real time. I hesitated. It would be nice to talk to a familiar face but what if Pierce returned in the middle. It felt like a betrayal. I just told him that maybe another time. He replied with a simple ok.

Then I sorted all the other emails. Today wasn't a good day. There were far more nasty mean crazies who wanted me dead than wanted me to find their loved ones.

It made my stomach clench. I shut down the computer and looked around the apartment.

The urge to look inside that stack of boxes was impossibly strong but I just thought about how I'd feel about him pawing through my underwear drawer back home. I decided with nothing else to do I'd clean the apartment because it really needed it.

Under the kitchen sink I found one bottle of cleaner and roll of paper towels. I started in the kitchen, wiping down all the cupboards, refrigerator and stove and then I moved on to the living room, where I dusted everything. I found a vacuum in a hall closet and dragged it around the carpet and laminate flooring but there was no mop so I hand washed the floor. Lastly I did my bathroom, which didn't look like it had ever been used before I came along. I stood outside Pierce's bedroom and paused. Finally I made a deal with myself that I would not touch his bedroom but if the ensuite bathroom needed cleaning I would give it a quick scrub. Opening the door to the bedroom, I tried to quickstep through it but stopped in my tracks at the picture frame on the nightstand. The three of them, Pierce together with his wife and young son, all sitting in autumn leaves somewhere looking impossibly perfect and happy. She had a bright smile and long dark hair. The son looked so much like Pierce it made my heart squeeze in my chest.

Feeling horrible even for looking, I gave my head a shake and marched straight into the bathroom off the bedroom. It was a complete disgusting disaster.

"Oh. My. God."

I just stood there blinking in surprise and attempting only to mouth breathe. I'd cleaned Gramps's bathroom often enough to know what happened when men gave up on even pretending to clean up after themselves. With determination and a strong gag reflex in check, I started with the toilet. Next I tackled the sink and countertop that was spackled with gobs of toothpaste and beard hairs. Finally I moved to the standalone shower. For a second I could smell Pierce. The scent of his body wash or soap was very intense in that area but it was also going to take an atomic bomb to get the soap scum off his shower doors.

"The man is a friggin' pig. Who would've guessed?"

Cleaner and roll of paper towels in hand, I took off my socks, rolled up the legs of my jeans and stepped into the shower stall. I sprayed and scrubbed and scrubbed and sprayed and, even with the exhaust fan running, could feel myself getting lightheaded from the fumes of the cleaner. I opened his bedroom window wide, kept the bathroom door open, then stepped back into the shower because, even though I'd given it a thorough cleaning, it would need another. I turned and coated the grimy tile with cleaner and lifted my hand to scrub.

"What the hell?"

I whirled around to find Pierce staring at me from the other side of his shower door.

"Um." I opened the door. "Hi."

"What are you doing?"

"Cleaning."

"I can see that." He grabbed me by a hand and pulled me out. "You don't need to be doing this."

"I'm sorry but someone should because it's gross."

He threw back his head and howled with laughter, and I felt my face go cherry with embarrassment. With the cleaner in one hand and what was left of the paper towels in the other, I sped out of the bathroom and went to the kitchen to stow away the cleaning supplies.

"You're not my maid, Julie," he said, all serious now. "I don't expect you to clean up after me."

"I was bored, okay?" I stuffed my hands into the front pockets of my jeans. "I'm basically a prisoner here."

"Oh, come on." He rolled his eyes in what was becoming a common and annoying look. "You are not a prisoner. You're just in protective custody to keep you safe and, yes, to help with the case if you can but—"

"But I can't leave. I can't call anyone besides Gramps." I felt suddenly a bit teary. "And I like to keep busy because keeping busy stops me from thinking about stuff that makes me want to drink."

I hugged my arms across my chest and stormed past him toward the living room. He followed.

"I'm sorry," he spoke to my back. "You're right. I should've thought about that. Of course being alone with nothing to do is horrible. I should've thought about that and given you a task or…something."

He touched my back and then his fingers recoiled as if burned. I wished he'd never seen those scars.

"Okay, well…" He cleared his throat. "I had things to do this morning but we'll get you the hell out of this prison now and go to lunch."

He walked over to the coffee table and picked up my long string with the faucet bit on the end and he held it out to me.

"What's this?"

"Nothing."

I snatched it out of his hand and brought it to my room, then changed my clothes to what I wore yesterday. There were few options because I didn't own a lot of clothing. I washed up but was still pretty sure I smelled like lemony household cleanser because that scent had burrowed inside my sinuses.

Pierce said we'd walk to a place for lunch and then head out. He didn't say where. I was just thrilled with the idea of getting out of the apartment. We took the elevator thirty floors down and walked for two blocks not saying a word. I saw a woman walking a Rottweiler and had to look away.

"Wookie is fine with your grandfather," Pierce remarked.

"Sure. He's feeding him table scraps and they're chasing rabbits." I tried to sound happy and upbeat but it came out deadpan. "Wookie used to be Katie's dog, you know. She got him as a pup and loved him to death until he became work and then she started leaving him with her mom when she'd skip town. Except her mom hated having Wookie around so one day she dropped him at my trailer for two weeks that turned into five years. Since then he's been my pal."

"Guess it was meant to be. He's lucky to have you."

I was the lucky one. Having Wookie had saved me from reaching for a bottle on many occasions.

Pierce held the door to the coffee shop open for me. It was cafeteria style and I grabbed a packaged sandwich and a coffee while he did the same.

"Gramps said Katie came back for Wookie while I was at work," I continued once we sat down. "She wanted to take him back to live with her but he wouldn't let her."

"That's crazy. She abandoned the dog and doesn't deserve to have him back. Besides, you love that dog and he loves you. Anyone can see that."

"She's just pissed I won't forgive her over the situation with Denny. She doesn't think she did anything wrong and she isn't used to anyone holding her accountable. She isn't as bad as this looks. She was always a good friend." That may have been stretching things a bit. "She was my only friend, really," I amended. "So she's pissed and wants to hurt me." I took a bite of my sandwich. "The next morning all the reporters were there. I'm pretty sure that was Katie's way of getting back at me."

"What an ass."

My head was down as I ate my sandwich. Yes, she was an ass but I'd been able to claim her as a friend before, and now I had nobody unless you counted Jonas, who might turn out to be a friend once all this was over.

"That string with the metal cylinder on it," Pierce began, interrupting my thoughts. "Was that for pendulum dowsing?"

When I looked up at him in surprise, he smiled.

"I told you I did my homework before I came to talk to you that first day."

"It didn't work," I told him. "I guess I'm not cut out…"

My words drifted and I thought about Grandma's face twisted with rage over a string with a fake crystal on the end. Quicksand. I shuddered.

"I hate it when you get that look."

"What?" I nonchalantly sipped my coffee.

"That look on your face that says there's only bad in the world because of what your grandmother did."

I flinched. Then I let what he said simmer a while until I replied with my voice lowered to a whisper.

"There isn't only bad in the world? How can you, with everything you do for a living…and what happened to your own wife and kid...how can you think anything else?"

He'd drawn first blood bringing up Grandma, and I'd cut him deeper with the mention of his family. He ate the rest of his sandwich with one hand while he looked through his phone with the other. I shouldn't have brought it up. His wife and son. That was mean and, just because mention of Grandma made me want to throw daggers, that didn't mean those knives had to go in Pierce's direction. We finished eating and walked back to his apartment in complete silence.

He curtly told me to grab my L-rods and I did. Then we took another awkwardly silent ride in the elevator down to the parking garage. I wanted to claw the words back but what was done was done. He was driving out of the city and I just kept my gaze out the window.

"Nowhere specific today," he mentioned suddenly, breaking the silence and forming a truce. "I thought we could drive to the area of each abduction and bounce ideas off each other."

"Okay." I nodded and felt good he wanted my ideas and felt better he wasn't going to be in a sulky silence all day.

"I've got our guys going through lists of every casino employee and delivery company that brings stuff to the casino. They're putting together a list of names that appear at all the locations near the abduction sites."

"That sounds like a lot of work."

"Ninety-nine percent of police work is sifting through details like that but, if we find something, it's like winning the jackpot."

We were on the I-5 heading north toward Arlington, Luna Quinn's hometown and where she was abducted.

When we drove under the overpass where his wife and son had been killed by a drunk driver, I stole a sideways glance at Pierce. His hands tightened a little on the wheel but otherwise you'd never know.

"So have you done the pendulum dowsing thing before?"

Pendulum dowsing held nothing but bad memories.

I will not stand by and let you bring Satan into my house!

"I don't think it's my thing. I could get a yes and no out of the pendulum but no matter how many different questions I asked about the missing girls, I came up empty. Sorry."

"Jesus, don't be sorry. You've helped us locate three girls."

"Dead, though," I said quietly. "It would be better if we could get them alive."

"You won't hear an argument from me about that."

The area where Luna Quinn was picked up was a stretch of road between a church and an office building. It had been after dinner but the exact time was vague because she wasn't reported missing for hours. Her parents thought she'd decided to go out with friends for coffee after work because that was an occasional routine.

Pierce pulled to the curb along that block of road directly in front of the makeshift memorial people had set up for her. Flower bouquets were piled three feet deep surrounded by votive candles. Someone had written RIP Luna in pastel-colored chalk on the sidewalk, and sad teddy bears stared back at us with shiny dead eyes.

"The office building at the corner does have security cameras. She was seen walking past the building at about seven-thirty. If she was continuing her walk home, she would've gone right by a convenience store up the road and would've been caught on their cameras. She wasn't."

It was an innocuous stretch of land in a small city of less than twenty thousand. Arlington was an hour north of Seattle so many people chose to live here and commute. Luna Quinn's parents probably thought it was a nice safe place to raise a family. Usually it was.

"All that stranger danger stuff they teach in school. Do you think she knew him?"

"It's a possibility," Pierce admitted. "But if he was strong enough he could've overpowered her or held a gun on her."

After a moment he drove from the abduction site to the closest casino. The drive was two or three minutes. A smattering of cars clustered around the entrance in the midafternoon sun.

"Your boyfriend, Denny, works at a casino, right?" Pierce asked.

"Yeah." I gave him a wary look.

"Did he work at just one or others as well?"

"The one up by me, he'd been there for months but he'd also worked at others. Just not at the same time."

It made me relieved to say that as if I'd just cleared Denny of suspicion. Yes, he'd screwed Katie and that hurt like hell, but he'd been good to me until things went to hellfire in a demonic handbasket.

"That makes sense but I hope to get the list later today of any and all people working at more than one casino. If there's a hundred people we'll have our work cut out for us the next while but what if it's only one guy?" He started up the car and began to drive away. His voice took on a faraway wishful tone. "What if there's just one crazy asshole who works at all the casinos near the abduction sites and he's our man?"

That would be good, I thought. I hoped it was that easy.

The drive to Maple Falls where Iris Bell went missing was almost ninety minutes. Pierce tuned the radio to a classic rock station and hummed along to a lot of the songs.

"You probably haven't even heard of any of this music," he said to me.

"What? The oldies but goodies?" I laughed. "Yeah, this is what we mostly played at the fill-up station."

"Really? Was that your choice or was the manager an old fart like me?"

I just laughed and looked out the window. Margie did set the station but I'd become used to the songs and tunes from the seventies and eighties and didn't mind most of them.

"You're probably missing your phone so that you could be listening to your self-help book."

"I don't mind listening to music."

But, even more, I liked hearing him talk to me.

"Did you find out anything from the DNA evidence off the girls, or are you not allowed to talk about that?"

"I think I'm past the point of trying to keep information from you about this case." He flashed me a crooked half-smile. "But, no, we don't have anything back on the DNA yet. Even with a big push it takes a while. In the meantime we can't hold our breath because it only helps if that evidence is a match to someone already in the system. This guy may never have been incarcerated."

I thought about that for a minute.

"How does someone just start killing people at random like that?" Then I laughed. "Yes, I know serial killers are more screwed up than the average person, but once upon a time this person was a baby and somebody changed his diapers and then he just evolved into a monster."

"I don't know the answer. Why some people can go through hell and become psychotic maniacs while others can be burned but not broken and..."

His voice faded toward the end and he cleared his throat. He was thinking of me. That I was burned but not broken. Or maybe he thought I was a closet psychotic maniac just because my grandmother was easy with her fists and whatever weapon she could get her hands on? He was probably right. At the very least I should come with a warning label.

Warning: Crazed dowser searching divine bones and the bottom of a wine bottle. May explode. Stand clear.

We were almost in Maple Falls when Pierce pulled into a station for gas. I waited in the car and happened to glance over at the fill-up store and my mouth dropped.

"I'll be damned."

Grabbing my purse I climbed out of the car.

"Do you want anything from inside?" I asked Pierce over my shoulder. He shook his head.

I hurried to the store and burst in through the doors with a big smile.

"Hey, there," I called out.

"Oh my God! Julie? What the hell are you doing here?"

"I should ask the same," I walked to the counter and asked Jonas. "Since when do you work at this location?"

He burst out laughing.

"Holy smokes, Julie, I almost didn't recognize you with the blonde hair. It looks good." He came around the counter and gave me a quick awkward hug and then went back to his cash register. "Margie asked me to help out at this station for a couple days when I told her I needed more hours."

He opened his mouth in a wide grin to expose the gap.

"I'm still planning on fixing my tooth but it'll cost a few hundred more."

"That sucks," I said, walking to the cooler and grabbing a Coke. "But you need to get it fixed. You're not going to catch yourself a pretty girl looking like a hockey player."

He snorted and as I paid for the Coke I looked over and saw Pierce leaning against the car watching me.

"Well, gotta run."

"That your dad or something?"

"An uncle," I said over my shoulder as I left the store. Once back inside the car I buckled up.

"Friend of yours?" Pierce asked.

"Actually, yeah, and a coworker. He worked with me at the station."

"I thought you were going into the store to buy something. From now on, you check with me before you just run off to say hi to someone. We're trying to keep you safe. There were threats made against your life and—"

"You know what? I don't need protecting. Not from Jonas. You know how many friends I have left?" I made an O shape with my fingers. "I have zero friends besides this lame-assed kind-of friendship with him. That's it. I'm sure you have a gazillion friends but I don't so you just concentrate on protecting all those girls who could get snatched by the killer," I huffed.

He opened his mouth to reply and then seemed to think better of it. He started the car and we just drove away without a word between us and only the music from the radio filling the car. We drove about ten miles farther down the road before we got to Maple Falls.

When a bunch of dumb commercials came over the radio, Pierce turned off the station.

"For the record I don't," he said.

"Don't what?" I looked at him.

"I don't have a lot of friends. Not real ones anyway. I… I mean *we* had friends together, my wife and me, but…" He shrugged. "They were other couples and afterward…that all drifted away. For the best, I'm sure. Who wants to be the fifth wheel, right?"

"What about Jill? She's certainly friendly toward you." I wiggled my eyebrows at him to lighten the mood.

"Oh you caught that, huh? Yeah, she's not very subtle." He looked over at me, completely bewildered. "For some reason, women find widows attractive. I swear I could have a horn growing out of the middle of my forehead and warts all over but the minute I announce that my wife died, they're on me like white on rice."

He looked comically dumbfounded.

"Maybe you should stop wearing that cologne," I joked. "I smelled it when I was cleaning your bathroom and it almost made me swoon. My knees may even have buckled a little."

He snorted good-naturedly as he steered the car to the curb in front of another pile of bouquets and teddy bears.

"Iris Bell," I said on a sympathetic sigh.

"Yes, we didn't have any cameras to let us know this was the spot but she walked partway home from work with a friend and they parted company right there." He pointed to a street up ahead. "She lives just a block behind us."

The street was quiet and tree lined but vacant of any buildings or houses.

"Was it late when he got her?"

"Evening. Just like the others." He looked up something on his phone. "There are two casinos almost equal distance from here. I'd like to take a drive to both from this location."

He headed north to the first one about thirty minutes away and then returned to the abduction site and went south to the other. There was no more music on the radio and he seemed intent on something that he wasn't about to share with me.

By the time we'd traveled to Alger and Burlington to see the sites where Kari Burke and Sue Torres were taken it was getting late. Pierce insisted on traveling from each site where the girls went missing to the closest casino. He asked me to let him know if I noticed anything unusual or if anything struck me as odd. I wanted to help the case but all streets and routes began to look alike. Many of the roads I'd traveled my entire life and nothing seemed strange or different about the drive. Finally, he reluctantly announced it was time to call it a day. The sun had gone down and there was no use driving around in the dark. A cloud of bleak abjection filled the car. Obviously, Pierce had higher hopes for the outing than I ever did. Right from the start I figured chances were low we'd find any clues just wandering somewhat aimlessly.

We got burgers at a drive-thru on our way back to his place. Although I enjoyed not being imprisoned in the apartment during the day, I was relieved when he finally pulled into the parking garage. My ass was half-asleep after so long in the car and it felt great to finally get out.

"I bet you're thinking that being an FBI agent is not nearly the exciting thing you thought it was," he said as we got off the elevator and walked down the hall.

It was boring as hell except for running into Jonas at the gas station but I wasn't going to tell him that.

He opened the door and I stepped inside.

"I sure as hell hope you get reimbursed for the gasoline if this is your normal day." I kicked off my shoes.

"Wow," he said, stopping short in the entrance.

"What?" I asked.

"It smells so fresh in here. I just noticed how much you must've cleaned this morning. I almost feel like I should mess the place up a bit."

"Don't you dare!" I said in mock horror.

He grabbed a couple glasses of water and brought them to the couch. I'd been ready to just head to my room but I guess he wanted company so I joined him on the sofa.

"Most of my job is like today," he admitted. "Boring paperwork, lots of legwork that leads nowhere. Chasing nothing leads and guessing about what to do next."

"You don't know it goes nowhere, though, right? That's why you do all this stuff because all you can do is try and find a link."

He leaned forward and sifted through the paper pile on the end of the coffee table and took out the eight-by-ten pictures of the missing girls. He fanned them out on the table and just stared at them.

"I'm missing something. I wish you could just wave a magic wand or hit me over the head with one of your rods and make me figure out what I can't see, because there's something big that I'm just overlooking. I can feel it."

He gathered up the pictures and put them back face-down on the other paperwork. Then he leaned back and put his feet on the coffee table and closed his eyes. I sipped my water for a minute and when he didn't open his eyes I got to my feet.

"Good night then," I said, walking away.

"Oh just a second."

He got up and headed off to his bedroom and returned with a stack of books that he put down on the coffee table.

"Ta-da. My self-help books. I thought you'd get a real kick out of these. Feel free to choose one if you want some light reading." He snagged one from the top. "Here's a good one, *Moving On: How to Heal Your Heart*." He tossed it aside. "It was a gift from someone or other but never mind that one because it put me to sleep in Chapter One. How about this one?" He picked up a thick hardcover. "*Mindfulness Exercises for Grieving*." He laughed. "I actually thought it was some kind of physical exercise regime."

I laughed and picked up the next one in the stack.

"*Exit Laughing: How Humor Takes the Sting Out of Death*," I read out loud and then looked at him with mock seriousness. "Well, did it? Did laughing take the sting out of death?" I put the book down and covered my mouth with my hand because I realized that was completely inappropriate but still let a giggle out. I started laughing so hard and I couldn't stop. I loudly snorted, then covered my face in mortification and bit the inside of my cheek to try and gain some control. It didn't work at all. Now I was snorting and giggling behind my hands as tears of laughter filled in my eyes.

"You find that funny, do you?" He took a step toward

me and waved a finger in my face. "I'll have you know that it was actually a *very* good book. I quite enjoyed it."

"I-I'm so sorry." I cleared my throat.

"No, you're not." He reached over and poked me in the ribs. "You're not sorry at all, are you?"

"No, I'm really not."

I squealed as he came closer and poked me in my ribs again, causing me to guffaw-giggle-snort in a really unladylike way. Suddenly he had both hands on my waist and we grew very quiet.

"You have a beautiful laugh."

The entire world seemed to cry *hush.*

I became very still as I looked up at his face. Licking my lips, I took a half step forward until we were only a breath apart.

"I'd like to kiss you," he said, his voice touchingly earnest. "I've wanted to kiss you for a very long time."

"Agent Pierce, I don't think Jill would like that very much," I breathed.

One of his fingertips traced up my arm to my shoulder.

"Then I should *definitely* do it," he murmured. "Please don't call me Agent Pierce."

"Garrett," I said, the name feeling strange on my lips.

He leaned forward, then added haltingly, "Are you okay with it, Julie?" He froze then and retracted. "I'm crossing the line here. I'm very sorry. Of course you're not okay with it. I don't know what came over me."

He went to turn away but I reached up and circled my arms around his neck, stood on tiptoe and drew him close to brush my lips against his. Hesitantly he returned the kiss and soon there was a fever of desire as he wrapped his arms around me and molded my body to his. His embrace was gentle, as if he was afraid I'd shatter into a million pieces if he squeezed too tight. I had zero interest in being treated like a delicate flower or an inexperienced virgin. My mouth opened and explored his. He was still hesitant until I took his hand and guided it under my T-shirt to my breast.

"Are you sure?" his lips murmured against mine on a low moan.

I reached for his zipper in answer and seconds later we were in his bed. There was no time to overthink the situation. All I wanted was to feel and concentrate on so many sensations happening at once. I met his need with a ferocious urgency of my own. Afterward, when he collapsed on top of me, I clutched him tightly and placed soft kisses on his chest before he rolled off.

It was inevitable, this frantic explosion between us, I told myself as I lay there trying to catch my breath. We worked closely together day after day and we both needed to obliterate the horrors of what we'd seen. I rolled onto my side and soon I heard his breath grow slow and even, so I opened the blanket to crawl out of his bed. I was sitting on the edge of the bed with my back to him when I heard the rustle of the blankets behind me.

"Stay," he said. "Please, stay."

He placed his hand at the center of my shoulder blades and his fingers traced and caressed my back from the top all the way down to the small indent at the base of my spine. I tensed as he haltingly touched the gruesome raised and knotted scar tissue. Then deliberately he put his lips to all of those old wounds, tracing the hideous keloid scars with his mouth and stripping away the ugliness. We made love again and it was as close to healing as I'd ever experienced.

EIGHT

I SLEPT HARD and long. The next morning I woke to voices. My hand went to Garrett but the sheets on his side were cool. I sat up and looked around for my clothes strewn haphazardly around the room and slowly began to dress. The woman's voice was louder, sharp. It was Jill. I zipped my jeans and just sat on the edge of the bed. I couldn't go out there and see her after breaking yet another one of her rules.

A biggie, I thought and smiled.

She left with the slam of a door and he walked into the bedroom. Things had changed. Immediately I could see that by the cut of his chin, the regret in his eyes and the way he hesitated to come closer. I got to my feet, smoothed my hair and went to leave.

"I guess I'll hit the shower," I said casually.

"We've got to talk."

Oh, brother. Cliché much? Get ready for it. He'll say it's not me it's him and last night was a mistake and blah, blah, blah.

He took me by the hand and brought me to the sofa. I sat, trying not to show fear and sadness in my eyes while he perched on the coffee table across from me, our knees touching. I steeled my heart and head from the hurt and then decided to go on the offensive.

"I know, I know." I put my hands up palms out. "You

don't have to say anything. It was a mistake. It's bad for the case because it could taint the evidence and—"

"Another girl is missing," he said.

I just blinked in surprise and wrapped my thoughts around the horror of that but also hid the glimmer of hope in my chest that he didn't regret the night before. Immediately I cringed with guilt because what does one night of lovemaking mean against the life of a young girl. I wanted to slap myself.

Garrett leaned forward and placed his hands on my knees.

"It's Katie."

"What do you mean?" I tilted my head in confusion.

"It's Katie. Your friend," he repeated. "We don't know exactly when she was taken because nobody reported her missing."

"No." I got to my feet. "That's ridiculous. Katie goes missing all the time. She is notorious for her disappearing act." I paced the room. "In eleventh grade her mom had every cop in the neighborhood convinced she'd been taken and then she showed up after three days wearing the same slutty dress she'd been clubbing in days before."

"We know it's the same guy."

"How do you know?" I demanded.

"Her car was found in the casino parking lot." He got up as he spoke and put his hands on my shoulder. "There was blood inside and a white ribbon."

"No."

I shook my head and continued to murmur "no" even as he put his arms around me and held me tight.

"Maybe it's not the same guy because he didn't leave ribbons on the abduction scenes, right? Could be just a prank. A copycat or it could even be that she set it up herself for attention, because that would be one hundred percent Katie," I said against his shoulder.

He let me ramble until I'd finally stopped and then he kissed the top of my head.

"They're bringing in someone to be interviewed so I have to go." He turned away. "I might be gone a while but, I'm sorry, you're going to have to sit tight here."

"A suspect?" I followed him to the door. "That's good, right? They caught the guy. We should celebrate."

"It's just a guy being brought in for questioning. It doesn't mean anything. We've interviewed a lot of guys over the last couple months."

"Okay." I nodded. He didn't want me to get my hopes up. I got that. "But it's better than nothing."

"Damn, you're probably going to hear it on the news anyway…" He shoved his feet in his shoes and reached for his keys off the counter. "It's Denny."

My mouth opened and closed like a goldfish.

He lifted my chin with the tip of his finger.

"It doesn't mean he did it but he was the last one seen with her so we've got to follow through, okay?"

He went to kiss the top of my head but I lifted my face to receive his lips on mine, and I kissed him long and hard, feeling overwhelmed and emotional. I wanted desperately to obliterate his words and simultaneously wanted Garrett to carry my imprint with him. He answered my need and for a flash of time I thought we'd be back in bed forgetting about anything as silly as Katie going missing and Denny being a murderer. Then he broke away and left in a whirl of apologies.

The minute he was gone I flipped on the television and watched the news. Replay after replay of Katie's nineteen-seventy-two blue Mustang surrounded by crime scene tape, and then a shot of Denny being brought out to a waiting undercover car. A hoodie covered his head and we only saw him from the back. The journalists only said it was an unknown person of interest but I knew from the stride, the set of his shoulders and a tangle of dark hair from the edge of the hoodie that it was Denny.

My head throbbed as I picked up my phone and called Gramps.

"I heard the news," he said when he answered the phone. "It's a mistake, of course. As big a numbskull as Denny is, I don't see him as a mastermind or criminal. Certainly doesn't have enough brains in his stupid head to be abducting and killing multiple girls."

"I know, it's crazy, right?" I rubbed the back of my neck. "But what about Katie? What do you think happened to her?" I swallowed nervously. "Do you think it was the same guy who took the others?"

"I don't know, hon, but you just calm down and don't worry about it. I'm sure Katie will come out right as rain. She always does."

"You're right. Katie's Teflon." I blew out a shallow breath. "I know I was pissed at her and Denny but that doesn't mean I wish them bad."

"Of course you don't. You've got a gold heart and you never wish anyone bad."

That wasn't true. I'd spent a lot of time growing up wishing I'd wake up and find Grandma dead on the kitchen floor of a sudden heart attack. At the end of the day, though, it had been her icy front steps that caused her to fall, crack her head open and die instantly. When I'd been at home it had been my job to chop away at the ice on the steps and then salt them. I shuddered when I remembered the glimmer of joy I'd felt when Gramps called me with the news of her death. I should've felt guilty but I didn't. All I felt then—and, to be honest, feel now—is unadulterated relief that the woman was now dancing with Satan and no longer on the planet.

I realized Gramps was going on about Wookie and so I gave my head a shake and tried to concentrate on what he was saying.

"You see, there's no truth to that saying you can't teach an old dog new tricks. This old dog learned how to bake dog treats from a recipe and Wookie learned to beg for the entire pan."

I closed my eyes and smiled at the thought of Gramps baking for my dog.

"I've never seen you cook or bake. Obviously I should've left you to your own devices long ago."

"Well, I've burned a few things already," he admitted. "Found out the batteries in the smoke detector work but that dumb mutt doesn't care."

Wookie was barking in the background as if in agreement.

"Gotta go take him for his walk. We have rabbits to chase. Big rabbits," Gramps said. "Don't be wasting your head space worrying about Denny and Katie. What will be, will be."

That wasn't good enough for me. I didn't want to just wait for the fates to bring Katie home.

We disconnected and I watched the television news again and again. Garrett had so many channels I could watch the same video clips on a half dozen different channels with varying opinions. In the end, though, they all said the same thing, which was nothing at all. There was a whole lot of guessing about this serial killer and

Katie's abduction. There was no mention at all made about blood in the car or the white ribbon. The law enforcement agencies were playing their cards close to their chests. It made me wonder what else they didn't reveal to the public. Or me. I was guessing that Garrett had a ton of information he wasn't about to reveal to some dowsing girl he happened to screw in a moment of weakness.

He kept his laptop on a credenza in the bedroom. I went in there and the scent of our lovemaking still hung in the air, making me feel guilty as I opened his computer to search for information. No matter what I tried, I couldn't get past the password request and I gave up after a few tries and turned it off. I decided to return to the living room and go through the stacks of paperwork.

I'd shuffled through the papers before but now I read all the notes and analyzed the pictures and reports. There was a ton of information on anyone who knew me and especially Gramps, Grandma, Katie and people who worked with me at the gas station. Also, I found a file that contained all the things that connected the girls besides the fact that they were from towns in Washington State. Each one had been a victim of abuse and had, at one time, attended a group therapy session at the community center for victims of abuse. I knew it well and had attended a session myself one time after I'd seen it advertised online. Went once but didn't go back. Bunch of doe-eyed girls who jumped out of their skin when there were loud noises. I wasn't like that and didn't feel right being there. I guess that was a connection they were keeping from the public. The killer must've seen them there or met them there.

There was a file simply marked with the initials POI.

I had no idea what that stood for but I opened it and realized that it contained almost ten pages about me. My throat grew dry as I read all the information: my date of birth, my mother's name, the fact that my birth certificate listed the father as unknown, the schools I attended, and more recent history of places I lived and who I lived with and where. Apparently the guy I'd roomed with just a few blocks from here during my waitressing days was doing time for sexual assault. Garrett had circled his name three times but notes farther on indicated the guy was definitely in jail at the time of the abductions.

Garrett had admitted the first time we met that he'd thoroughly checked out my history, but seeing my life sprawled out in front of me in black and white still made me feel violated. His final notes were his interview with Mrs. Buchanan. She'd hired me years ago to help find her little girl presumed drowned in the Nooksack River. His notes said the dad refused to be party to my search even though the girl had gone missing and then died while out fishing with him, but the mom told Garrett she would be forever in my debt for giving her closure.

Closure. I always cringed at the word even though I understood the need people had to have someone to put inside the casket.

Altogether I saw at least one hundred pages on the missing and dead girls, trying to draw a connection. Everything from every dentist any had ever seen to every single teacher, boyfriend, schoolmate, neighbor and cell phone provider. Beyond the fact that each girl had been a victim of abuse, I saw little connection between the girls other than they all lived north of Seattle in the west half of the state. Suggesting the killer was also a local.

Once I found a blank piece of paper, I wrote down

everything I knew about Katie to see if any part of
her life crossed with the other girls. Nothing I could
find matched. I slammed my fist on the coffee table
out of frustration. On the off chance Katie had sent me
any kind of message, I started up my laptop and went
through my emails. Nothing from Katie but there was
a message from Jonas.

Great seeing you with your uncle yesterday. What a
fluke to run into you like that! I'm so sorry to hear about
Katie. ☹ I know you used to be friends so I'm sending
you hugs and kisses.

The attached picture was of him making a moronic
kissy face. His comment that Katie and I "used to be
friends" hurt. He hadn't heard of the disagreement from
me so that meant that either she had told him we'd fought
or he'd heard it around town. Probably heard all about
Denny and Katie being together and me catching them
playing hide the salami. A part of me still wanted to
be too angry with Katie to care about her going missing but nobody deserved what happened to those girls.
Katie had been a part of my life for so long that her abduction felt personal and I had an ache of worry sitting
heavy in my chest.

Deciding maybe a hot shower would help clear my
head, I closed my laptop and got to my feet just as my
phone chimed. It was a text from Jill telling me to open
the door. The second I opened it she walked past me with
a sack of groceries. She took out random salad fixings
and a bottle of dressing and some chicken breasts and
stuck it all in the fridge.

"If you're going to play his mistress the least you can

do is cook for him," she said snidely. "Oh, don't worry. He's too sweet to kiss and tell. I guessed when I showed up early this morning and the door to your room was wide-open and, guess what, you weren't in it."

"It's really none of your business."

"That a fact?" She put her hands on her hips. "Your name is all over this case. Just because Garrett is the lead investigator doesn't mean we don't all go down with him if the evidence is tossed out because he's sleeping with a witness. I use the term *witness* loosely because, in my opinion, this entire investigation revolves around you." She poked a sharp fingernail in my chest and I took an involuntary step backward. "Your best friend is missing. Your boyfriend is being interrogated as we speak, *a-a-and* you've found three bodies." She laughed meanly. "For all I know you're sleeping with Garrett *and* the killer. Wouldn't surprise me one single bit actually."

"You should go," I said, trying to sound tough.

"You're throwing me out of his house now? That's priceless." She laughed. "Don't ever forget that you were a person of interest on this case long before you became his roll in the hay."

She slammed the door so hard when she left that the floor shook. I turned the dead bolt and exhaled loudly. It took me ten minutes in the shower just to wash away Jill's venom.

The words *person of interest* ricocheted inside my head. My file was marked POI. At least now I knew what that stood for.

When I climbed out and dried myself off I remembered I'd seen a washer and dryer in a closet off the kitchen. I put the small amount of clothes I'd brought from home into the washer and then I took the sheet off my bed and wrapped it around myself when I returned to my laptop.

There were two emails from Katie's mom, Mrs. Cole. The first one was a message that she sent to everyone on her email list. It had a Missing Person poster attached with a picture of Katie. She was pleading with everyone to put them up all over town. The second email was a personal message to me:

I know you and Katie had some kind of falling out but I don't care about that right now. Katie told me a long time ago that you have some kind of witching talent. If you have the power to help find my baby girl please try. Please, please try. Love, Mrs. Cole.

The message twisted my heart. Mrs. Cole was the only person who ever stood up to Grandma. She'd seen marks on my legs one summer and told Grandma that she would call the authorities if it didn't stop. Grandma was a lot more careful about where she landed her blows after that, but it was nice of Mrs. Cole to try.

With all the other crazy emails that had flooded my inbox I nearly deleted a reply from the woman who was a self-proclaimed expert at pendulum dowsing. She suggested multiple reasons why my pendulum dowsing might not be revealing results.

Perhaps the questions you are seeking are not for you to know. If that is the case, you may not ever get your answers. I do not know if you are using metal or crystal for your pendulum but some find that divining with a more personal object with emotional ties helps to relieve blockages. Also, I suggest you remove all emotions you have tied to the outcome.

She went into great detail describing her own methods of dowsing. It felt strange having someone describe so matter-of-factly something I'd always kept somewhat quiet and deemed to be my own weirdo talent. I left the email open in order to think about the suggestions while I went to throw my clothes from the washer to the dryer. Garrett walked into the apartment while I was standing there with only the sheet on.

He looked positively miserable but then he stopped and his eyes grazed over me.

"That's the best thing I've ever seen you wear," he said, walking toward me. Then he pulled the sheet from my grasp and it pooled at my feet. "Correction, this is."

We didn't make it to the bedroom this time and the lovemaking was frantic and hurried and felt more like a cathartic purging of all that was broken in both of us. Afterward he lifted me and brought me naked to lie on the sofa. He crawled in behind me and covered both our bodies with the thin sheet.

"I need to rest my brain for a while," he whispered and his hot breath caressed my neck. "Please lie with me."

It was midafternoon and I wasn't tired at all, but feeling needed and cherished was the most powerful drug I'd ever experienced. It was much stronger than all the wine I'd ever had and I wouldn't have moved out of that spot for the world. When he draped his arm around me and I could feel his heart beat against my skin, I finally understood what all the love songs and poets raved about. My head knew that we were just seeking refuge in each other. This could not possibly be love. Still my soul ached for him and for the possibility.

Oh my dear gawd I was love drunk.

After an hour he stretched languidly behind me and cupped my breast.

"Did you sleep at all or just wait for me?"

"I closed my eyes for a minute."

Not a complete lie. I had rolled toward him and buried my face in his chest with my eyes closed and enjoyed the rise and fall of his chest and the steady rhythm of his heart.

"I see you've been getting more information on pendulum dowsing," he said, obviously reading my email on the coffee table.

"Yeah." I sat up reluctantly. "I don't know if it'll help at all but thought I'd get advice from a so-called expert." I turned to him. "Are you hungry? Jill dropped off some more food."

He sat up and dragged his fingers through his hair. "I'm sure she was her usual polite self."

"She definitely has a big hate on for me. What were the terms she used?" I tapped my chin. "Oh yeah...*person of interest* and also your roll in the hay."

"Damn," he muttered. "I'm sorry."

"Don't be. Strangely enough only one of those insults bothered me and it wasn't the part about rolling."

He laughed then but got up in search of his clothes across the room. Once he was dressed, he pulled his cell phone from his pocket and typed on it. "There. I've asked her not to come by the apartment anymore. Her services as your keeper are temporarily on hold."

"I appreciate that."

I walked down the hall, pulled my clothes from the

dryer and dressed on the spot and then brought the spare couple of outfits to my room, folded them and put them back in my bag. When I came back to the living room he had my computer on his lap.

"Have you tried all these suggestions?"

"No." I sat down next to him. "I don't have a personal item to use for dowsing. Obviously part of your bathroom faucet that I was using is not what she'd call personal. I don't own any jewelry so..." I shrugged.

"Yeah, I wouldn't think so." His phone kept beeping with incoming messages. "I have to go back out," he said. "I'm sorry but I can't take you with me and I might be quite late."

"Sure. I get that." I nodded. "How'd it go with Denny?"

"He's been released and he'll be watched over the next while but he was working inside the casino at the time we think the attack happened. The casino has cameras everywhere and he seemed to be on the casino floor and on camera throughout his shift. Outside cameras showed him coming into the building at the beginning of the day and leaving at the end of his shift and not leaving otherwise."

"Did the cameras pick up anything in the lot around Katie's car?"

He shook his head. "Her car was parked just out of range of the cameras."

"She loves that stupid car," I mumbled. "She always parks it far away so nobody will accidentally ding it."

Garrett had walked to the door then and I followed to say goodbye. After he slipped on a jacket he turned to me. "I feel like I need to be saying something here about you and me."

"You really don't have to."

Please don't ruin it by trying to classify it and make it fit into a square box. And also please don't say anything that makes this happy feeling dancing in my gut turn into a diarrhea cramp.

Before he could say anything I dragged him into a kiss. I really didn't want him to try and fill the air with words that might sting or, worse, pacify. After a couple of minutes of tongue tango he wordlessly left the apartment to go and be the big bad agent he got paid to be. I hoped he did his job well and found Katie before anything bad happened. I locked the door and returned to the computer where I re-read the dowsing expert's opinion about using a personal item as a pendulum tool. She'd attached a link that had a video of her performing pendulum dowsing. Her technique was similar to mine but she used a gold chain and her wedding band. On the video she claimed that oftentimes a ring held the most intimate emotional value and that it was always a truer instrument for her, adding that the ring of anyone interested in the outcome of a question could work.

It made me wish that I wore jewelry and it also made me think of that white circle on Garrett's finger. It might not be an impassioned token of mine, but it would belong to someone who was emotionally invested in the questions I needed to ask. I drummed my fingertips on the table for a few seconds while I thought about all the reasons it would be totally wrong for me to use Garrett's wedding ring. In the end, though, I decided to look for it and was able to find it in the first place I checked— in the drawer of his nightstand. Next, I looked for floss and found it in his bathroom cabinet.

After I tied the ring to a length of floss I took it into

the living room. I sat cross-legged on the floor and held the ring to my heart.

"Please allow me to use the energy of this ring in order to help others," I said.

Lifting the string up, I steadied the ring until it was completely still.

"Show me your yes."

The ring moved from left to right slowly and then picked up speed in a wide arc. I stopped the motion and waited for it to settle.

"Show me your no."

The ring moved toward me and away in a deliberate line, slowly at first and then more quickly. Once again I stilled it.

"Is Katie still alive?"

The ring moved left to right in a perfect affirmative manner.

"Whew, thank God."

I blew out a breath and swallowed against the lump that formed in my throat as I steadied the ring.

"Is Sue Torres still alive?"

At first the ring remained motionless but slowly it swung toward me and away.

No.

"Damn."

NINE

KATIE WAS ALIVE but Sue Torres was dead. Things were speeding up. He was no longer keeping them alive for weeks. I got out the map and flattened it out on the floor in front of me then smoothed the creases. I started calling out names with the ring poised to answer.

"Is Katie in Anacortes?"

The answer came back no.

"Is Katie in Bellingham?"

No.

"Is Katie in Everett?"

No.

I recited town after town and the answer was always no which could mean the entire pendulum thing was complete crap. Or I had yet to guess the right town. So I kept guessing. Eventually my stomach clenched from hunger and I made myself a sandwich. I ate it over the sink and washed it down with a glass of water while I thought of another step to find Katie alive.

When I returned to sit cross-legged at the map, I picked up the string again.

"Is Sue Torres dead?"

The ring swung left and right in confirmation.

I looked over the map, at the rivers and casinos and abduction locations and possible bridge areas.

"Is Sue Torres's body in the Samish River?"

The pendulum returned a no.

I asked three more rivers and all came back as a no. "One more." I sighed then promised myself a break. "Is Sue Torres in Thomas Creek?"

A wide swinging arc back and forth. I gasped. Yes.

Oh my God! I closed my eyes and let a silent tear fall because we were too late again and I was still better at finding the dead than the living.

When Garrett walked through the door in the wee hours of the morning, I was sitting on the couch in just a T-shirt. I had the television on to a sitcom rerun that I wasn't watching. I'd already placed his wedding ring back in its resting place because it felt like a betrayal to tell him that I'd used that symbol of love to find a body.

"You didn't have to wait up," he said, shuffling into the living room as if the weight of the world was on his shoulders. "I expected you to be in bed long ago."

"Katie is alive," I said quietly. "At least she was a few hours ago according to the pendulum of doom." I sighed. "Unfortunately, Sue Torres is dead. She's in Thomas Creek. Where the old ninety-nine highway crosses over."

He stopped in his tracks. "You should've called me."

"I thought about it, but she's dead and Katie's alive and I wanted to find where Katie was and I couldn't." I looked away and blinked back a tear.

He got on his phone then to pass along the message. When he ended the call he reached out a hand to me.

"We'll head out as soon as it's light. Come to bed."

The next morning I was out of the shower and dressed ready to go by six although the sun had yet to poke up from the horizon. Garrett was making phone calls. Near as I could tell the phone didn't leave his ear even while he showered and dressed. I'd made coffee and toast and handed him one of both. My body was apprehensive and tense with the weight of a secret.

"Ready?" Garrett asked, which was a foolish question because I'd been standing at the door with my shoes on for fifteen minutes.

"I used your wedding ring on a string of dental floss to do the pendulum dowsing," I blurted. "I'm sorry. I know that's an invasion of your privacy but it was the only object I could think of that had emotion tied to it. I should've asked. I'm very, very sorry."

"My wedding ring?" He stared at me. Dark emotion crossed his face and then was gone.

"Yes. I put it back in your drawer."

He nodded. "Let's go."

Once we were in the car he told me that he'd called investigators to meet us on the scene. Every other time he called the technicians to come after the body was found. I fisted the L-rods in my lap and hoped the pendulum could be trusted.

We'd been battling Seattle traffic for half an hour when he said suddenly, "I don't want you to be afraid to tell me anything, or ask me if something's okay. Like the ring." He turned to look at me. "You were afraid to ask me."

"I wasn't afraid… I just…"

"You were afraid to ask me and then you were afraid to tell me afterward."

I swallowed and turned away. He reached to grab my hand and held it tight. My eyes were moist and I couldn't look at him. Fear had been part of my makeup for so long I didn't know how to turn it off.

The area a hundred yards from the bridge was abuzz when we arrived. Agents were standing around with coffees in their hands and just leaning against their cars. All were men except for Jill, who stood out like an angry sore thumb. Garrett parked the car behind the others and asked me to wait. He got out and talked to the others while I held tight and counted the minutes. Simultaneously all heads turned to look at me and I felt myself grow small and worried.

Garrett returned to the car and opened my door.

"Nothing like an audience," I complained.

"I can send them away if you think that—"

"I'm fine. It'll be good." I stepped out, rods in my hand.

"Some of them have already gone down to the water. Stomping all over a potential crime scene like the stupid asses they are."

"Well, they have every right to be here. I just have to put on my big girl panties and do what needs to be done."

He bent down and whispered in my ear, "I'm going to get you out of those big girl panties before the day is out."

I turned away so the others couldn't see my smile or guess about the blush on my cheeks. Straightening my spine, I cleared my throat and blew out a long breath.

"You've got this," he said.

I nodded, put on my game face and put out the rods. While everyone watched and Garrett walked behind me, I stepped into the grassy ditch and followed it in the direction of the creek. I could hear the water rushing and a curious crow cawed his dislike at my intrusion. The rods remained still. The bank was covered in blackberry brambles nearly five feet high.

"Hey, Garrett, we looked over the bridge," Jill called out. "There's nothing down there."

I licked my lips and followed the edge of the bramble.

It was silly because nobody would've dragged a body down this way.

"Could we drive over to the other side?"

"Absolutely."

Garrett held up his hand to stop the questions that pelted us as we walked back to the car and then drove only a couple hundred feet forward. It was embarrassing. I should've been able to stroll right on past all those agents with my head high but there was no way I had that level of confidence. Plus, even though the bridge was small, it was still high over water and gave me the willies.

I climbed out and started my walk again. Almost immediately I felt a tremor and the rods pulled away in the opposite direction of the bridge. The ditch was filled with runoff from the creek. At one point my right foot slid on the mud and water filled my shoe, but the rods were pulling. I followed a gravel farm road that crossed the quick-flowing creek. I climbed up the bank and stood on the gravel over the ditch. The rods crossed. I took a couple of steps forward and they uncrossed. From the corner of my eye I could see the clutch of dark suits that had followed along the road side to watch. There was complete silence when I backed up and the rods crossed again.

Garrett was behind me.

"Where?" he asked.

In answer I walked back down the short grassy bank, where water flowed under the farm road through a concrete culvert. I shuffled down, pushed the tall weeds aside and bent to look. I caught a glimpse of a delicate white hand just inside the tunnel. Garrett put his hands on my shoulder and stopped me from going farther.

"It's okay. We've got her from here."

"In the culvert!" he shouted to the suits as he walked me back to his car.

There was a great deal of scrambling then with guys popping their trunks and grabbing evidence bags and cameras. Jill stood outside Garrett's car and stepped forward as he opened the door for me.

"I can sit with her awhile, if you'd like," she offered in a saccharine tone.

Please say no. Please say no.

"Take off, Jill," he said coolly as he shut my door.

I covered my smile with my hand but Jill caught it anyway and the daggers in her eyes chilled me more than my soaking wet foot. She didn't follow Garrett and the others down the slope into the culvert. I imagined it wasn't in her job description as babysitter of the dowser. When I looked up, I noticed something white fluttering in the distance. I squinted and leaned forward.

"Damn."

I climbed out of the car and looked around for someone to tell. Jill was closest so I called her over. She sulkily came and I pointed up the road to a cluster of thorny blackberry bushes.

"I think that might be a white ribbon."

She followed where I was pointing.

"Oh God," she muttered and chased off down the road.

A couple of the other left-behind agents followed her but she got there first. I watched her don gloves, whip out her phone to snap some pictures, and then step right into the thorny branches to retrieve the ribbon, holding it up as if it was a trophy.

She carried it importantly in her gloved hands and placed it in an evidence bag another agent handed her.

Then she came up alongside the car, opened my door and said, "Good eye, Julie." And shut the door again.

It was a big deal for her, I could tell.

It had started to rain and the agents were pulling out tarps and canopies on stands trying to protect their crime scene. Garrett climbed into the car and was drenched.

"Whew," he said. "I'm done here. Ready for lunch?"

He was pumped and it jostled me.

"Why wasn't the ribbon attached to her?" I asked. "All the other girls..."

"It was attached. On the wrist. Just like the others." He started the car up and blasted the heat.

"Oh I guess the one I saw was just a random piece of trash?"

"No, it definitely looked like the same kind the perp is using on the girls. Maybe a bit that got away from him while he was tossing her over the bridge?" He smiled over at me. "He's getting sloppy."

"And that's a good thing."

"Very good. It means he's feeling the pressure and he's more likely to get caught. We may even have a witness this time." He nodded up the road to a large bungalow. "Guy up the road said his dog was going nuts around one in the morning. He saw a car stop on the bridge."

"Really?"

"Unfortunately, all he could tell the investigators was that it was a dark four-door. Possibly older model. He thought the guy might be having car trouble so he was going to come out and offer some help. By the time he got his shoes on, the car was gone."

He turned the car around and we were heading back toward the highway.

"But it means he's killing them sooner." I licked my lips nervously. "Katie won't have very long."

His mouth pulled into a serious frown. "Hopefully, long enough."

We were quiet as we headed back down the highway.

"Where would you like to grab a bite to eat?"

"Could we just have something at your place?"

"Home it is," he said.

But it wasn't my home. It was far away from Gramps, Wookie and probably from wherever Katie was being held.

"You're upset," he said as we neared the city. "Julie, I want you to know that we've got literally hundreds of guys searching every clue and all the areas for Katie."

"I know."

But I felt in my bones it wouldn't be enough, and now he was going to bring me back to his apartment and I would sit there and fret and pendulum dowse and let the quicksand thoughts and monsters creep under my skin like an infection.

He parked the car and came around to open my door. He always did that and it was strangely sweet. I knew it was an old-fashioned gentlemanly thing but it made me feel weak. He grabbed for my bag.

"I've got it," I snipped.

Then I felt petty and annoyed at myself because all I wanted at that moment was him and I didn't want to push him away. The second the elevator doors closed, I dropped my bag and ravished him. I pulled his shirt out from his pants so I could run my hands up his chest and feel his warmth as my mouth devoured his. He met my need with his own and when the doors slid open we stumbled down the hall, not wanting to let our lips part. He kicked the door shut and pulled my shirt up over my head as I frantically wriggled out of my jeans.

There was nothing tender or subdued about our wild and raw encounter. I wanted to expunge all thoughts of white ribbons, dead girls and Katie, and Garrett, no doubt, had his own demons to bury.

Ultimately we both slid onto the cold kitchen tile trying to catch our breath.

"Wow," he said exhaling loudly. "I was wrong about one thing," he continued as we both struggled, gasping to our feet.

"What's that?"

"Age *does* make a difference. You're killing me."

"You don't seem to have a problem keeping up." I slapped his bare ass as he walked into the bedroom to dress. "And I mean that both figuratively and literally."

He chuckled softly then went to his laptop in the corner of the room and checked a few things before heading for the shower.

I climbed naked on top of the covers of his bed and lay there languidly, fingers laced behind my head, trying really hard not to think of anything—particularly four dead girls and missing Katie. When he entered the bedroom with a towel wrapped around his hips, he slowly shook his head and his eyes darkened with desire. He bent and kissed me tenderly.

"Wish I didn't have to go out again but I have to go meet with the medical examiner." He began to dress and I enjoyed watching him move.

"If you keep looking at me like that, I'm never going to leave this apartment."

"Promises, promises," I joked.

He slipped a belt through the loops of his pants and grabbed a new shirt. He sat on the bed as he did up the buttons.

"I don't know how long I'm going to be," he admitted. "This may well go into tomorrow so order a pizza or Chinese if you get hungry and—"

"Don't worry about me. I'm fully capable of feeding myself. Just do what you have to do."

"Once this is done, I want to spend a week—no, make that a *month*—in bed with you."

That was a wonderful, marvelous thought that felt like a fairy tale. I didn't pin hopes on it. He'd begun to mean so much to me and I honestly couldn't say if that was real or circumstances. I needed to protect my heart.

He brushed a kiss against my lips and then got to his feet.

"Oh yeah." He opened the bedside table, pulled out his wedding ring and squeezed it in his fist for just a second before he placed it in my hand. "If it will help, feel free to use it."

His laptop still glowed in the corner of the room and once he was gone, I set his wedding ring on the table and sat down with his computer. I began to look for anything that could give me an idea of where to start looking for Katie. I wanted to know who, for example, had given him hints about where the first couple of bodies were located.

It took me only a few moments to uncover the fact that the tips had come anonymously by handwritten letters in the mail postmarked in Oregon. Who wrote letters anymore? The notes had been fingerprinted and the envelopes checked for saliva DNA but both revealed noth-

ing. Although the notes described the letters, the letters
were not in the file.

I saw documents from the medical examiner's office
for Iris, Luna and Kari but it was too soon for Sue's. In
every case the cause of death was listed as asphyxiation. They'd been strangled and, based on traces of evidence on the bodies, it looked as though a common type
of rope had been used. A long list of debris collected
at all the scenes was itemized. Every cigarette butt and
random trash from a single shoelace to bottle caps had
been bagged and itemized. Reading the long list caused
my eyes to twitch.

There was a large document written about me but it
was basically the same thing as what was contained in
the folder on the coffee table. One note had been made
that I seemed to have no medical records beyond a broken wrist and no dental records.

*If you're not dead or dying there's no reason to pay
money for a quack*, Grandma used to remark. Because
there was no way she'd want a doctor taking a close look
at the marks on my body. I didn't catch many flu bugs
growing up and the couple times I did, I went to school
anyway. It was always better than being at home.

A few things added to my file recently included interviews of Margie and Jonas. An agent had gone by
and asked them about my character after I'd gone out
that first time with Garrett. It felt like something that
had Jill's name all over it but Margie and Jonas didn't
have much to say besides that I never missed a shift and
customers liked me.

"Go me," I murmured to the room. "When this is all
over, I'd better get hired back and get a big fat raise."

Quickly I scanned through the rest of the document

on Delma Arsenault slash Julie Hall, interested to see if Garrett had made any personal observations about me. Not that I expected there to be mention of my superior skills at lovemaking but the thought did make me smile.

I was still smiling when I turned to the last page of the document about me. The final entry was a picture labeled Molly Arsenault. My mother. It was like a punch in the gut.

"Oh. My. God."

The words came out on a gut-wrenching gasp. My lips began to tremble and my hand reached to touch the screen. The only photo I'd seen of her was when she was in her late teens, probably around the time she had me and ran away. This picture wasn't that old. The face staring back to me was maybe forty years old but I'd recognize those pale blue eyes and that full bow mouth anywhere. I'd memorized those features years ago. There was a notice at the bottom of the page giving the last known address in the town of Marysville.

Abruptly I got to my feet. I rubbed my hands on my arms as if they were freezing and I walked in circles. What if she still lived at that address? I was breathing heavily and sweating. Forcing myself to calm down, I got a pen and paper and took down the address. Then I googled the address and Molly Arsenault to see if I could find a phone number. Nothing. I did a street-view map search of the house and found myself staring at the small white wood-framed house.

That could be her house.

There was a blue compact car parked out front.

That could be her car.

The yellow house next door had a For Sale sign out front.

Those could be her crazy-assed neighbors who always annoyed her but now they were moving and she was relieved. I followed the street view down the road and imagined her walking to that corner store and stopping to mail a letter in that mailbox or catching a bus at that bus stop. I might be pushing the boundaries of imagination just a bit too far but I couldn't stop myself even if I wanted to try.

My mind ate up every visual and fabricated every scenario possible for a chance encounter. Eventually, I closed the laptop and rubbed my temples. As I sat on the edge of the bed a thought occurred to me. Garrett asked me if I'd ever searched for my mom. He asked and yet all this time he knew where she was! He should've told me about finding her last known address and given me the opportunity to decide whether or not I wanted to pursue it instead of playing God and not giving me the information. Annoyance pricked my skin and made me edgy.

Now that I knew her address I couldn't erase it from my head and I had no choice. I just had to go there.

A few seconds of googling and I found I could take the 421 bus and be dropped a block away from her house. A ninety-minute bus ride and it was possible I'd have all my answers. I cracked my knuckles nervously. Garrett would probably not be home for hours. I grabbed my purse and paused. Jill mentioned that there was tracking on the phone they gave me so I took the cell out of my bag and left it on the counter as I headed out the door. I had no key and couldn't lock up. Here's hoping nobody would be stupid enough to break into the apartment of an FBI agent.

Heavy ash-colored clouds spat cold rain on my head as I ran to the bus stop just in time to catch the bus. For an hour and a half the bus bounced and jostled down the road and out of Seattle, and I frowned out the window while I thought. Many of those thoughts were fueled by anger filled with a powerful rage at this woman…my mother…who'd abandoned me. She left me behind to be abused. As much as I tried over the years to tell myself that perhaps she didn't know she was dropping me into hell, I knew now that wasn't true. People didn't change who they were and nothing could convince me that my grandmother had been a kind and gentle mommy when my own mother was growing up.

The only thing that had stopped me from hating my mother and becoming embittered over the years was possible circumstance. I covered and blanketed layers of justifications like a pretty parfait over the abandonment to excuse her for her actions. Perhaps she was extremely ill with cancer and so, riddled with the disease, she didn't know what else to do. Then again, maybe it really was to be a temporary drop-off for just a few days, like I was told, but she'd come to a catastrophic ending herself. Both of these scenarios had been favorites of mine because in both she'd wound up dead. Perfectly acceptable reasons for not rescuing me.

As the bus lurched down the highway closer to Marysville, all my jangled nerves gave way to an edge of excitement. I felt driven by an inexplicable need to see my mother's face and hear her voice even though I knew there would never be a rationalization or apology big enough.

When I climbed off the bus in Marysville, a light rain was falling but the sun was peeking through the thin clouds. I slipped the hood of my sweatshirt up over my head and walked up Sixth Street. There was a coffee shop at the corner and I desperately wanted to just grab a coffee and sit while I memorized the speech I was going to give her or, better yet, I'd love to stop at the store and buy a bottle of wino courage to help me be strong. Instead, I just kept walking.

The house was a small bungalow with faded green-painted wood siding. A rusted tricycle lay on its side in the middle of the sidewalk, and my head swam. I'd never considered the possibility of half-siblings. What if she'd had a whole new family and that's why she never came back? The idea felt like a slow burn under my skin as I walked up the steps and knocked.

Voices inside, male and female, argued about getting the door and I held my breath and strained to listen. Was the female voice my mom? While I cocked my head and leaned in to hear, the door was yanked open. I released the breath I was holding. The woman in front of me was the right age but Asian.

"Hi," I blurted. "I'm looking for Molly Arsenault."

"Not here."

The woman went to slam the door and I put my hands up to stop it.

"Do you have an address where she could be?"

"No." She narrowed her eyes at me. "Are you a bill collector?"

I shook my head. "I'm her daughter."

Her gaze scraped over me first with doubt and then with curiosity.

"Ted!" she screamed over her shoulder. "Some girl's here saying she's Molly's kid."

A scrawny bald man with a long braided goatee came from the back of the house. He was about fifty and wore jeans and a stained T-shirt.

"Molly's kid?" He spoke with a cigarette dangling out of the corner of his mouth. "What's your name?"

"Delma Arsenault." The name felt foreign on my lips.

"Well, I'll be damned." He stepped aside. "Come in out of the rain." He looked at the woman who'd answered the door and snarled, "Don't just stand there gawking, get us both a beer."

The Asian woman skedaddled toward what I assumed was the kitchen and the man waved me inside.

"Come in. Sit."

Even though the carpet looked filthier than the bottom of my shoes could possibly be, I slipped off my runners and followed him inside. He sank into a faded recliner and I took the sofa next to him, choosing a spot between a pile of laundry and a stain that looked suspiciously like cat vomit. The woman brought out two cans of Pabst and shoved aside an overflowing ashtray to put them on the coffee table.

She stood there grinning at me until the man she'd called Ted glared at her pointedly and then she hustled off again. Once she was gone he cracked open a beer and handed it to me.

"Oh. Um. No, thanks."

He shrugged and took a long swig from the can before he said, "Molly ain't here. She left maybe two years ago."

"Oh." My heart fell. I licked my lips, tempted by the other can of beer on the table. One fast gulp would take away the edge. I forced my gaze from the beer to his face. "Do you know where she went?"

"No. Strangest thing though. She took the car but didn't pack a damn thing. I figured she went for smokes or beer but she never came back. They found her car on the side of the road up by Sedro-Woolley."

I straightened and frowned. "You filed a missing person's report?"

"Tried." He took a drag from his smoke, then guzzled his beer and wiped a few stray drops from his beard. "But cops said the car was working fine and it looked like she walked away of her own accord. No sign of anything bad and she'd run off before so…" He shrugged. "They just figured she'd gotten the hell out of Dodge, you know? We didn't have the best history." He took another sip. "Cops were called on occasion so…yeah, they figure she just left and then I got to thinking that they're probably right." He tilted his head and shook a nicotine-stained finger at me. "You look like her, you know. Same eyes and mouth. Same kind of line between your eyebrows like you think too much."

"You knew about me." I stated it as fact.

"Oh sure, but never thought I'd ever see you." He flicked an ash of his cigarette in the ashtray on the table and tossed his now empty beer onto the table beside it. Then he sat back, linked his hands behind his head and grinned. "Molly told me she had a kid who got adopted out."

"Adopted out?" I sat forward and, when I did, almost put my hand on the vomit stain.

"Yeah, she said she dropped you at her parents' place because she was headed into rehab."

He fondled his braided beard a bit, then snagged the second beer off the table and lit another smoke. "She said she had an issue with coke back then but that was long before I met her. I wouldn't have put up with that kind of crap."

Right, because your sense of integrity and high moral fiber wouldn't have allowed it.

He puffed hard on his cigarette and took long pulls on the next beer and I just sat there trying to absorb what I'd learned so far. When he finished the beer, he dropped what was left of his cigarette butt into it. It made a sputtering sound as he put the can down.

"Anyway," he started up again. "She said the rehab was a couple months and when she got back, her ma said she'd dropped you off at Child Protective Services and that you'd been adopted."

"I wasn't adopted." My throat was so dry that my voice cracked as I spoke.

"Yeah, well, when I met her that woulda been maybe ten years after that happened. She didn't talk about it much in the six years we were together." He picked at his teeth with his fingernail. "She wasn't doing coke anymore when we met but she could put away a bottle of vodka without any trouble at all." The thought made him smile in memory. "Once, though, she got sober for a few weeks and that got her straight enough to get thinking about it. We started talking about you and she did some digging and realized her parents could've turned you over to Child Protective Services but nobody woulda been able to adopt you without her permission." He leveled his bleary eyes on me for a second. "We shoulda come looking for you and we talked about it but figured you would've been old enough to be on your own and long gone so we just let sleeping dogs lay." He shrugged. "She didn't want to talk to her folks."

"I appreciate your time." I got up from the sofa and my fingernails bit half-moons into the palms of my hands as I struggled to keep my voice even. As I slipped my feet back in my shoes I asked, "By the way, the name Arsenault. Any idea how I ended up with that?"

"Sure." He nodded. "Molly was married to some guy when she had you." He quickly added, "Don't know his first name so, sorry, I'm no help there."

My heart thrummed painfully in my chest. "Really? Any idea where I might find him?"

"Sorry, dahling." He blanched and stroked his beard. "Your daddy died in the Gulf War just after you was born." He shook his head slowly and mumbled, "God bless America," while oddly looking at his feet. Then he perked up and added, "Molly said the marriage wouldn'ta taken anyway but it was worth it just to have a different name than her parents."

"I can relate to that."

My hand was on the door when I realized I did not want to go back to Garrett's apartment and be on my own with quicksand thoughts and this ache in my chest.

"Do you have a phone I could use?"

"Sure."

He took a cell phone out of his pocket and handed it to me.

"Excuse me while I go use the facilities." He bowed comically and left the room.

I thanked him for his time and then dialed the number for the fill-up station and was relieved when Jonas answered the call.

"Hey, any chance you're available to pick me up in Marysville after your shift?" I asked, trying to keep emotion from my voice and failing miserably.

"You okay?"

"Yeah," I whispered on a choked sob. "So, can you?"

"Geez, I would if I could but my car died this morning and I had to tow it to the shop." He sounded sincerely upset. "If you want I can see if my brother will loan me his, but he works until seven."

I had an idea.

"How about I call Gramps and get him to pick you up in my Jeep when you're off? You could drop him back off at his place and then drive down here and get me. Okay?" I added, "I'd ask him to come get me, but it's a bit of a drive for him. I don't like him on the highway much."

And I didn't want Gramps to know I'd been searching for my mother. I wasn't ready for that conversation.

"Sure. I'm off at four," Jonas said.

I gave him a meeting spot in town.

"As soon as I can get there, I will," he promised.

I ended the call and then dialed Gramps, letting him know what I arranged, adding a little white lie about wanting to have my own wheels and Jonas offering to deliver the Jeep to me. Gramps said it was no trouble at all to bring the Jeep to Jonas and get a lift back.

"Wookie and I are done our rabbit hunting for the day anyway," he added.

After I disconnected the call, I looked up to see Ted's girlfriend standing there.

She looked over her shoulder nervously, then whispered to me, "I heard a rumor that Molly got into the crack and OD'd. Ted couldn't handle that so I kept it to myself. Thought you deserved to know."

I started to thank her but then Ted reappeared, his hand out for his phone. I handed it to him and he hugged me awkwardly.

"Molly meant something to me." He exhaled hot beer breath onto my neck. "If'n we'd found you, we could've been a family and all."

"Thanks for letting me in and clearing up stuff about my mother," I told him, untangling myself from his hug.

"No problem." He tugged on his beard. "Don't suppose you have a couple bucks you could loan your almost stepdad, now, could you? Things are a little tight."

I opened my purse, handed him a twenty and walked out the door.

I'd seen a Jack in the Box fast-food outlet close by when I got off the bus and I told Jonas that's where he'd find me.

The fast-food restaurant was five minutes away and it would be at least a couple hours before Jonas would show up. I sat down on a bus stop bench and cried hard for a few minutes.

"You're being stupid," I admonished, scrubbing my hands across my damp eyes. "You've been without a mother your entire life. This makes no difference. Bubkes. Snap out of it."

After a few deep cleansing breaths I forced myself to my feet and walked the rest of the way to the Jack in the Box. I ordered a burger and fries and then sat there not eating while sickly thoughts moved through my head. At first I was furious for coming but then I reasoned that it brought a level of closure I wouldn't have been able to get otherwise. *Closure.* I chuckled softly to myself. How I hated that word.

I dipped a cold fry into a coagulated blob of ketchup and stuffed it in my mouth. At least with Jonas bringing my Jeep I wouldn't feel as much a prisoner. I'd drive him back to his place and then call Garrett and let him know I was okay but needed to go. Part of me wanted to run back to his apartment, crawl under the covers in his bed and just wait for his body to be next to mine, but now I needed to focus on Katie and it didn't feel like that was possible from his apartment.

Jonas arrived and bustled into the restaurant out of breath like he'd been running.

"I got here as fast as I could. You sounded upset." He slid into the booth and pointed to my uneaten burger.

"Help yourself. I'm not hungry," I told him. "It's just been a sucky few days, you know?" I blinked back tears.

"Horrible about Katie." He nodded as he unwrapped the burger and took a bite. "Do they think it's the same guy who took her? Same guy as the others? I mean, she's older than those girls so maybe it's not, right?"

"She looks young, though," I said. "She's always getting carded."

"True." He took another bite out of the burger and smiled. "I was really surprised that you called me of all people. And kind of honored."

With a half-smile I said, "Don't be too pumped about it. I'm not exactly Miss Popular these days, except with the local media."

He'd devoured the burger and was licking the tips of his fingers.

"Do you want me to get you something else? It's the least I could do after you drove all this way to help me out."

"Nah, that was perfect." He crumpled up the wrapper.

"Well, that money I loaned you before? The fifty bucks? Consider it more than repaid," I said.

"Nah, I'll still pay you back for that eventually. I just like to think we're friends and that you'd come and pick me up an hour away if I called you up crying."

"I don't think I was crying."

"No, but you sounded like you were about to cry. You wanna talk about it? I got small shoulders but big ears."

No, I really did *not* want to talk about it. The spot inside my heart was too tender.

"I'm just really worried about Katie." Which was true.

He nodded seriously. "Okay, so where am I taking you?"

"Can we just drive back to your place and I'll drop you off? I'm not sure if I'm going to take a chance of bringing all the news reporter Armageddon onto Gramps so I don't want to go home or his place. Just need a place to clear my head for a few hours while I think of what to do."

"No problemo."

We got up from the booth and I followed him outside. He held up the keys but I shook my head.

"Do you mind driving? I'm beat."

He climbed behind the wheel and started the Jeep.

"For what it's worth, your grandfather seems to be doing great. Every time I see him he's talking about fishing. He said that since I was doing you this favor, next time he sees me he'll tell me one of his secret fishing spots."

"He must really like you then because he doesn't tell *anyone* his favorite fishing holes."

There was a bottle of cola in the cup holder that Jonas said was for me, and when we exited onto the highway the sun glinted off something shiny next to the drink. I lifted the bottle out and saw Katie's favorite gold hoops exactly where she'd left them the night we went to the casino together. I scooped them out and squeezed them in my hands for a minute and offered a silent prayer that she would be found alive. Then I stuffed the earrings into the front pocket of my jeans for luck.

"I like driving your Jeep," Jonas said. "It handles really well. Maybe I should just trade in my piece of garbage for one of these."

"You'll want to get a newer one than this though. This thing has cost me a few bucks in repairs this year."

There were signs indicating road construction on the highway and traffic began to narrow to one lane. The sun broke out of the clouds and was baking us through the car windows. My air-conditioning was sketchy at the best of times and today it felt more like the sputter of a drunk's hot breath.

"I'm going to exit and go route nine," Jonas said, rolling down his window a bit.

"It'll take longer."

"Yeah, but I'd rather keep moving than inch my way in traffic for the next twenty miles. Besides, the guy behind us has been riding my ass since Marysville."

He took the off-ramp and I grabbed the Coke out of the cup holder. It was still somewhat cold but didn't fizz when I unscrewed the lid. My first thought was that it was flat but I was thirsty so I guzzled about half of it in one go. There was a bitter taste in my mouth and I made a face and put the drink back. A few minutes later I began to feel dizzy.

"You okay?" Jonas asked, giving me a sideways glance.

"I'm… I'm…" My tongue was thick and my thoughts were jumbled.

"You're what?" He glanced in the rearview mirror and threw up his hands with exasperation. "I'm going to pull over and let this guy pass."

The Jeep swerved to the shoulder, and my body flopped against the door but I couldn't straighten. I had a sudden very clear thought.

I'm roofied. Damn! Jonas drugged me!

TEN

When I woke up, I was lying on a cold wooden surface. My eyeballs felt gritty and when I tried to move to a sitting position, my wrists and ankles screamed in pain. They were bound tight with nylon rope. I wanted to shout but there was duct tape over my mouth.

I wriggled to a sitting position and immediately the world spun out of control. I choked back vomit as I leaned back against the rough walls. I squeezed my eyes shut and waited for the world to stop spinning. If my experience with binge drinking and hangovers was any kind of indicator, I'd be fine in a few hours. Not reassuring considering Jonas could be back in minutes and I could end up dead and at the bottom of a bridge with a white ribbon tied to me at any second.

A fresh wave of nausea washed over me.

When I felt I could open my eyes again without throwing up, I slowly blinked them open. My heart pounded wildly against my chest as I looked around the place of my confinement. I strained my eyes in the dim space but there wasn't a helluva lot to look at. It appeared that I was in a small windowless wood shed; maybe four by five feet. In the corner was a small tangled nest of old fishing line. A slim ray of light creaked in through a knot in the wood in a top corner. I listened hard for noises from outside but heard no cars or highway traffic sounds, only birds and, somewhere close by, a creek or river. My gaze fell onto a bucket in the corner that reeked of stale urine. I wasn't the first person to be held prisoner here.

God, I felt so stupid. I pressed the back of my head against the wood, looked up at the low dark ceiling and tried to swallow the panic. Never once had I suspected Jonas of being the killer. I'd been safe and far away from him and what did I do? I called the guy to come and get me.

Anyone who spends five seconds with you knows you're so stupid you can't tell your ass from a hole in the ground, Grandma would say.

Gawd, the crazy old bat was right.

The grades I got in school were always half-decent. Some As, mostly Bs. I'd leave the report cards on the table and she'd toss them in the trash without bothering to read them. The message had been clear all along; there was absolutely nothing I could ever do to please her. The only thing I ever hoped for was to fly under her radar and avoid her wrath.

She's having a good ol' knee slap at my predicament now. She's cackling in her grave.

The thought spurred me into action. Using my shoulder to rub against the corner of the tape on my mouth I was gradually able to peel it away. Immediately I took a large gulp of cold air and began screaming at the top of my lungs.

"He-e-elp!"

Over and over I yelled until my throat burned from the effort. A few feet away a half-filled water bottle lay on its side. I scooted on my ass to reach it with my bound feet and drag it toward me but when I bent and scooped the bottle up with my teeth I noticed bits of white grounds floating inside. It was laced with something.

"Damn."

I dropped the bottle and used my bound feet to kick it to the side. It rolled and bounced off the pee bucket. It took some effort but I managed to scrape myself over to the door, then leaned back on my knuckles behind my back and kicked my feet against the door with all my might. It did not even shudder in response. Still I tried over and over.

The twine that bound my feet at the ankles cut painfully into my skin as I kicked. Using the wall as leverage, I managed to wriggle to my feet and then slammed my entire body against the door but it refused to give. There were two double dead bolt locks on the door, one near the top of the door and the other midway. This wooden hut might have been built to resemble an ordinary fishing shack, but it was too solid and reinforced for only that purpose.

After a while I sat back down in the corner to rest and gather my thoughts. Suddenly I heard the crunch of feet on the brush outside.

"Hey!" I shrieked. "In here! He-e-elp!"

The footsteps stopped outside the shed. Abruptly a tiny hinged opening maybe four inches square popped open. It was located on a corner wall near the ceiling and I hadn't noticed it before.

"Hey!" I screamed. "Let me out. Please!"

Two water bottles were flung in through the little hatch and bounced off the wood floor near my feet.

"Jonas?" I screamed. "Let me go, Jonas. You don't have to do this. I won't tell a soul. I swear to God. Just let me out."

No reply. The opening was slammed shut and latched, followed by the sound of footsteps leading away.

The water bottles that were thrown inside contained the same white floating bits and crumbs as the other.

He doesn't kill them right away, I reminded myself. Then I remembered reading how much weight the girls lost before they died, and I cringed. He knew eventually they'd start drinking the water or die of thirst.

Instead of kicking and slamming into the door I concentrated on loosening the ties around my wrists. The shred of light was long gone from the tiny hole. Evening had faded to night and I was in complete darkness. My wrists were slick with blood from wriggling and squirming within the ropes. After a while, though, I was rewarded when one strand loosened.

"C'mon," I pleaded.

My throat was burning and dry. I wanted to take just a single sip from one of the water bottles but didn't chance it. I just kept focusing on getting my hands free, but the more I forced, the tighter the knots felt and the more painful my wrists became.

After a minute I relaxed my arms completely. An angry curse escaped my lips and my chin fell against my chest in despair. There had to be a way. I began to concentrate on only my right thumb. The area near the base of my thumb felt looser so I twisted and bent the lower joint until abruptly it slid under the rope. Once that thumb was out, I could squeeze the rest of my hand and then both hands completely free.

Covering my face with my hands I screamed loudly for a few seconds and then I freed my ankles. The charcoal darkness inside the shed was so complete I couldn't see my hands in front of my face but I raced to my feet and pummeled the door once more to no avail.

"Think," I growled in the air.

Not a brain in that stupid skull of yours, I heard Grandma say.

"Go to hell!" I shouted in reply.

Then a flood of quicksand memories washed over me. Grandma locking me in the garden shed on a freezing cold winter night. The recollection was so overwhelming that it enveloped me and swallowed me whole. It was too hard to just keep pulling myself out of that deep quicksand. I could not just keep pretending to be whole when I felt like I was shattered in a million pieces.

"You win!" I shouted to Grandma who, even in death, seemed determined to fry my brain.

I fell to my knees and pounded the floor with my fists over and over until I was completely exhausted. My forehead touched the coarse wood floor and my breathing came in hard gasps as I fought my emotions.

Then I got mad.

There is no way I survived countless beatings at the hand of that vicious woman only to be killed by a serial killer. I refused to think that was my entire wasted life. If I did nothing now, I'd be dead. If I'd done nothing in that garden shed when Grandma locked me up in winter, I would've been dead of hypothermia by morning. No doubt she would've claimed it was an accident and that I must've gotten myself locked in and fallen asleep. I squeezed my eyes shut against the memory but it persisted.

A brief glimmer of something sparked inside my head. The kind of detail that often got buried in trauma because of the need to obliterate all the pain. The reason

I didn't die in that garden shed was because I'd managed to pop off the cover plate and unscrew the bolts of the dead bolt using an old trowel that I found near a bucket of garden tools. My fingers had been numb with cold as I worked the edge of the trowel into the screws.

Sadly, there were no gardening tools in this hellish prison.

Still, I began groping around on the floor in the dark for something…anything…that could be used as a screwdriver. My hand bumped the bucket of piss in the corner and I gagged as it sloshed over the side. I considered whether or not I could use the water bottles. Maybe the lids or even the bottles themselves could be used as a tool? But after I squeezed them in my hand I realized the plastic was too thin and flimsy.

Perhaps a loose piece of wood? My hands ran along the boards on the floor and in the corner became tangled with the fishing line. I shook the line off and heard a small solid noise that was far different than the sound a filament of string should've made landing on wood. I patted the palms of my hands along the fishing line until I felt something hard. I picked the object up and fingered the details of the thin, smooth and unmistakable shape of a fishing lure blade. I remembered saving up one Christmas to buy some of these for Gramps.

"They give the lures a sparkle," he said excitedly. "You tie these to the rigs and it's like diamonds to a girl. Fish can't resist 'em."

The thin oval metal might bend, twist then break when used as a screwdriver but I had to try. I groped around along the door until I found the circular plate for the lock and then blindly wiggled the blade into the edge. I pried and coaxed and jiggled the blade until the plate popped off.

"Yes!" I cried and swallowed the nervous lump in my throat.

Next, I used the opposite, more pointed, end of the lure as a screwdriver. It took less than a minute to wiggle the first screw out and that bolstered my enthusiasm to unwind the next one. Again, it turned easily and before long I was prying off the inside plate and using my fingers to prod the outside plate until it fell out on the other side. It took some maneuvering to slide the bar out of the lock using my fingers. If I came out of this alive, I promised myself the luxury of my first manicure to fix my splintered nails. Excitedly, I tried to push the door forward but it held fast. I'd forgotten about the second deadbolt above my head.

"Damn!" I moaned.

With a quick intake of breath I stood on tiptoe and felt around for the lock. I could feel it but couldn't manage the leverage needed to position the metal correctly.

"Damn!"

If only I was a few inches taller. Then I remembered the pee-filled bucket. I gagged as I spilled out the contents of the pail into the farthest corner of the shed. Once I'd brought it over to the door, I turned it over and prayed it would hold my weight. It did. The top dead bolt was identical to the lower one and the plate came off easily. However, while unscrewing the screws the blade broke in half. I jammed the bits into the screw and prayed as I applied pressure and turned. I have no idea how long it took me to get the screws to turn even a minute fraction. It felt like hours. My fingers stung and ached from the effort but, eventually, the screw came out far enough that I could work it the rest of the way out with my fingertips.

I was free!

I burst out of the shed and ran. Branches scraped my arms and face as I ran blindly through the thick brush in the dark. I went as fast and as far as I could. Thankfully, it was a clear night, and the moon and stars allowed enough light through the trees for me to find my way to a dirt road. Once I reached the road I back-stepped into the brush alongside. If Jonas came back I did not want to be easy to spot. Unfortunately, I had no idea where I was and could only hope that I'd eventually find a busier road if I followed this one.

The wind rustled through the trees as I walked. Many times I stopped and strained my ears to listen. I was never quite sure if the sounds that reached my ears were the crash of my own footsteps through the bush, the wind through the leaves, or Jonas hot on my trail. It was the last thought that propelled me faster. I'd never been good at track-and-field in school but there was nothing like the thought of being strangled then chucked over a bridge to make me want to break a land-speed record.

After walking what felt like miles and miles in the dark, I was out of breath and needed to rest. An icy wind had kicked up, and the stars had begun to be covered with a veil of clouds. I hunkered down against a large rock to get a break from the breeze, and when I crouched something in my front pocket dug into my leg. Katie's earrings! I cried softly for a minute while I clenched them in my fist. Had she been initially brought to that same fishing shack? Was her urine what was collected in that bucket? Sadness stung my eyes and I wished there was a way to find out if she was okay.

Then I realized that there was a way.

Deciding to put my faith in dowsing, I pulled a shoe-lace from one of my shoes and tied one end to the heavy gold hoops.

"Show me your yes," I whispered and watched the earrings swing left to right.

"Show me your no."

They began to swing toward me and away. I stilled the earrings with my hand and drew a deep breath.

"Is Katie still alive?"

There was a moment's hesitation and then slowly the pendulum swung in the yes direction.

"Thank God," I breathed.

"Will I find help?" I asked.

The earrings stilled completely. No answer at all.

"Is Garrett looking for me?"

The earrings wildly swung to a yes.

"Is Jonas looking for me?" I asked.

The response came back as a no and I felt my body relax a little. I had time. At least I hoped I did.

"Is Katie nearby?" I asked.

The earrings swung to no.

"Should I continue in the direction I'm going?"

The answer was yes.

After a few more minutes I re-laced my shoe and struggled to my feet.

"I don't know how and I don't know when, Katie, but I'm going to save your lying, cheating ass," I growled. "But first, I've got to save my own."

My legs protested the push forward but I knew I had to keep going. At one point the dirt road reached a fork, and I once again used Katie's earring and my lace to find the answer to use the road veering right. Luckily, after

less than half a mile, the dirt road opened ahead onto
one that was paved and sure to have traffic. Hopefully.
Eventually. At least maybe once it was the butt crack of
dawn and not the middle of the night.

There was just one problem getting onto that paved
road just ahead.

A bridge. A nasty-looking rusty trestle bridge that
looked like it had stood the test of time but would most
likely collapse under my weight and send me plummet-
ing into the ravine below.

I sank back into the dark bushes and gathered my
courage. It wasn't safe to stay in one place. I had to keep
moving forward. I imagined Katie nagging me.

"Get your ass going, Jules!" she'd say.

"You're not the boss of me," I grumped in return.

It was thinking about Gramps and Wookie that got
me on my feet. They needed me. Thoughts of Garrett
helped to propel my feet forward once I was on the edge
of the bridge. I remembered the time I did it by following
him and I did it the same way this time. I walked down
the center of the road on shaky legs that threatened to
buckle. It was almost impossible to encourage my feet
to go faster but I crossed the bridge deck as quickly as
I could. I tried to ignore the small voice inside me that
wanted to pull me to the railing. The voice that said that
Grandma was right all along and I wasn't worth the bag
of skin I was born in.

An eerie sense of déjà vu hit me when I was halfway
across. Quicksand thoughts that wanted to drown me
in the creek below.

I bit down on my lip, fisted my hands at my side and
pushed my trembling legs forward by imagining Garrett on the other side coaxing me onward like a tod-

dler learning to walk. Once I reached the other side of
the bridge, I rushed to the side of the road. My nausea
was so great that I had my hands on my knees as I dry
heaved. A dozen deep cleansing breaths helped me to
find a little calm inside.

"You're almost done," I told myself. "You got out of
that shack and you're on the main road. You've got this."

Just after my little pep talk I straightened and began
the arduous task of once again putting one foot in front
of another. Suddenly, headlights were coming over the
bridge. I ducked behind a small tree until I made out that
the vehicle approaching was a large dump truck. Definitely not Jonas. I jumped into the middle of the road
and waved my arms in the air until the driver screeched
to a stop.

A middle-aged woman climbed out and glared at me,
hands on her hips.

"I could've run you right over!" she exclaimed. Then,
"Oh my God!" as she took in my disheveled appearance
and blood-caked hands.

I'd sunk to my knees right there in the middle of the
road with my arms wrapped around myself as if I'd break
apart if I let go. It probably took her ten minutes to get
me calm enough to explain who I was and what had happened. Once I said I'd been taken like the other missing
girls, she helped me crawl inside her truck, locked the
doors and called for police.

State Patrol arrived on the scene first and the officer
took me in his car.

"The entire friggin' state's been looking for you,"
he remarked with entirely too much happy enthusiasm
in his tone.

I was shaking in the back of the car and couldn't

muster the energy to say a word of protest at his upbeat attitude. He handed me a scratchy and smelly wool blanket from his trunk and told me to sit tight. As if I was capable of doing anything else. Once I was cocooned inside the blanket, I sprawled out on the back seat and passed right out.

What woke me up not too long afterward was the commotion caused by an ambulance and half a dozen black-and-whites as well as a couple unmarked cars. Even though my eyes had blinked open I didn't want to leave the safety of that back seat and the coziness of that stinky blanket.

However, a federal agent who was not Garrett did not understand my need to sleep until next year. He asked me questions in a rocket-fire pattern but my head had an army of tiny men with jackhammers pounding a horrible beat and my mind had a hard time computing the answers as quick as he'd like them. I explained as best I could the direction from where I came and the location where I'd been held.

Apparently, telling him I had no idea how long I'd been walking and that I'd just followed the directions of a pair of earrings was not going over well. Haltingly, I described Jonas and gave a description of my Jeep. I was informed that they'd all been on the lookout for both since I'd been reported missing.

"I'm sorry but I can't tell you much. I was drugged. It was in the Coke bottle in the Jeep."

He accepted that for now and then waved the paramedics over. As they wheeled me on a stretcher toward the ambulance, I craned my neck but didn't see Garrett's sedan anywhere. My heart fell. I should've asked the other agent for him but now I was ushered into the ambulance before I could.

"You're a miracle girl, that's for sure," the paramedic remarked as he jabbed an IV needle into my arm. "The entire state was looking for you and *bam*, here you are!"

"Yeah. Bam," I said weakly.

I didn't remember much except there were too many people asking me too many questions and all I wanted was to be left alone with a couple bottles of wine. I said as much and the doctor slapped his thigh as if that was the most hilarious thing he'd ever heard.

It felt like hours before I was brought into a room where I could blissfully close my eyes. I opened them again only a short time later because of the familiar smell of a manly soap. Garrett.

I bolted upright so quickly I nearly toppled the IV pole.

"It's okay." He rushed to me. "It's only me."

And I couldn't find the words to tell him that I knew it was him and that I hadn't jumped because I was startled but because I wanted to run to him. He sat on the edge of the bed and held me while I sobbed uncontrollably.

"I thought I'd lost you forever." His voice was rough and ragged in my ear. "I was tearing the state apart."

"I-I'm sorry." I cried. "I shouldn't've left. I just… I just…"

"You went to find out about your mother. I know because that's the page you left open on my laptop. Thank God you did. It gave me a place to start." He hugged me even tighter. "That page brought me to Marysville and to Ted who said you used his phone to call Jonas and—"

I pulled myself back to look in Garrett's face.

"Did you catch him? Jonas?"

He shook his head. "Not yet. We will though." He pulled me close again. "I promise."

"Because Katie's still alive."

At least she was the last time I checked. I hoped it was still true.

My wrists were bandaged since they'd been cut badly from the ropes, but they didn't hurt me as I clung tightly to Garrett, not wanting to let him go. I knew, though, that he'd have to leave if he was ever going to do his job and catch Jonas and pull him limb from limb while, hopefully, covering him with acid, fire ants and giving him a colonoscopy. Preferably, all at the same time.

"Jill is downstairs with your grandfather. She went and told him the entire story and he's a bit of a wreck and blaming himself over giving your vehicle to Jonas."

"I asked him to," I said.

"I know."

Garrett kissed my face all over from the top of my head to my chin and every spot in between until I laughed and pushed him away.

"I know you need to get out there," I said. "It's okay. Go and find Katie and catch Jonas. Just be safe."

Just as Garrett was walking out, Gramps was walking in. His usual broad, muscled shoulders were hunched. He looked like he'd aged a dozen years since I saw him last. Jill gave me a hello wave and said she'd been returned to the job as my minder and would be sitting right outside my room if I needed anything.

"The police told me it was Jonas…" Gramps began but I shushed him. "I should never have left you alone with him."

"Not your fault and everything's okay."

He pulled me into an awkward hug and lowered himself into the chair next to the bed. He'd always looked sturdy and strong like an ox but now he looked weary and it pained me.

"Maybe you should give up those long walks with Wookie until you get your energy back," I suggested. "You're looking a little under the weather."

"I'm good as gold. Chopped wood for hours and then hauled it near the woodshed like it was nothing."

"Yeah, I know you're strong but you still don't look good as gold." I squinted at him. "You're a wreck. I'm sorry for doing that to you."

"Well, sure, I've just been sick with worry these last twenty-four hours." He shook a finger at me. "But you're safe and that's all that matters. Wookie and I love our long walks. Gave me something to do while you were away. Went out fishing with the guys a couple times too but nothing was biting. Probably Wookie barking his fool head off scared the fish." He chuckled good-naturedly but it was forced. This had been a huge strain on him and I felt horrible.

"Well, I'm breaking out of here tomorrow and coming back home so I'll take that big mutt off your hands and you can go fishing all you want. You should probably take a week straight and fish to your heart's delight. It'll do you a world of good."

"You're coming home?" He looked up in surprise. "I thought for sure they'd be keeping you under lock and key."

"What for?" I shrugged. "Between you and Wookie I have enough eyes on me."

The fatigue in his eyes worried me.

"I could've done more." He looked at his feet.

"Don't be silly!" I said. "The FBI is far more qualified in this situation than you so don't think for a second you could've done more."

"I'm not talking about this. I'm talking about before. Grandma."

My stomach rolled at the mere mention of her name. Yes, he should've protected me from her but that was water under an ancient, dilapidated bridge.

"Look." I struggled to sit up straighter. "There is nothing that can change what happened."

"I love you. You know that, right?"

"Of course! And I love you." My voice broke just a little.

"Your grandmother…well…she knew things that…"

While Gramps fought to verbalize his thoughts, I battled the demons in my head that wanted to dredge up stuff I wasn't strong enough to deal with.

"The past is the past!" I shouted and then lowered my voice. "We don't need to talk about it."

And even if the quicksand swallowed me whole, there was no way I wanted Gramps to worry himself sick over something we couldn't change now.

Jill came into the room and looked at both of us. She'd obviously heard my shout.

"You should be resting," she said.

I agreed and told Gramps to go on home and take care of my dog.

"Once you're up to it, I'm gonna take you to my favorite fishing spot," Gramps said. "Clackamas River, just outside of Portland."

He patted me on the arm and headed out the door.

Once he was gone, Jill asked, "Need anything?"

After a pause I nodded.

"Can you arrange for my bag to be brought here

from—" I hesitated to call him Garrett in front of her "—Agent Pierce's apartment? I'm going to head home after they discharge me."

To her credit she didn't ask questions or make any snarky remarks but just nodded and said she'd make sure it was taken care of. The nurse came in and gave me a shot of something deliciously soothing that made me feel like nothing was wrong with the world. When I woke up in the morning Garrett was sitting in the chair next to my bed holding the bag.

"Good morning." He smiled.

I yawned and stretched and he got up to sit on the edge of the bed and drop a kiss onto my forehead. I noticed for the first time that the worry lines between his eyes had deepened since we met.

"I hear you're moving out?" He nodded to the bag.

"It's time I went home." I sat up and he moved to position the pillows behind my back. "I want to keep an eye on Gramps and, besides, Wookie will keep me safe."

"And your shotgun." He smiled. "First time I met you I thought you were going to blow my head off."

"It's a good thing you're so good-lookin'." One of my arms still had an IV but I put the other one around him and brought him close. We rested our foreheads against each other. I closed my eyes and breathed in his scent.

"You can come and stay with me," I murmured. "My trailer is closer to everything that's happening out here than your apartment anyway, and I promise not to shoot you or let Wookie bite you."

"Maybe once all this is done. I have to catch this guy first. Until then, I won't be doing much sleeping. We have a command center set up in town." His mouth was an angry line. "I checked Jonas out myself and I cleared him as a suspect early on. Obviously, I'm to blame for—"

"No, you're not to blame." I tightened my arm around his neck.

He kissed me far too quickly and got to his feet.

"We're using a hotel in town for our base while the investigation is going on and I need to be with the other agents while the hunt for Jonas continues." He nodded to the door. "Jill will be keeping an eye on you and there'll also be at least one other agent on duty at your premises when you get out of here." He pointed a finger at me. "No more random trips without checking with me."

"No worries there," I promised. "I can't imagine going anywhere or doing anything besides sleeping." I quickly added, "Unless you need my help... You know... have rods, will travel."

He shook his head and made for the door but just as he was leaving the doctor walked in the room and Garrett stood near the door and waited.

"So what's the good word, Doc?" I asked. "Am I free to go?"

"All your blood work isn't back yet but, yes, I think a couple hours longer on the IV and you can check out."

"The toxicology report?" Garrett asked. "Do you know what he used to drug her?"

The doctor shook his head. "It won't be available until later today or tomorrow."

The doctor came closer to the bed, his eyes softened and he lowered his voice.

"As you know, before we bandaged up your wrists and ankles we took a lot of X-rays."

"I'm surprised I'm not glowing from the radiation," I joked but the doctor didn't smile.

"There were a number of poorly set bones. Old breaks and—"

"Accidents," I snapped.

"I couldn't find any medical records and all those scars on your back…" His voice was a hesitant whisper. "We have a very good psychiatric team here."

Well, this was really embarrassing.

"I'm good. Really," I said hastily, my voice thick with bravado and my lips offered up a quick, bright smile. "Just wanna go home, Doc."

"Okay, but anytime you want to see someone, then—"

"I got it. If things change, I'll give you a call."

The doctor looked like he wanted to say more but stopped himself. Instead, he took my vitals and told me that after one more saline bag in my IV I'd be free to go. They'd send me home with a change of bandages for my wrists.

After he left, Garrett returned for another quick kiss. It was a chaste and brotherly peck that left me wanting to call him back for more. I didn't want him to go but I couldn't ask him to stay either. Part of me felt like we'd lost our moment for happiness. I could feel it slipping away like water through my fingers. The killer had thrown us together and now he was pulling us apart.

Jill drove me home. There were reporters and news vans down the street. Even though they'd been pushed far back from the entrance to our driveway, I could feel their telephoto lens scrutiny on me when we stopped in to see Gramps. Wookie went absolutely nuts with happiness when he saw me. Surprisingly, Jill loved big dogs and didn't mind him snorting her crotch and drooling on her good shoes. I never would've figured her for a dog person but it just goes to show you can't judge a woman by her occasional grumpy behavior.

Gramps still did not look like his usual self. His large frame felt smaller somehow when I hugged him, but he put on a good show when he served us up some chicken noodle soup from a can and grilled cheese sandwiches which were only somewhat black.

"You're going to be glad to see this mutt go," I told Gramps as I was leaving with Wookie.

"He's a pain in the ass but I didn't mind the company."

"You can bring him hunting bunnies anytime," I remarked.

"You like to hunt, Mr. Hall?" Jill asked. She'd been looking over the small house with curious glances.

"Nah, that's just what we call it when I take Wookie for our long walks, and he runs off to chase rabbits in the tall grass."

"Plenty of area to walk here," Jill said. "This property goes on for, what? A dozen acres?"

"Used to have many times that," Gramps said. "Slowly sold it off to those with the energy and youth to work it. Kept what I could though. Don't like feeling closed in."

Jill dropped me back at my place, and my trailer felt strange and small but that faint smell of dusty curtains and old linoleum was all mine. Definitely not the posh surroundings of Garrett's Seattle apartment but it felt like home. Wookie ran around happily sniffing the rooms to make sure everything was the same and then collapsed on his bed. I took my bag and dropped it in the corner next to my shotgun.

"So what's the plan?" I asked. "Are we roomies now? It's not the Ritz but I do have a spare room."

"Oh no-o-o," Jill replied, not bothering to hide her disdain as she took in my cramped quarters. "I'll be in my car keeping an eye on your place and it'll go in shifts. Every few hours you'll get a new agent watching you. I'm on until ten. I'll poke my head in occasionally to check on you and when the next guy arrives, we'll give you a heads-up."

She reached into her purse and tossed me my old cell phone and gave me the names of two other agents who would spot her. Then she left and waited on the steps outside until I locked the door behind her. I looked out the window and watched her climb into her car and get comfortable.

I took my laptop out of my bag and opened my emails. I was not prepared for the assault of hundreds of messages from people who were worried about me when they thought I'd become a victim. Apparently being abducted by a serial killer was akin to celebrity. Everyone I knew or kind of knew wanted to send me a note but, as I scrolled through, there were hundreds whose names I didn't recognize. It was overwhelming. I gave up and powered on my cell phone. A lot of messages there too. I replied to the text messages from Denny and Margie, who'd heard I'd been found alive and were glad. Denny went so far as to apologize for banging Katie and being so mean to me. He even hinted at a rekindling of our relationship. That would happen only once the devil was serving Grandma iced tea in hell.

A couple of older text messages from Jonas stopped me in my tracks. The messages were from before we'd begun communicating via email. There was nothing evil in his remarks. Nothing to indicate he was a psycho killer wanting to imprison me in a fishing shed and then choke me to death and toss me into a river. His texts just asked how I was and further texts were statements about how many reporters were at the fill-up station. After that, he'd begun emailing me and I just fell into his trap. My finger paused over the delete button. I resisted only because I knew it could be evidence.

My heart pounded when I got to the old messages from Katie begging my forgiveness and then steadily becoming more pissed with me for not responding.

Her very last text to me read: Jules, don't let Denny come between us. He wasn't that good a lay.

It was so typically Katie that I smiled in spite of myself.

I sat there thinking of Katie and reminisced about the good times rather than the not-so-good-you-screwed-my-boyfriend time. Abruptly, in a moment of panic, I put my phone down, got up from my seat and started looking through the stuff that had accompanied me home from the hospital. My filthy clothes from my grim ordeal were bagged. I tugged out the jeans, reached in the front pocket and found the earrings. I closed my eyes in a thankful prayer, then went to my bathroom and pulled a box of dental floss from the drawer.

Wookie eyed me curiously as I pulled out an arms-length string of dental floss and tied it to one of Katie's earrings. After a moment of deep cleansing breaths, I began the pendulum questioning.

"Is Katie alive?"

The earrings hung very still before swinging slowly left to right, indicating a hesitant yes.

"Thank you," I whispered.

The slow swing of the pendulum hinted that time was running out.

ELEVEN

THERE ARE A LOT of different cities, towns, and counties in Washington State. Asking a pair of earrings to tell me where Katie was being held felt like a hopeless and ridiculous task but I pushed on because I had no choice.

There were a lot of nos.

Until there was finally a yes.

When I asked about Whatcom County I got a positive indication from the pendulum.

"Great," I said on a long exhaled breath. "Now we just gotta narrow that down a tad."

Whatcom County was home but it was also twenty-five hundred square miles. If I wanted to get near streams or bodies of water that didn't help because fifteen percent of the county was water. Also, I was hoping that the water would only come into play once he killed her. And I was going to do everything in my power to make sure that didn't happen. I was tempted to call Garrett and tell him what I'd learned but, until I got it narrowed down, it seemed an impossibly useless clue. It would take Garrett an entire army to search that much area. I rubbed my bandaged wrists and felt a helplessness wash over me.

Even though I knew it wouldn't help, I wanted to call Garrett and ask how the investigation was coming. I wanted all the details, even the smallest minute indication that they were one step closer to catching Jonas and finding Katie. I couldn't call, though, because I couldn't be distracting him from doing his job. I knew he'd check in with me when he could.

I busied myself with my pendulum dowsing, asking about specific locations and remote possibilities until my eyes were crossing from fatigue and my stomach was grumbling, demanding food. Unfortunately, I had an intense craving for a pizza made with sausage, roasted peppers and provolone from Serious Pie. There was a very good chance that what I was craving wasn't pizza at all but the naked body of a certain FBI agent. And that agent was definitely *not* Jill.

Thinking of Jill made me realize that I'd been home for several hours and she had not poked her head in to check on me once and it was after nine. She had not even asked to use the bathroom all day. That woman must have an iron bladder or else she'd chosen to squat in the tall grass rather than use the washroom in my trailer. I went to the window and squinted into the darkness. Jill was not in her car. No doubt she was out patrolling the perimeter like the badass agent she was.

Wookie went to the door and whined.

"Aw, sorry, big guy. You probably need to get out to pee, right?"

I went to the back room to get my runners that were lodged under my bag. When I moved my bag, my divining rods tumbled out onto the floor. As I stuck my feet inside my runners, I noticed the rods vibrating. At first I thought they were trembling because they'd been knocked to the floor but then I picked them up. They simultaneously swung around to point behind me.

"Oh shit."

My first thought was that Agent Jill had managed to

nab and kill Jonas. But, if that wasn't the case, there was a body out there and I'd better tell her about it. I stuffed the rods in my back pocket and opened the door. Wookie bounded outside, ran to Jill's car and peed on her front tire. I caught up to him just as he took off into the field behind my trailer, happily barking as if on the trail of something that had the potential to be rabbit stew.

The wind kicked up a notch and whipped my hair straight back from my forehead as I followed Wookie into the night. My nerves jangled as I waded through the tall grass. The dog was headed into the back forty and he was already almost out of my line of sight.

"C'mon, Wookie!" I called. "Let's not do this tonight!"

There was a sick feeling in the pit of my stomach, and when I pulled out my rods and they immediately pointed in the direction Wookie was headed, that feeling turned into full-blown panic. I froze to the spot while I considered my options.

I could just go back to the trailer and wait for Wookie to return and wait for Agent Jill to come and tell me what was going on. Besides, it was not like the dog would get lost on our acreage or beyond. Whenever he'd wandered out of eyesight before, he'd always returned after a few minutes. He could be dropped off ten miles away and still find his way back home.

"I'm going back inside!" I shouted to Wookie but the wind tore my words from my throat and buried them in an angry howl. As I shouted and turned away the rods whipped to point behind me.

"Damn. Damn. Damn!" I did *not* want to follow the rods.

And I sure as hell did *not* want to find whatever body they were indicating, even if it meant that body was Jonas's and this entire horrible ordeal was over.

With a sigh and a loud colorful curse, though, I turned back around and followed where the rods were pointing. After all, maybe a girl's body was out there on my property. I sure hoped not but Jill was probably out patrolling the perimeter nowhere near where the rods were saying a body could be, so I needed to be sure. Maybe Jonas was making some sort of a sick point by tossing the victim near my house.

And maybe that victim was Katie.

The thought hit me like a punch to the gut, and it took me a second to recover my breath. If it was Katie, I owed it to her mom and out of respect for all our years of friendship to not let her body sit out in the elements for longer than necessary.

So I put one foot in front of the other, following the rods and listening to Wookie's distant bark. The area I was headed was one of the sections of land sold off when Gramps began downsizing his property. Whoever bought the acreage had allowed most of the land to go fallow and had only farmed less than half.

I did *not* want to head off in the direction of that acreage. Quicksand thoughts rolled around in my head and made me want to run home, lock the door and hide under my covers. But the rods pulled me forward and Wookie barked off in the distance. I kept wading through the grass and followed. In the dim light I could already make out in the distance the garden shed Grandma had locked me in when I was just a kid. I'd hoped the new owners of the land would bulldoze the building but they never had and now I was nearly upon it. The gray silhouette of the narrow building looked ominous against the night sky.

"There is nothing sinister about a garden shed," I

told myself as I walked. "It's just a building for hoes and rakes and…and…"

And whips with metal bits tied on the ends of the strands of leather to inflict the most damage and pain.

"Rotten little girls with sluts for mothers don't deserve a roof over their heads," Grandma hissed in my ear.

"Shut up!" I screamed until my throat was raw.

I shook my head but her voice persisted and the memories came in waves. The worst night ever had been when she'd discovered me pendulum dowsing, and now it was divining rods that were leading me right there. Soon I'd reached Wookie, who was standing directly in front of the garden shed, his head low, ears back and the rumble of a growl emanated from between bared teeth. The rods crossed.

"Jesus, Wookie." I blew out a nervous breath. "C'mon, boy."

I whistled for him and patted my thigh but Wookie never even lifted his head or turned in my direction.

"There is nothing inside that old shed," I said, my voice angry now. "Nothing but bad memories so come o-o-on!"

Even though I said the words I knew they were a lie. The rods didn't make things up. There was a body in there and, even though it could be Katie's, I couldn't bring myself to open the door.

With a grab of Wookie's collar, I attempted to yank him away but he whipped his large head around and snapped at me; something he'd never done before.

"Jesus, Wook. What's got into you?" I ran my hand through my hair. "Did a rabbit get inside that shed? Is that what this is all about? Some stupid friggin' bunny?"

But there was no rabbit. Maybe he realized that Katie, his previous owner, was in there and he had some kind of misplaced loyalty to the girl who didn't care a rat's ass about him. Well, if a dog could be loyal to her, I sure as hell didn't have the right to walk away.

"Fine."

I pushed past Wookie and put my hand on the door handle. "I'll open the shed. I hope you're happy."

Wookie growled low and deep in reply. I sighed and went to turn the door but, of course, it was locked.

"Guess we can't get in."

I released a long relieved breath but even as I took my hand off the knob I knew what I had to do. If this was a dozen years ago the key to the lock would be a yard away under a rock but this lock looked newer.

That gave me pause. There was only one reason why a new lock would be on this old shed, and that was because it was being used for a new purpose.

I walked a few feet to the right of the shed looking for the rock that used to be the hiding place for the old key. I'd found it as a kid and had thrown the key far and wide into the field. Grandma had laughed at that because, of course, she had spares. Many spares.

In the dark and tall weeds I actually tripped over the rock before my eyes could adjust enough to see it. I bent and lifted the stone and, sure enough, there was a silver key with hardly a speck of dirt on it.

When I slid the key in the lock I said a mental prayer that the rods were wrong for once and that the only thing inside was a poor trapped rabbit hiding from Wookie. I wasn't prepared for what I saw when I flung the door open.

Agent Jill lay in the center of the small shed, her hands

and feet bound by rope and a white ribbon tied tightly around her neck.

She was dead.

A scream burst from my throat and died there as I was hit on the back of my head so hard it brought me to my knees and I bit through my lip. I attempted to turn around and face my attacker but even as I fought to get to my feet I was hit again and again. The world faded to black.

Lights out, Julie Hall.

WHO KNOWS HOW long later, my first thought was that I must be dead because I couldn't see a thing. The second thought I had was that I couldn't possibly be dead because I had pain. A load of mind-blowing pain in my skull that was far worse than I'd had even on my worst benders. I realized something was over my head and that was why I couldn't see. Some kind of cloth hood. My wrists and ankles were bound, and the rope cut into the familiar abrasions from earlier. I tried to find a voice to scream but only a garbled groan passed through my lips. When I struggled against the ropes they didn't budge.

Think! I ordered my brain but the response I got from my head was: *No thinking. Let's just take a lo-o-ong nap.*

The urge to give in to sleep was strong but, instead, I tried to focus on what was happening. I was being bounced around in some kind of hard open trailer. I could feel the cool night air on my skin and hear the loud motor of the vehicle pulling it. Occasionally the trailer would bounce or lurch in a rut and my body would slam painfully into the sides, or worse, I'd slide against something soft and fleshy that I knew had to be Jill.

Dead Jill.

I tried really hard not to think of that. Instead, I focused on sounds.

Jonas had somehow gotten on the property, killed Jill and then commandeered Gramps's ATV and trailer. Gramps kept the keys for the ATV on a hook inside his door.

I hoped Gramps was okay. The overwhelming emotion that accompanied that thought threatened to swallow me whole.

"Jonas! Don't do this!" I shouted against whatever hood covered my head but my scream was blown away by the wind.

I used to know this part of our land like the back of my hand but having no vision fooled with my head. Near as I could figure we were heading west, and the only thing in that direction was a creek that was normally just a trickling line of shallow water but now, with spring runoff, it was a few feet deep and across.

Would he tie the ribbon to my body before or after he strangled me?

The thought iced my veins just as the trailer came to an abrupt stop. Footsteps sounded and there was the rustle and grunt and dragging sounds that had to be Jill's body being hauled out of the trailer.

"Please…" My voice came out on a whimper. "Don't… don't."

No response came. The only sounds were heavy, solid footsteps accompanied by a slow dragging sound that stopped after a few minutes. He was tossing Jill in the creek. Poor Jill. Nobody deserved that. I blinked back tears and struggled to free myself. I hoisted my body over the edge of the wagon and wriggled and writhed until I'd flung myself over the side, landing on dirt and rocks with a solid *umph*.

Now what?

My ankles and wrists were bound and I had a cloth tied over my head. I found a large rock, placed my wrists on an edge of it and fought against my ties. If I could get the ropes off my wrists I could remove the hood and free my feet and then run!

The ropes finally felt like they were loosening when abruptly I was hauled upright by my armpits then dragged and flung back into the trailer.

My lips parted to protest but then I heard an electronic hum and my entire body went rigid. I couldn't form thoughts or move.

I knew I was put back in the shed but just when I began to feel like I could protest, I heard the hum and my body went rigid again. After a while I regained control of my body and my thoughts enough to realize I'd been tased. What roused me was someone trying to remove the cloth from my head. At first I remained very still but then I decided to head butt my attacker. I was probably going to end up dead anyway. There was no way I was going down without drawing blood! Fingers fumbled with ties around my neck and just as the hood was being lifted off I pulled my head back and slammed it forward connecting with Jonas's face.

"Ouch! God dammit!"

But that wasn't Jonas.

It was Katie!

I shrugged the hood the rest of the way off and there she was in all her glory. Except not very glorified at all. Her feet were bound and so were her wrists. Her hair was caked with old blood and she now had fresh red that ran down her chin from her nose.

"Katie! It's you!" I screamed. "Oh my God." I shuffled on my ass to get closer to her. "I'm so happy to see you."

"Sh-h-h!" she hissed. "He'll hear you. You're happy to see me, huh? You've got a funny way of showing it. I figured you were in on this little episode but…" She looked me over and shook her head. "I guess not."

"You thought I was in on this?" My jaw dropped in surprise. "Just because we had a fight doesn't mean I wasn't doing anything and everything to try and find you!"

"Fine. You obviously did a fine job. You found me. Now what? We're both stuck." She blinked back tears. "There's no way out of here. Lord knows I've tried. The closest I came was rubbing the duct tape off my mouth and loosening the rope on my wrists enough that they didn't cut off the circulation. I've been tased so many times I look like I've got chicken pox from the barbs, and drugged so much my brain doesn't work. It's been days, Jules." Her voice broke. "I wish he'd just kill me already instead of making me starve to death."

"You're not going to starve to death and he isn't going to kill us. We're getting out of here just as soon as I get the ropes off my wrists. After the ropes are off I'll snap the back off the dead bolt and use something to undo the screws and then we're free."

"You got some superpowers besides finding dead people?" Katie remarked coolly. "'Cuz I don't see any of that shit happening. I've been here for days. I get water bottles drugged with his sleeping pills as he told me but that's it. There's no way out of here."

I explained to her how I'd been abducted before and how I'd managed to get out but she was only half listening. The look on her face said she'd given up and made her peace with dying. The girl in front of me wasn't my irreverent, plucky and wild half-friend. This girl was broken and it killed me to see it.

"Don't give up," I whispered.

"Your grandma knew all about it. How screwed up is that? She knew all along he was killing and she just held it over him so that she could keep beating you. That's what he told me. Started with some poor baby in a well. How messed up is that?"

Baby in the well? The first time I'd used my rods I'd found that toddler. Could Jonas have been killing that long? He would've just been a kid himself.

"I don't know what you're talking about. You're delirious but you're going to be okay. We just need to get out of here. We're going to fight and get free. There's no way we're going to let Jonas win."

Katie's face screwed up into a skeptical sneer. "Who the hell is Jonas?"

"Jonas. You know…" I nodded at her. "The guy I worked with at the gas station. Guess you didn't see who took you but that's who it was. He's been taking all those girls and—"

"Jesus…" Katie muttered. "I saw who took me, Jules. Looked him right in the eye while he pointed a Taser at me. It sure as hell wasn't any guy named Jonas. It was—"

But the name never left her throat because there was the unmistakable sound of a key in the lock outside. I looked at the door in fear but struggled to my feet hoping I could perform my head-butting maneuver again, this time on Jonas when he opened the door.

The door flung open and the figure was backlit by the bright moon behind him.

Gramps.

"Thank God!" I cried. "You gotta be careful. He's still out there and—"

But even as I spoke I realized he had a roll of white ribbon in one hand and a handgun in the other.

TWELVE

"No-o-o!" I CRIED.

But Gramps ignored my protest. He had Katie by her ankles and was dragging her out of the shed, ignoring her screams of protest. He hauled her out of the shed and then there was the fumbling sound of a key going back in the lock, but I rushed the door before he could lock it again and it sprang open. With my ankles bound I couldn't run. I fell out through the door and landed on the rocks outside while I screamed and screamed.

"Shut up or I'll blow both your heads off right here," Gramps hissed.

This was impossible! How could the man I'd loved my entire life be a monster?

"Wh-why?" I murmured. "Why are you doing this?"

"I love you, Delma," Gramps said fiercely as he wiped sweat from his forehead. "I'm not gonna hurt you. Once I deal with this brat you and I can go live in the woods and fish and—"

"No! Leave Katie alone. We'll…" I swallowed my fear. "We'll get you some help."

"You wait here," he told me. "And you let me deal with this nasty business. Stay put, no matter what."

He'd put the gun down in his waistband and was dragging Katie by her wrists down toward the creek. In his back pocket I could see the black outline of a Taser.

Quicksand thoughts swam in my head. A memory

came into focus. Gramps telling me to stay put no matter what. *No-o-o! Don't think about it.*

Me getting bored sitting on a rock holding my broken wrist and carefully following him through the woods. Watching him drag something in a large plastic bag out of a shed in the woods, then huffing as he dragged it through the woods. The bag tore as he dragged it. Something pale and white and fleshy inside.

Stop it! Don't think about it!

Gramps was sweating as he dragged the bag onto the deck of an old bridge and heaved the bag over the railing. As he did, something that looked like a hand slipped out of the bag. I ran back to the rock where he'd told me to sit. I ran and ran, and at one point my shoe got stuck in sticky mud. Quicksand.

Quick! Hurry! He'll find you!

It took me forever to free my foot from the sticky mud and, once I did, I tripped only a few feet from the rock and I banged my arm hard as I went down. When Gramps reappeared a few minutes later he thought my sweating and tears were because of my sore wrist that was obviously broken.

It's okay. It was nothing. He was littering. Just throwing out trash. It's okay. No quicksand to get you now.

I wanted to curl up in a ball because that memory threatened to swallow me but, instead, I struggled to my feet. Katie needed me. I took a step and saw one of my dowsing rods on the dirt nearby. I got down and scooted in the dirt toward it, got it in my hands that were bound in front of me and then got back to my feet. I began to hop which was ridiculous because I'd never be able to outrun Gramps while hopping but I had to at least try and convince him not to kill Katie. As I took a couple hops toward them my right foot lifted out of my runner and I was able to immediately wriggle both feet out of the ropes. Then I was running toward Gramps and Katie.

When I reached them, Gramps was on his knees and had his hands around Katie's throat. He was squeezing so hard her face turned purple and eyes bugged out. Before I could change my mind, I raised my bound hands in the air with the dowsing rod and brought it down full force into Gramps's back.

He turned to look up at me and blood spread quickly across his back. Even though he clawed at the rod and removed it, he couldn't stop the bleeding. Blood was flowing quickly and soaked the T-shirt I'd bought him last Christmas. As Katie and I looked on, he got to his feet then stumbled a few feet before finally falling facedown in the dirt.

"Let's go!"

I helped Katie to her feet and we began to run back to the shed.

"We'll get in the ATV and drive it back to the house and call for help."

Once we reached the ATV, though, we couldn't find the keys. Gramps had them. We both collapsed on the dirt and lay there on the ground staring up at the stars. My hand reached for hers and squeezed.

"Thank you," Katie said, and the words came out on a choked, raspy cough.

I didn't reply right away because my head had no words. The wind was whistling through the grass and the rustling sound was loud in my ears.

"We've got to head back," I told her.

We got to our feet and there was Gramps.

Katie screamed and began to run as he reached into the waistband of his pants and pulled out the handgun.

"Don't," I whispered.

"I'm tired, Delma. I shouldn't've let your grandma hold it over my head just so she could torment you. I shoulda turned myself in and got you help and—"

"Put the gun down," I said.

"I never wanted to hurt you," Gramps said.

He brought the gun to his chin and pulled the trigger.

I dropped to my knees and couldn't stop screaming.

AT ONE POINT there were shouts and flashlights and Katie screaming in Garrett's arms. Then I realized it wasn't Katie screaming, it was me.

"Quicksand," I whispered in Garrett's ear.

"No more quicksand," he replied, hugging me so tight it hurt my ribs.

It was a good hurt.

THIRTEEN

BY THE TIME they let me out of the psych ward, the blond in my hair had grown out three inches from my scalp. I didn't go back to the trailer. Wookie and I moved right in with Garrett. I thought it would be awkward but it wasn't. Except maybe for Wookie, who missed Gramps and rabbits and having hundreds of acres for his toilet.

Katie wrote me nearly every day when I was locked up but I didn't reply and I didn't see her. I just couldn't. The psychiatrist told me it was okay to cut those ties. He also taught me that there was no reason I should've known about Gramps's predilection as a serial killer.

The doc *told* me that but, of course, the guilt had wormed its way into my heart.

Doc also said that it was okay that I hadn't remembered about Gramps killing someone way back when because I'd been protecting my own self until it became suddenly important to remember. After weeks the doc said my world was full of potential and I was ready to live my life moving forward instead of back.

What he didn't know was that not everyone is ready for the full potential of their own future. Some would rather cocoon themselves in the maybes than move forward, and there's heated comfort in the devil you know. But I knew I was never going back to my old life. I needed to set fire to everything about that life.

But I did see Jonas when he came by even though

I cried nonstop for two days after hearing he'd been found in a fishing shack very close to the one where I'd been stashed. They'd found three other similar shelters in the area and one in the Clackamas River area of Oregon, Gramps's favorite fishing spot, from where he'd mailed letters to the FBI. They said Gramps used the Taser on Jonas. He'd borrowed a car and followed Jonas when he went to get me, and got him when he pulled the Jeep over. He'd also used the Taser on Jill and the girls to overpower them. I thought back to when Gramps had suggested I get a Taser. He told me, *they're easy to use*. I never once thought to ask how he'd know that. So much I didn't figure out before it was too late.

Mostly I spent my days watching television and taking Wookie for long walks in downtown Seattle. Garrett would come home and tell me about his day and would sometimes bring pizza.

It was a nice life.

A simple life.

And boring as hell.

When I tired of licking my wounds and figured I'd done enough navel gazing to last a lifetime, I cracked open my old laptop and ordered myself a new set of dowsing rods and some proper divining crystals. Then I opened my emails. There were hundreds of new ones. Maybe even thousands. I didn't look at any of those but went straight to the email folder labeled Jobs.

I clicked on an email I'd received a while back. The one where a man said he wanted help finding the body of his dad who was an Alzheimer's patient who'd wandered into a Colorado forest the year before and was presumed dead. He wanted help finding his dad's body. I sent a simple reply:

Thank you for your email and I apologize for my delay in replying. I'm so sorry for your loss. I have recently started a new business to help people find their deceased loved ones. If you still wish to hire me to find your father, I'd be pleased to assist you.

I signed the email with my new company name:

Divine Reunions

I had a feeling, deep down in my bones, it was going to be a hit.

* * * * *

ACKNOWLEDGMENTS

THANK YOU TO SARAH, Daniel, Donovan and Devin, who love and support their crazy mother.

I am grateful for the tireless support of super-agent Melissa Jeglinski.

Big smooshy hugs to my editor, Deborah Nemeth, as well as Stephanie Doig, Tasneem Dasoo, Stephanie Van de Vooren, Melissa Anthony and the countless others on the Carina Team who helped with this book.

ABOUT THE AUTHOR

WENDY ROBERTS IS an armchair sleuth, fan of all things mysterious but a huge chicken at heart. Her mind is often in a secretive cloak-and-dagger world of intrigue while her physical presence is usually at home feeding feral cats and a demanding guinea pig. Wendy resides in Vancouver, Canada, where she happily writes about murder and is always at work on her next novel.

You can find Wendy on the web here:

Website: www.WendyRoberts.com

Twitter: www.Twitter.com/AuthorWendy

Instagram: @WendyRoberts_Author

Facebook: www.Facebook.com/WendyRobertsAuthor